TRAPPED SOULS

AN ELENORA BELLO MYSTERY

JACINTHE DESSUREAULT

Demiurge
Underground

Legal deposit – Bibliothèque et Archives nationales du Québec, 2022
Legal deposit – Library and Archives Canada, 2022

ISBN 978-1-9994431-4-6 (paperback)
ISBN 978-1-9994431-5-3 (ebook)

CHAPTER ONE

Of all the spirits to summon, did it have to be the grisly one carrying her severed head against her hip?

Queasiness pooled in Elenora's stomach as she anticipated seeing Mary Gallagher's ghost. Even in broad daylight, the prospect was daunting. Beheaded in 1879, Headless Mary was a local legend. The murdered prostitute was rumored to reappear every seven years. The location of her scandalous demise, once a scuzzy tenement, had become a vacant gravelly lot lined with wild shrubs and cinder blocks in the Griffintown neighborhood of Montréal.

"Tell me if you feel a warm chill," said Yukiko, a laid-back woman in a flowing summer dress. Her long, straight black hair swayed as her hands moved fluidly over a circle of five lit candles. As the resident medium at the Off-Path Office—a clandestine organization dealing with supernatural threats—she'd been tasked with helping Elenora decipher her newfound psychic abilities to get better control over them.

Yukiko had chosen Mary Gallagher as a test subject since

Elenora had felt puzzling "warm chills" months earlier while walking by Mary's turf. No one at the OPO knew what the incongruous chills were, but the medium thought the spirit was trying to get Elenora's attention. She suggested they try to connect with the notorious ghost to get answers.

"The warm breeze and Aubrey's heat are confusing my senses," Elenora replied.

She'd felt the mysterious warm chills for the first time on a frigid April day. The contrast between the unexpected warmth and the chilly weather had been jarring and impossible to miss. Whereas now, the same chills would be harder to detect, considering the balmy breeze blowing through the lot and her eight-month-old daughter asleep against her chest in the baby carrier—a little furnace on this hot July evening.

Elenora focused harder on her senses to catch any sign Mary Gallagher's ghost might give her. A distracting aroma of fried chicken wafted by. They'd been attempting to coax the specter into the open for over an hour, and Elenora was getting hungry. And despite her sitting on a cushy picnic blanket, her legs were numb, and sharp bits of gravel dug into her backside through the layers of fabric. She couldn't wait for the unfruitful séance to end.

Maybe they would have a better chance of success after nightfall, but the lot was located across a university campus in a populated area. The sight of two middle-aged women meditating with candles in a spot famous for its haunting would easily attract the attention of campus security and lookie-loos eager for content to share on social media. Yukiko had thought their séance would be more discreet on a quiet Tuesday night before sunset, and she'd been right. A few people had walked by, but no one had given them a second look.

"One last try." Yukiko also looked ready to call it a night. "Mary Gallagher, I respectfully summon you. Please show yourself."

The flames on the five candles flickered lightly. That was new. Hope surged in Elenora, and she held her breath.

Another wave of fried chicken scent floated past, followed by a group of students boisterously debating an engineering lecture. Elenora willed them to pick up the pace and disappear. Not that it did anything—she wasn't a telepath. Though she briefly wished she were so she could make them leave faster. If Mary Gallagher was finally considering showing herself, they couldn't afford to spook her.

Thankfully, the kids took their loud argument elsewhere, and the flames kept fluttering.

Come on, Mary.

After a few long minutes, Mary was still a no-show.

Hmm...

"What if it's not Mary Gallagher who's trying to get my attention?" Elenora mused.

"You think we're barking up the wrong tree?"

Sudden shimmering above the candles caught their attention. A light fog materialized. Elenora gasped.

"You can see that?" Yukiko's voice held a hint of surprise.

Elenora gave her a distracted nod. "Is that her?"

"It's someone."

The fog wavered, faint against the setting sunlight.

"Let's see..." the medium muttered to herself.

She moved her hand in a random pattern over the flames,

and the fog further solidified. It took shape, unveiling a dim apparition.

Mary.

It was impossible to mistake the local legend for anyone else. The specter held her severed head at waist level, and her dress sported generous blotches of blood. Chills, both warm and cold, ran through Elenora. The sight was both frightening and fascinating. It didn't help that the departed's attention had snapped to her. Mary's haunting stare bored right into Elenora's eyes, searching and intense.

"She's staring at me," Elenora whispered, unsure of what to do. She certainly didn't want to piss off the scary lady.

"You can see her?"

"Yes." Elenora glanced sideways at Yukiko.

The medium stared at her with a baffled expression. "You can see her eyes? Her face?"

"Yes. Am I not supposed to see her?"

"Well..."

"Should I take that as a no?"

"Yes, you should take that as a no." Yukiko scrambled for an explanation. "Usually, a non-medium needs a revealing spell to see a ghost. Maybe your abilities—"

A guy wearing a backward baseball cap drove by in a convertible blaring "Cotton-Eyed Joe," sending the skittish specter back into hiding. The car's tires squealed as it turned a corner, and the frantic tune waned as fast as it had scared Mary off.

Elenora let out a frustrated groan, startling Aubrey awake.

"Shhh, it's okay," Elenora comforted her little girl before the abrupt awakening made her grumpy.

Surprisingly, neither the yahoo's musical ruckus nor the explosive backfiring of a motorcycle earlier had interrupted her sleep. No, it had taken a quiet groan of frustration to wake her up.

"Well. That's that," Yukiko said with the resigned wisdom of someone used to dealing with finicky ethereal beings.

The medium blew her candles out and started packing while Elenora struggled to process what had just happened. She had seen Mary Gallagher's ghost, confirming the rumors of her presence in the lot. But more importantly, Yukiko seemed baffled that she'd seen the woman without a revealing spell. After all, their plan had been for the medium to translate any interaction between Elenora and Mary. They hadn't expected Elenora to see Mary.

"Did I see Barlow's spirit because of a revealing spell?" Elenora asked.

Months earlier, while discovering her psychic abilities and working on her first paranormal case, Elenora had witnessed an exorcism when her friend Rolland had been possessed by the evil spirit of a killer named Oliver Barlow. She'd seen the murderer's spectral form come out of Rolland's body.

"Yes. The girls always cast a revealing spell during an exorcism to see what they're dealing with. But possessions are special cases because the spirit entwines with a living body, grounding them to our plane of existence. With ghosts, if no medium is present to summon them, to coax them into our realm, most witches are blind to them—regardless of spells. There are exceptions, of course."

"And today?"

"Today..." Yukiko fussed with the contents of her backpack, as if buying time. She finally zipped it and met Elenora's expectant gaze. "I should have been the only one able to see her. Unless..."

"Unless?" Did Elenora even want to know?

"Unless you have channeling abilities too."

CHAPTER TWO

"Mommy's pulling my leg, isn't she?" Serena asked Aubrey in a high-pitched voice.

They were in their favorite meeting spot, the newly rebranded Café Jackalope. The owners had remodeled the place from a nondescript hole in the wall with a decent but small coffee offering to a swanky hole in the wall with a drink menu a mile long and a camera-ready, urban-cabin feel. Wide planks of black-painted shiplap contrasted with mounted heads of the shop's namesake mythical animal surrounded by silver light fixtures and other shiny accents.

Serena lived nearby, and when she'd heard Elenora would be in the neighborhood to summon Mary Gallagher with Yukiko, she had insisted they meet afterward for an evening snack and decaf beverages. They had become best friends and hadn't seen each other in a while.

Sitting in a high chair, Aubrey eagerly waited for the witch to feed her more applesauce, little arms flailing in a gimme-now fashion. She shrieked, revealing a dimple in one of her reddened cheeks. She'd been teething up a storm, and her nonstop drooling irritated her sensitive skin. Two thin pigtails shot up from her head like miniature palm trees. At birth, her hair was dark, but it had since paled considerably to a light-chestnut color. When Elenora had become pregnant, she'd had a vision of a little girl with nearly white hair and had been convinced that would be her future daughter. She often wondered if she would eventually be proven right.

And if so, what would that mean?

"I wish I were pulling your leg," Elenora answered Serena after swallowing a bite of abricotine.

"But you saw her, just like you're seeing me, right?" Serena zigzagged a spoon full of applesauce toward Aubrey's mouth. "Open wide for the flying broomstick!"

"Kinda. She was really faint though, and honestly, if I hadn't been focusing on the fog, I could've missed her entirely."

"But you still saw her without a revealing spell." Serena shook her head. "That's amazing."

Elenora felt special to get the respect and awe of powerful women such as Serena and Yukiko. She also felt privileged to have seen Mary when hordes of ghost chasers wished they could. Not to mention she'd seen a spirit without a revealing spell—a big deal, apparently. Unfortunately, this also meant that, once again, she was different, in a puzzling way. And *that* made her uneasy.

Why me? She hadn't asked herself the question in a while, but here she was again.

"Do you think you might have encountered other spirits before but didn't notice them?" Serena asked, refilling the spoon to appease the wiggly eater in front of her.

"It's possible, but I don't remember feeling warm chills before the vacant-lot incident. And Yukiko's convinced they're linked to my psychic abilities. She thinks I have a peculiar connection to spiritual matters."

"So, maybe you seeing Mary Gallagher unassisted isn't all that far-fetched."

Elenora took another bite of her apricot pastry.

"That said, I still can't believe you saw her without help. That's so cool." Serena grinned and teased, "Soon you'll be doing spells, too, and I'll be out of a job."

"Serena Winston! Take that back!" Elenora laughed. "Like I need more craziness in my life."

Serena laughed, too, scraping the bottom of the apple-sauce jar. "You got another one of these?"

Aubrey stared at her with a ravenous gaze, as if she hadn't eaten in days.

"Nope, and that's more than enough, kiddo," Elenora told her daughter.

"Brace yourself for mutiny, then." Serena leaned closer to the baby. "It's Mommy's fault, all right? Your witchy godmamma's on your team. Never forget that, toots."

Elenora shook her head and distracted Aubrey with a rubber zebra while cleaning her sticky face with a wet wipe. She then lifted her daughter, wiggling her gently to dislodge her legs from the high chair before dipping her toward the stroller.

"Wait, I'll take her," Serena volunteered.

Elenora changed course and plopped Aubrey on her friend's lap.

Gnawing on the rubber zebra's neck, the baby tilted her head back to scrutinize Serena's pretty face and auburn hair from below. The witch swept her ponytail away from the impending death grip.

"Did you ever consider having kids?" Elenora took a sip of her decaf latte, now lukewarm. It still tasted like heaven. She lifted her eyes from the cup in time to catch a subtle wince on her friend's face and regretted asking. Was that a sore subject?

"Maybe in my next lifetime. Right now, I'm too busy dealing with evil assholes," Serena replied with studied nonchalance.

Evil assholes... Elenora didn't like the sound of that. She dropped her voice to a whisper. "Did another evil spirit appear?"

"No. I meant Kéven in accounting. The guy's a real douche."

Aubrey giggled.

"Oh, what's so funny? The *douuuuuche?*" Serena pitched her voice high again for the baby's benefit, making her giggle some more. "I totally agree. He's a funny douche. Wait until you meet him. You'll totes agree, girlfriend." She fist-bumped Aubrey's tiny fist.

"So, what did evil Kéven do?"

"Well, he knows I've been working around the clock on this demonic case—"

"Demonic? So there *is* evil around..."

Serena swatted the air dismissively. "It's just a mild succubus case. She's inoffensive. Kéven's way worse."

Elenora tried to wrap her head around a so-called *mild succubus case.* "Wouldn't that be sexual abuse?"

"Not if it's all very consensual. The objects of her attention are all hitting the sack by, like, eight o'clock for long nights of kinky dreams. Trust me, nobody's calling 911."

Elenora snorted at Serena's snark. "Then you're pursuing this because...?"

"Because we can't let her set a precedent. That's the problem with evil—once it gets away with something, it always tries to see how much further it can go without getting caught. If we let this slip, it's gonna be harder to take down the next serious abuser."

"Makes sense. So, what did douchy Kéven do?"

"Kéven. Right. So, he knows that I'm swamped—I barely have time to go to the bathroom. But I still bothered emailing him to let him know my time sheet might be late. And he said, 'No prob.' Then things got even crazier because I have to help with two other cases on top of the succubitch, and I missed the deadline—sue me. So the next time I'm actually able to check my phone, it's blowing up with messages from freakin' Kéven telling me in every language ever known to man that I didn't submit my time sheet. Seriously?"

Elenora waited for her friend to go on, but Serena reached for her fancy twelve-instructions-with-extra-whip-and-sprinkles coffee instead and took a long sip.

"So, that's it?" Elenora bit her lip to keep a straight face.

"I had to wade through every single one of his inane messages—voicemail *and* email—in case there was anything of *actual importance*! Do you know how much time I wasted because of that jerk?"

"Maybe he likes you?" Elenora teased her.

Serena made a gagging noise. "Oh, God and the devil forbid."

Aubrey squealed and launched into a fit of giggles, turning the witch's sour mood on a dime and making her laugh. "You're right, girl. Maybe I overreacted a little. But he's still a douche."

Elenora chuckled.

"Speaking of nightmares, how's your sleep lately?" Serena asked, her expression turning serious and attentive.

"Much kinder to me. The heart-wrenching dreams are muffled, and none of them have required my attention lately."

"Awesome! That sucks so much less."

"It sure does. Now, if only Aubrey's teeth could leave her alone, I'd stand a chance of getting some truly restorative sleep."

Back when Oliver Barlow's spirit had wreaked havoc, Elenora's dreams had been filled with gruesome premonitions linked to his murderous actions. Soon after the spirit's demise, her nights had become less trying but still emotionally taxing. Most dreams felt like an SOS in a bottle washing up to shore just a hair too late.

Like the dream she'd had of a drunk woman in a red coat getting hit by a white car. Elenora recognized the downtown intersection. And judging by the squealing of the brakes before impact, it seemed like an accident rather than a premeditated attempt to run the woman over.

The dream felt like a premonition, so she woke Tom, her homicide detective husband, at two in the morning to tell him about it. They puzzled over what to do with the insight. But how could you prevent such a car crash? Put a police roadblock on the busy downtown strip to slow traffic until a drunk woman matching the description safely crosses the street?

Such a disruptive fishing expedition would be unrealistic and hard to justify.

"What if it's already happened?" Tom wondered.

He called Station Twenty, and they confirmed that a woman had been pronounced dead at the intersection of Crescent and de Maisonneuve moments earlier. She wore a red coat, and the car was white. Elenora remained awake for the rest of that night, torturing herself. If only she'd gone to bed a little earlier, maybe it would have made a difference.

The nights were filled with haunting maybes.

Thankfully, other similar dreams were not all as troubling and frustrating. Some were bittersweet. Like the one she'd had of an old man dying in his bed at home, alone. As Elenora entered his bedroom, his departing spirit—sitting in a chair by the bed, standing guard over his body—stood to greet her with a serene smile.

"Thank you so much for coming." He handed her a piece of paper with an address on it. "Willem's food is at the bottom of the pantry. I'll be on my way now. It's been a good one." He tipped his head in a silent farewell and vanished.

Elenora instantly memorized the address, knowing she would soon be yanked away.

The next morning, Tom and his detective partner, Alex Bélanger, went to check the address. They found Mr. Albert Leclerc lifeless in his bed, a poofy silver cat at his feet. The man had died of natural causes the previous night. Thanks to Elenora, they discovered his body quickly. They also fed the cat kibbles from the bag that was indeed at the bottom of the pantry. Tom had brought Willem home until long-term care could be arranged. They'd ended up adopting him.

While both the feline and the stirring memory of her

brief encounter with Mr. Leclerc made Elenora smile, she still wished she'd received the man's address earlier. Maybe he could have been saved. At the very least, he wouldn't have died alone.

The cruel timing of Elenora's insights affected and aggravated her. Why have premonitions at all if she had no chance of preventing these tragedies? Were they only meant to taunt her?

Elenora had discussed this with Dr. Brent, the OPO psychologist helping her recover from the Barlow trauma and understand her new reality. The good doctor was of vampiric descent and had seen many things over several lifetimes. She had a theory about Elenora's insights and abilities. She compared Elenora to a radio receiver that captured spiritual frequencies floating around the island of Montréal. Some airwaves reached her instantly while others traveled more slowly, as proven by a dream Elenora had of a decades-old death.

Yukiko thought Dr. Brent's theory had merit. It had inspired the medium to teach Elenora to mentally dial down the spiritual frequencies so the visions would stop crippling her emotionally. The technique consisted of Elenora picturing a radio dial in her mind and turning it down before falling asleep. This simple solution muffled the intrusive airwaves in her dreamscape, enough for her to finally sleep without mortifying interferences.

"But what if I miss an important premonition that could prevent a tragedy?" Elenora asked the medium when the uncomfortable thought struck her.

"That's a valid and caring point. But since Oliver Barlow

—who would have popped up on the OPO's radar sooner or later—how many of those dreams allowed you to prevent an unfortunate event?"

They both knew the answer to that. "None. But—"

"Then how is that fair to you?"

Elenora had never thought of it in terms of unfairness to herself. The dreams were intrusive and debilitating, but it was no one's fault.

"Your mind is still mending from what Barlow did to you. If you want to help others, you need to take care of your mental health first. You can stop dialing your mind down when you're ready."

Elenora accepted the compromise with reluctance. Her mind badly needed a break. Fortunately, Yukiko had taken her qualm to heart and had soon come up with a solution. She and Dr. Brent retraced an old magic-assisted visualization technique used by former OPO psychics. With Serena's help, they customized it using the radio receiver approach to suit Elenora's mind. The resulting procedure would train her subconscious to sweep for elements of imminent danger in her premonitory dreams. If any were found, her mental dial would turn itself back up, making her receptive to the relevant vision.

However, there was a caveat.

"The upside is this will open your mind," Dr. Brent said.

"And the downside?" Elenora braced herself.

"It will open your mind..." Dr. Brent gave her a rueful look over the rim of her glasses.

"What Meredith means," Yukiko jumped in, no doubt noticing the growing alarm in Elenora's face, "is that this could further stretch your abilities. We know you're trying to put a lid on what you already have. But this should also give you more control in the long run. So, not a bad thing, right?"

Sugarcoated or not, it was a bummer. Elenora was trying hard to rein in and diminish her abilities, not expand or intensify them.

Damn it.

"Think about it," Yukiko said gently. "It's ultimately your choice, of course. And no one will try to sway you or judge you. You're the one living with your powers. Just consider this a viable option to getting both the important premonitions *and* sleep."

Kind words didn't make Elenora's decision easier. She had mixed feelings about this, especially the risk of further expanding her abilities. Would she be fixing one problem only to create another? Some cans of worms were best left unopened. But if she turned down the risky opportunity to play it safe, she would be doomed to suffer from a perpetual flow of misplaced guilt.

Elenora had ended up taking a leap of faith and accepting the new technique.

"Baaabaaaaaa!" Aubrey's ear-splitting declaration sliced through Elenora's thoughts and brought her back to their table at Café Jackalope.

"Girl, I totally agree," Serena deadpanned. "Oh look, Mommy's back with us. Just in time for us to get kicked out."

A glance around the coffee shop confirmed it was on the verge of closing. Serena stood and set Aubrey down in her stroller while Elenora collected her purse and the diaper bag.

"I'm glad the dreams are giving you a break," Serena said.

A break.

Elenora gave her friend a weak smile. She suspected it was only a matter of time before she channeled another dreadful case.

CHAPTER THREE

Montréal, 1899

"Do you think it wise to welcome the departed into our home?" A frown appeared on Jane Gill's delicate face as she took in the back of the newly built Queen Anne mansion. It was stunning and perfect, an elegant match for her loveliness.

"The departed are dead, my love," Joseph, her husband, replied. An award-winning postmortem photographer to the city's upper class, he was determined to offer his young wife the very best his fortune could afford. "They are harmless. And you know I would never put you in harm's way. If I didn't think this was entirely safe..."

His words didn't seem to reassure Jane one bit.

"Would it help if I had a hedge planted on either side of the studio's entrance?"

As a strategic move, Joseph Gill had their house built right next to a high-class mortuary so his clients could easily be wheeled to his basement photography studio and back.

Jane craned her neck daintily toward the side of the house. "Hmm. I suppose it wouldn't hurt."

"Consider it done. I don't know why I hadn't thought of it already. I hope you'll forgive me."

She offered him a reserved smile that did little to mask how unsettled she still felt.

"Have you seen the roses?" He pointed at a row of rosebushes near the house. Jane gave them a cursory glance before turning her attention to the mortuary next door.

Joseph sighed inwardly and forced himself to sound enthusiastic. "Once we've moved in, you'll be too delighted with the house to worry."

"Will people even dare to visit us? Those with a pulse?"

It was a fair concern, but he would make damn sure Jane got as many visitors as her precious little heart wished.

"I assure you we will be the talk of the town, my dear, and anyone will consider it a privilege to be invited to our soirées."

Joseph had spared no expense in building the magnificent home so his wife would be happy and his booming business could become even more profitable—in that order.

When he met Jane, he was already wealthy from birth and famous for his photography. He was also known for his artistic temperament. In contrast, Jane was an orphaned, penniless beauty with an agreeable character. On most days, the photographer wondered how she'd ever consented to be his and feared she might come to her senses one day and leave him.

As for his photography business, Joseph had made sure the new place had the best amenities and the latest inventions. He would still do the occasional house call, but he planned to immortalize most of his deceased clientele in his home from now on. He was already well-known for his spectacular results, but the studio would bring his artistry to new heights. His pictures would be even more realistic and dazzling in that controlled environment. It would be child's play to capture the dead's essence.

At last, Jane stepped closer to the rosebushes to admire the budding flowers. Her gaze surveyed the roses but then lifted to the house's vaulted gable roof. She looked back at the bushes, and her shoulders slumped. Gracefully.

Joseph's heart sank. "What is it?" he asked, despite knowing exactly what was on her mind.

"This is where he landed, isn't it?" Her voice was sad.

Joseph took in a sharp breath. How he wished a construction worker hadn't fallen off his roof to his death when they were building the house. The clumsy fool. His death still upset Jane. Joseph hoped their home's modern amenities and exquisite woodwork would be enough to make her forget the inconvenient tragedy.

"Landed, yes. But not buried, of course... I assure you the lovely young man is nowhere near here. Remember, this was nothing more than an unfortunate accident. Construction work can be perilous and unforgiving. You have nothing to fear."

Joseph had thrown a significant amount of money at people to keep the tragedy off the news to not alarm Jane, but she'd still found out about it. What a bothersome turn of events. His wife was already awfully skittish about his post-mortem-photography endeavors. She was a fragile little doll, and death made her uncomfortable. And now, the mere memory of a dead young idiot threatened to ruin everything.

"What if his spirit is still here?" Another frown appeared on Jane's pretty face.

"He wasn't pronounced dead until he reached the hospital," Joseph fibbed. "They rushed him away promptly. I am certain that a lovely fellow such as himself was reunited with his departed loved ones. His spirit wouldn't care to return here."

She nodded absently.

"I heard he was very charitable. He certainly wouldn't hold a grudge against our home." Joseph knew of no such thing, but it *could* be true. After all, he had employed only hard workers with good references. But at any rate, if the thought soothed Jane...

Her face lit up. "The roses are to commemorate his death, aren't they? How thoughtful."

The rosebushes had been planted to distract Jane from the lad's death and the mortuary. But if it pleased her to think they were a memorial, that worked too.

"Indeed. Aren't they stunning? I hope you'll enjoy them. And this entire garden." He made a sweeping gesture at the lush backyard. "Your own little paradise. My love, let's not allow trivial matters to prevent you from feeling at home."

She gave him a placating smile, then her gaze shifted to the mortuary. Again.

CHAPTER FOUR

Elenora had seen a ghost. Without help. The formidable thought was sinking in.

Granted, the apparition had been really dim, almost transparent, and Elenora had barely interacted with Mary Gallagher. But she still had *seen* her. All by herself. According to Yukiko and Serena, the feat was nothing short of miraculous.

I should be freaking out, Elenora thought as she tackled a fragrant diaper. Her nostrils flared, and her focus snapped back to the task at hand as she reached for the wipes.

She had just arrived home from the coffee shop with Aubrey, and her mind swirled. Tom was working late, so Elenora was alone with the baby, the cat, and her thoughts. She prepped her daughter for bed and hoped Aubrey would sleep well. At least one of them wouldn't be dreaming of Mary Gallagher.

Elenora had seen a ghost in all of her horrific glory. Why wasn't she freaking out more?

Not long ago, she would have been beside herself with

worry. But now? Sure, she was freaking out a little—who wouldn't? But not that much, considering the magnitude of the event. Maybe she had finally internalized that freaking out was futile. If one thing had remained constant since her first premonition, it was that her countless hours of fretting and stressing hadn't changed a thing. Why would it this time? She had an undeniably strong connection to the spiritual realm, and no amount of worry would change that.

You saw Mary Gallagher. Come on! How special is that?

A small smile appeared on Elenora's lips. Had seeing Mary been a sign that her psychic abilities were expanding, like Dr. Brent had warned her could happen? If so, the expansion hadn't been exceedingly scary so far. A tad gross—because Mary—and certainly unsuspected. But if Elenora was being honest, the brief spectral encounter had intrigued her—enough to disappoint her when the ghost vanished before they could truly interact.

Would Mary have talked to her if she hadn't been spooked?

Imagine having a conversation with a departed soul...

Elenora felt Aubrey's gaze on her, an awestruck, adoring look only babies seemed able to muster. She smiled at her daughter and was rewarded with the biggest single-toothed grin.

"I love that smile so much, Aubrey," she cooed. "Such a pretty smile."

The baby giggled. After a long bout of raging gum pain and gut-wrenching tears, the sunny reprieve was welcome.

"Are you being a giggle puss?"

More giggles.

"What's so funny? Is it the *douche?*" Elenora caught

herself. With her luck, *douche* would be Aubrey's first favorite word. "Never mind I said that, cutie. Please forget I said that." She blew a raspberry on the baby's soft tummy, enjoying the sound of one last giggle before securing the bottom snaps on the onesie.

Soft fur rubbed against Elenora's calves. Part of Willem's nightly routine was to say goodnight to her before he curled up at the foot of Aubrey's crib. As if the cat's new mission in life was to guard Aubrey in her sleep. He had taken a liking to Elenora's daughter despite her occasional eardrum-piercing cries, and he followed her around all day.

Elenora picked up Aubrey, and the little one snuggled against her. Serena seemed to crave baby snuggles. As Elenora sat in the rocking chair with Aubrey, she mulled over her friend's bristling reaction when she had asked her about kids. Maybe the witch simply didn't want any and was tired of being asked. Elenora could understand and respect that choice. But it seemed to be something else. *Does she want kids but can't have them?*

While her vivacious friend looked like a college kid, she wore a glamour that masked several hundred years of age. In purely human terms, that made her too old to have kids. But in Serena's case, Elenora had no idea what the fine print was, especially since the witch had a smidgen of vampire blood running through her veins. If she could have kids, would the baby inherit that blood and her magic? Or would it depend on the father? Both of Serena's parents had had magic. But what if the dad were human? Would the baby then be a regular mortal and potentially grow old and die before their mother?

Maybe those concerns had occurred to Serena.

Had Elenora known she might pass down her psychic abilities, would she have done things differently? Would she have been comfortable getting pregnant knowing that her child might grow to have horrific visions because of her?

Elenora's powers had revealed themselves only during her pregnancy, so she hadn't had to make that hard decision before conceiving. But once she knew, she'd agonized over Aubrey's welfare in the womb and had kept at it even after the pediatrician had declared the baby healthy and normal in every way.

Normal for now.

She had no way to know whether Aubrey would eventually develop psychic abilities. How much of her so-called gift had her daughter inherited? The question was a source of perpetual anguish. Every time a well-intentioned friend or stranger enthusiastically called Aubrey "special," Elenora couldn't help but cringe—and worry that they might be right.

If Aubrey turns out to be special, I will love her just the same.

What about her own mother? How would Muriel have felt about Elenora had she known she would become psychic?

That reminded Elenora she hadn't seen her in a while. They were overdue for a visit.

The thought bummed her out. She loved her mother—or more accurately, she had fond memories of her mother. Muriel had become a ghost of her former self. After the traumatic loss of her husband in a freak car accident when Elenora was only three years old, she'd lost mental contact with the outside world and had been committed.

Since Muriel was physically unresponsive, visiting her

was a frustrating and heartbreaking task. The only time she'd reacted to anything in the past two decades was when Elenora and Tom had announced the pregnancy. Muriel had made a fist, and a disturbing expression had flared in her eyes. Her briefly sharp gaze had been a stark contrast with her usually dead stare. After this puzzling episode, she had returned to her catatonic state.

Fur tickled Elenora's legs again. Willem gave her the hairy eyeball, clearly impatient for her to leave. She took his insistent cue and put Aubrey in her crib.

Elenora read in bed for a while but soon had to reread too many sentences and gave up. Barely after closing her eyes, she fell into a deep sleep. A tug at the edge of her consciousness demanded her attention.

A premonition worth considering, perhaps?

Blurry shapes came into focus, and Elenora found herself in an old mansion under renovation. Roaming around, she searched for signs of life. A pounding made her perk up. As she approached a staircase, the noise intensified, echoing from above. The sound of a hammer? She went up the stairs to investigate.

The more attuned she became to her dreams, the more sensory details she picked up. Wearing a light summer nightgown—the same one she wore in bed—she noticed a breeze caressing her face and bare arms. With each step, the airflow became stronger.

The stairs led her to the attic, a large space with nooks. The high ceiling had impressive dark wood beams and was vaulted in several places. A scaffold stood against a wall. The source of the breeze became obvious—a good chunk of the house's exterior back wall was missing. Visibly under construction, the hole would become a large window, maybe. A sheet of plastic covered it, the only thing protecting the room from the great outdoors.

Movement at Elenora's periphery caught her attention, and she spotted a young construction worker in jeans and a dust-covered black tee. He was about to swing a sledge-hammer at an interior wall.

As the tool hit the wall, the man flew backward across the room, as if propelled by an invisible force. He went through the plastic sheet and the hole in the exterior wall.

Whoa!

Pushing past her surprise and the dread filling her, Elenora willed herself to approach the hole to see if the worker had survived the fall. She could force herself to wake up—something Dr. Brent had taught her—but the vision seemed relevant and compelled her to do her due diligence and collect clues.

She pulled the sheet of plastic aside and looked below. The construction worker had landed flat on his back over a patch of roses in bloom. His lifeless eyes stared back at her, his limbs at unnatural angles. She ignored the pang of sadness to absorb the scene. Oddly, a second pair of arms and legs shot out from underneath the young man, as if he had fallen on top of another person. Had there already been someone else in the bushes?

Tom and Alex approached the victim at ground level, entering Elenora's view.

And then she woke up, convinced the premonition was

indeed a meaningful one. She'd seen Tom and Alex, so it had to be. Her psychic filter had worked and let in an important vision.

Elenora's breathing was short, her heart beat so fast it threatened to jump out of her chest, and the back of her neck felt damp. Yet she was barely rattled, though she had witnessed the death of a young man. She had likely witnessed a paranormal event. Because if not, then how else could he have shot across the room like that?

Her mental filter must have let the vision through because something about it was supernatural.

Crap. Here we go again.

Pale-blue light spilled from beneath the blinds. A glance at the alarm clock confirmed it was early morning. Elenora slipped out of bed—careful not to wake Tom just yet—and headed to the bathroom. She splashed cold water on her face and latched onto its coolness to anchor herself in the present and calm her racing heart.

She tiptoed back to the bedroom and found Tom stretching and smiling at her. The guy could function and look refreshed on very little sleep. He'd always given early birds a run for their money, but this was ridiculous. These days, when Elenora woke up feeling *only slightly frazzled,* she considered it a good night. She found her husband's sleeping superpower unfair, though it sure came in handy when Aubrey partied all night long. She couldn't hold too much of a grudge.

Tom took in her disheveled state. "Did Aubrey give you a hard time last night?"

"No. Just a poor stranger who fell to his death." She sat

on the bed and told him about the premonition. "Does a recent case match?"

"Not that I know of."

Just then, Tom's phone rang on his nightstand. They exchanged a concerned glance. He reached for the cell. "It's Alex." He answered the call and put his partner on speakerphone. "Let me guess: a construction worker fell out of a window."

There was a brief silence. "Hey, Tom. Chief's on the line with us."

Police chief Manuel Costa was the only other person at the precinct who knew about Elenora, Tom, and Alex's involvement with the paranormal and the existence of the OPO.

"How'd you know about the death, Madigan?" the chief asked, his voice gruff despite him being the gentlest human being one could meet.

"I told him," Elenora said, both to inform the chief and signal her presence on the call. She'd worked as a police social worker at his precinct for a long time, and they had a close working relationship.

Another silence was followed by a grunt. "That doesn't bode well. No offense, Ele."

"None taken."

"So, what happened?" Tom asked.

The chief told them about the bizarre death of a young construction worker named Jérémie Marsan the day before. He had fallen to his death from a hole in the exterior wall of the attic of an old house being renovated and had suffered a considerable blow that was hard to explain. The victim's coworker swore he didn't do it and said it was as if a tornado had thrown the kid outside.

Elenora was about to confirm the witness's account when the chief said, "The body's at the morgue. I'd like you two to take the case since..." He cleared his throat. "You are *aware* of things."

"Okay. But aside from the weird blow, what makes you think the case involves something *abnormal?*" Alex asked. *Abnormal* was his favorite word for anything paranormal. It allowed him to avoid saying the word *paranormal.* "The coworker could be lying."

"There's a pentacle in the basement," the chief added.

"A *pentacle?*" Alex choked on the word.

"You heard right."

"The coworker might be telling the truth," Tom said. "Elenora saw what he described."

"Yeah. I saw the victim hit a wall with a sledgehammer, and the next thing, he was flying across the room. I didn't see anyone push him. It was truly bizarre."

Alex's groan traveled over the line.

"It's an interesting coincidence that this occurred on our turf," Tom said.

"Actually, it happened in the West End, but the case file triggered an alert because of the house's history. Otherwise, I wouldn't have known about it," the chief replied.

"Lucky us," Alex mumbled.

"What's wrong with the house?" Tom pulled the covers aside and swung his legs over the side of the bed.

"I'll send you guys what I got," the chief said.

Elenora almost asked about the extra limbs she'd seen in her vision. But surely the chief would have mentioned a second victim if there was one. Since the case was bizarre enough, she chose to remain silent for the time being.

They wrapped up the call, and Tom headed for the shower.

***

"Maybe there's a reasonable explanation for what happened," Tom told Elenora as he entered the kitchen, accepting a cup of coffee from her.

"But we don't really believe that, do we?" She took a sip of her coffee.

He laughed. "No...but maybe it doesn't have to be like the last time?" He gave her a sympathetic grimace and took a plate from the cabinet.

Tom must have thought she was upset, and he was trying to sound supportive, which was sweet but unnecessary. Not only did Elenora still feel fine, but she actually looked forward to hearing more about the case. Maybe having gone through a multitude of tragic visions for which she could do absolutely nothing had made her grateful that in this instance, they had some power to act. Solving the case wouldn't bring back the young victim, but something fishy had happened in that house—which had been a crime scene before—and they might have a shot at stopping its mystery threat before it claimed another victim.

"I know you want to reassure me, and I appreciate the effort. But allow me to put you out of your misery right now," Elenora said.

He quirked a brow at her.

"Oddly enough, I feel okay about this," she added. "Not

about a young guy dying, obviously—that's horrible. What I mean is I'm coping. I'm not traumatized like I would have been before. I feel...objective?"

A relieved smile spread over Tom's face as he reached for two slices of oatmeal bread. "I'm so glad to hear it."

"Please tell me what you find."

"I'll be happy to." He popped the slices in the toaster and went hunting for the peanut butter in the fridge.

Elenora wondered what Tom and Alex would find and truly couldn't wait to hear all about it. But then it occurred to her: if the death was indeed supernatural, would they find anything on their own?

"You know what?" she blurted out. "Let me ask Pierre if he can meet us there and watch Aubrey. Maybe I can help expedite things."

Tom stared at her, speechless for a moment. "Are you sure?"

"Don't make me change my mind."

CHAPTER FIVE

Montréal, 1911

"The house might be haunted," Irène de Montbleu whispered between clenched teeth to her sister, Angéline, as they studied the attic of the grandiose mansion for sale.

I most certainly hope so. Angéline wanted more than anything for her dearly departed fiancé to be haunting the home. Anselmo had worked on the house twelve years earlier when it was built and had fallen to his death. Since then, Angéline had often tried to summon him at his grave in the cemetery, but he'd never shown. She was convinced his spirit had remained at the house because of the violence of his passing. The spiritualist spinster had kept an eye on the property ever since, hoping to acquire it someday.

Someday was today.

"Dear sister, I've needed a big change of scenery for a long time. You know that better than anyone," she replied to Irène.

"I understand. But do you need one as *creepy* as this?" Visibly appalled and scared, Irène tugged on her sister's arm to lead her back down the stairs.

Angéline let out a quiet, disappointed sigh. She wished she could have done a quick séance in the attic to test her theory, but now was obviously not a good time. It would be improper to summon a spirit with her nosy sister glued to her side and an eavesdropping selling agent only paces away. There was also the tiny detail that no one in Angéline's posh family knew she was an accomplished medium—and that she'd been secretly engaged to a modest construction worker from an immigrant family before his premature, accidental death. Holding a séance now would raise a few eyebrows.

She mouthed *Anselmo?* at the attic space.

Irène tugged harder on her arm. "This whole place is drenched with death."

Angéline gave in and followed her sister down the stairs. Her hand glided over the stunning banister. She loved the smooth craftsmanship. Her gaze took in the wonderfully rich woodwork, the plush exotic rugs, the regal furniture. Clearly, Mr. Joseph Gill had spared no expense on the aesthetics of his home, but Angéline's appreciation went beyond beauty. Her beloved had been a talented carpenter, and she couldn't help wondering which parts of the house were of his making. Her heart squeezed longingly as she entered every new room. She needed this house for herself.

Irène shivered and stopped next to Angéline. They were now facing the stairs leading down to the infamous basement that had housed Mr. Gill's postmortem photography studio.

"Masses of dead people have been down there. Every newspaper said so," Irène protested.

Angéline snorted and waved off her sister's concerns. Every news outlet had printed articles about the photographer's house being up for sale after its well-known owner, who was traveling the world with his family, had decided to sell it. They all emphasized the curiosity-arousing studio, where Joseph Gill had artistically photographed countless departed clients in lush décors. The selling agent's advert had offered a poetically gothic take on the space, no doubt to appeal to the extremely limited pool of buyers: the handful of people rich enough to entertain the purchase while having no qualms about the place's funereal heritage. It made business sense to adopt a romantic view of death to entice. Or at least reassure.

"Indeed, dead people have been in the basement. But the papers like to be dramatic because drama sells. And you make it sound like the dead marched in here in droves, taking over the place. In reality, it was *alive* members of *elite* families who brought their departed loved ones here to have their likenesses immortalized."

"Semantics."

"I should remind you that the photographic results were always tasteful, magnificent, and often award-winning."

From the moment she'd lost Anselmo, Angéline had studied the postmortem work of Joseph Gill with interest and had reluctantly been impressed, given her mixed feelings about the man. While she knew he wasn't responsible for the death of her betrothed, thinking about the eccentric photographer and his home still made her heartbroken and bitter. She also felt an infuriating affinity to the man since they both worked with the dead.

"An artistic genius lived here," she said.

"A morbid, somewhat-talented businessman," Irène countered.

Angéline let her sister have the last word. Their verbal sparring was of no consequence to her, especially since she was so close to getting a piece of Anselmo and a chance to reconnect with him. The opportunity might never present itself again in her lifetime. Her heart did a little flip.

She absolutely needed this house for herself.

"Are you certain I cannot convince you to have a cup of tea? We have a wonderful new blend from England," the selling agent said enthusiastically to Angéline.

He's trying to steer the conversation away from Irène's pessimistic attitude.

Even though Angéline and her sister were the only visitors, an expansive spread of delicate pastries and beverages had greeted them in the kitchen as part of their viewing experience. It paid to be rich. She had heard that a substantial number of thrill-seeking lower-class folks had unsuccessfully attempted to get a tour of the house. It was one of the rare times she was grateful to be a daughter of the great Albert de Montbleu.

"Thank you, Mr. Small, but I must politely decline." *Again.* She didn't care about distractions right now. She was there with her senses wide open to *feel* the house as much as she could. Not to lose focus by sampling the latest fashionable drink.

Earlier in the visit, she'd had to tell the agent she did her best thinking when given room and silence to stop him from fawning over her and drowning her in insipid details about the remarkable qualities of the overpriced fixtures. Thankfully, he'd promptly understood her meaning and had given her space, keeping his spoken contributions to a minimum for the rest of the tour, even if it had pained him to do so.

Angéline brushed her hand over the velvety texture of the wallpaper lining both sides of the well-lit staircase leading to the basement before she headed down.

"I will have a pastry." Irène rushed to the safety of the departed-free kitchen.

Angéline chuckled. Her sister's evasive maneuver was for the best. She didn't need spooked disapproval to complement her visit to the most intriguing part of the house.

On her way down, she heard tentative footsteps behind her. She turned and saw a hint of discomfort on the agent's face as he followed her. She bit her lip to stop from asking if he, too, would like a pastry in the kitchen.

He raked his throat and struggled to keep his voice even. "The professional space was very well maintained and contains no remnants of previous activities. We had a priest conduct a cleansing ceremony."

Angéline hummed instead of expressing her disappointment over the clergyman's interference. She suspected his effort would do little more than give prospective buyers an artificial peace of mind, but she still would have preferred for the space to remain untouched. Establishing a spiritual connection was already tricky enough.

At the bottom of the stairs, a massive, beautifully carved mahogany door stood ajar. Angéline pushed it open and stepped into a large antechamber. *A former waiting room for the studio?* To the left was another mahogany door.

"This is a side entrance." Mr. Small opened the door to reveal a steep ramp going up to an outside door. He closed it quickly with a small shudder.

Angéline pointed to an elegant set of French doors. "And these lead to the studio, I presume?"

"Indeed. And to an adjoining darkroom. Over there are a lavatory and a storage room. This space would make for a fine servant's quarters."

Angéline held back a laugh. As if one could find a servant in town willing to live down there.

She opened one of the French doors, and an impressive room appeared before her. Fieldstones covered the walls, and gold sconces complemented them. The wood floor had gorgeous inlays. The opulent space conveyed the right amount of gravitas. Unlike the rest of the house, which came furnished, the studio was empty. *Probably not to irk buyers.*

Angéline poked her head into the former darkroom, where no photography equipment had been left. Back in the studio, she took a moment to feel the room. As she had predicted, she didn't get any vibes. Since Joseph Gill's departed clients had been thoroughly dead at the time of their visit, Angéline hadn't expected to find or feel anything eerie.

Mr. Small waited for her by the stairs, looking relieved that she was done and ready to bolt. Still, he invited Angéline to lead the way.

Irène poked her head at the top of the stairs. She, too, looked ready to go. "This place is positively too large for just one person, let alone a woman living by herself. Papa will worry sick," she whined when Angéline landed on the main floor.

"I will bring Adèle with me."

"Adèle couldn't kill a dead fly."

Angéline shrugged. "I appreciate your concern for my

safety, but I doubt I'll be in any danger here. And Papa doesn't care enough to worry sick, dearest. He just pretends to."

Irène pinched her lips at the truth. "*I* would worry. And so would Mama."

She had a point. "Your mother will worry sick!" was an argument her father might very well use against her to veto the purchase. *Fiddlesticks... But thank you for the warning, Irène.* Angéline intended to be well prepared to plead her case to the patriarch, and this meant expecting every potential argument against her purchasing the house.

"You're right. This place is ridiculous for one person," she said after careful consideration.

"I'm glad I could talk some sense into you." Irène gave a little smirk. "Mr. Small, we thank you for your help—"

"I will let rooms to other women. Spinsters of independent means. We will keep each other company and safe." Angéline liked the idea. It would make a powerful argument, whether or not she acted on it.

"That is not what I meant, and you know it."

Angéline turned to the agent. "Mr. Small, thank you, indeed. Please draw up the papers."

"You think Papa will sign?" Irène's face fell with incredulity.

"I will not relent until he does."

She would move heaven, earth, and hell to get the house. Her father didn't stand a chance.

CHAPTER SIX

"Jérémie Marsan was twenty-three years old. He had a criminal record—petty theft, narcotics...." Elenora read bits out loud from the passenger seat as she browsed a document on her phone.

Chief Costa had emailed them everything he had on the current case and the old house with the intriguing past. She, Tom, and Aubrey were headed to the scene of the accident.

"He was recently let out for good behavior. He'd also been a juvenile delinquent..."

Elenora could already read between the lines of the victim's past—a kid from a poor family falling in with the wrong crowd, exposed to violence, influenced or bullied into committing petty thefts. Before anyone knew it, Jérémie Marsan was facing jail time and a destroyed future.

Thankfully, he had found the strength to turn his life around while behind bars. *Smart kid.* He had taken courses, been active in therapy, and made himself useful to convince the parole committee that he deserved a second chance, which he'd gotten. Until death had taken it all away.

The timing's cruelty saddened Elenora. The kid must have worked so hard, and then he'd barely enjoyed his reward.

"What else?" Tom brought her focus back to the file.

"Hang on." She moved on to the next document—one about the house. "Now, let's see. 34 Maple..." She scrolled down, taking in details to give Tom a summary. She made a low whistle. "The chief was right. The house has more history than Greece. This address was already known because of an unsolved suspicious death in 1973. Jean-Luc Rivard, also twenty-three and a satanic cult leader... That's a new one."

"I wonder what you need to major in for that."

Elenora laughed and went on, "Another death occurred before his—a natural one. In 1962, Angéline de Montbleu died of a heart attack in the house. She was eighty-one. And before that..."

Elenora scrolled down some more. "No other deaths. However, the original owner of the house was a famous post-mortem photographer. He used to take pictures of his dead clients in the house's basement."

"Okay, wow."

"You took the words right out of my mouth."

"Was the house built on an ancient sacred burial ground while we're at it?"

Elenora snorted. "Doesn't say, but we shouldn't rule that out just yet. Do you think Alex is filling out papers to request a transfer?"

Tom chuckled. As a previous skeptic, Alex had hated every minute of their first brush with the paranormal. He was already uneasy about the pentacle in the old house and must have been beside himself reading the case files.

"Are *you* considering a transfer?" Tom gave Elenora a half-serious look infused with humor.

"I'm not considering it yet, but the day is young," she said dryly. She did feel some jitters, but they were more positive than not.

He gave her a warm smile. "I'm glad you're here. I missed working with you."

Elenora returned the smile. "Me too." As much as she loved being at home with the baby and appreciated her generous one-year maternity leave, she craved adult stimulation, and working with Tom and Alex never failed to provide that. Being on a case again, even if only for a brief contribution, was exciting.

"Do you think Marsan's death could be related to Rivard's?" Tom asked.

"At a glance, the two deaths have nothing in common other than the location and their age at death. Marsan presumably died from a fall, whereas Rivard was found inside the pentacle in the basement. Traces of 'spontaneous bleeding' marked his chest, but no signs of trauma. The ME—"

"Poulin?"

"Yes. Poulin concluded he bled to death but couldn't pinpoint the exact cause. Rivard had no cuts, no wounds, no signs of a physical blow, suicide, or murder."

Thoughtful silence filled the car as they pondered the facts.

"The house is being renovated, right?" Tom sped through a yellow light.

"Correct. And my premonition was right about the enormous hole in an external wall in the attic. A window is being put in, and Jérémie Marsan fell through that opening."

"Any sign of negligence on the contractor's part?"

"No mention of it. But the report indicates a delivery snafu with the new window after the crew had already taken out the old one and enlarged the opening."

"Hmm... Rivard died in the seventies. Has anyone lived in the house since?"

"Hold on." Elenora further browsed the house report. "Doesn't look like it. After Rivard's death, it seems like the property was empty and left to rot. It stayed in the family—a niece inherited it recently. She lives in Toronto, and she's the one investing in restoring the house. She probably intends to sell it."

"I wonder why she doesn't just sell the land. An old house like that, neglected for decades, sounds like. I can't even imagine how complicated and expensive it will be to restore it and bring it up to code. But the lot must be worth a fortune."

"Maybe she has both deep pockets *and* an appreciation for older architecture. I wish more of those people were around."

Elenora belonged to a local history Facebook group, and it often aggrieved her to see before-and-after pictures of beautiful old buildings destroyed to make way for overly modern or depressingly dull constructions—often both. Especially the boxy beige or gray buildings predominant in the sixties and seventies. *Cold War chic*, she and Tom liked to call those. It was frustrating to lose architectural gems for those monstrosities and sad to think the damage could never be undone.

"So, we have three deaths in an old house falling apart," Tom recapped. "One of a natural cause and two that are suspicious and hard to explain. You and the chief already suspect a paranormal element in Marsan's death. And to this day, a very competent medical examiner is still scratching his head over how Rivard died. I assume he didn't take the satanic part seriously."

"You think Jean-Luc Rivard's death might be paranormal too?"

"I think we're gonna need a mega whiteboard to keep the details of this case straight. How do you feel about us repainting the dining room walls in a few weeks?" Tom beamed her a huge teasing grin.

Elenora swatted his arm. "I'd like to see you try to bring a marker anywhere near those walls."

"I can use a pencil."

"Stay away from the dang walls! I hate painting."

He laughed. "So, what do you think?"

"About you assaulting the dining room walls?"

"About the satanic guy's death. Any gut feelings? You think Satan might have killed the president of his fan club?"

Elenora groaned. When she'd decided to come to the party, it hadn't crossed her mind that the devil might be there. Hopefully, Tom's joke would remain just that.

"No gut feelings, and you shouldn't joke about these things."

"Maybe you'll pick something up at the house."

She shuddered at the prospect of coming across anything satanic. Maybe she should have stayed home. "Maybe we should've asked the witches to meet us there."

"Trust me, the moment we find proof of anything paranormal, I'll call them. And I'll get you home the minute you want out."

"You think you can get rid of me that easily?" she said, half-joking, half-serious, and entirely unsure how she felt about stepping aside. She was already invested in the case. Though, if the devil came out of the woodwork, she should stay the hell out of the way.

"You don't have to shoulder anything you don't want to. That's all I'm saying." Tom reached for her hand and squeezed it. "What about the limbs you saw in the rose-bushes? Any mention of them in the files?"

"Not that I can see."

"Maybe you'll learn more about their owner at the house. They could reveal a connection between the deaths."

Tom tapped the horn to warn a distracted jaywalker that the light had turned. The kid wore headphones and didn't even react. He kept crossing the busy street despite other cars honking at him much more aggressively.

Tom took in a long, frustrated breath. "Little..." He grunted.

Elenora brought down her visor to check on the back seat. Aubrey was still asleep, her head slumped to the side against her car seat. She would go on a stroll with Pierre while her mom and dad investigated the premises. Pierre had entered Elenora's life when she was a kid and had just lost her father. A retired police detective and eternal bachelor, he had become a father figure to her and took his duties as honorary grandfather very seriously.

"Now, what about the killer?" Tom asked. "You think we have another Barlow situation?"

"I sure hope not." Elenora wasn't ready to face another

murderous spirit wreaking havoc through an innocent person's body. Nor did she want Tom and Alex involved in a similar scenario.

"Here's an insane theory," he said. "You know how, in some action movies, the good guy and the bad guy grab each other while fighting, and they fall off a building together?"

"And keep fighting? Yeah. That's always so realistic."

"You said it looked like Marsan was lying on top of another person in the rosebushes. What if the mystery dude is a ghost that pushed Marsan to his death and got tangled up with him? What if he's the invisible force?"

"They would have fallen together from the attic?"

"That could explain them landing one on top of the other —and why you saw him, but he wasn't found at the scene."

Elenora had to blink at Tom's theory. "That kind of makes sense...if you ignore the insane part."

Tom's phone rang, and he hit the answer call button on the steering wheel. "Hey, Alex. What's up?"

"Hey. I'm at the house." Alex's voice came out rough and filled the car. He sounded tense.

Hopefully, he wouldn't wake Aubrey. Elenora pressed the volume down button a few times just to be on the safe side.

"Great. We just crossed Cavendish. We'll be there in five," Tom said.

"Okay. I'll wait for you in the car. Any thoughts on the case?"

Tom filled his partner in about the mystery limbs Elenora had seen under Marsan in her dream and told Alex his crazy theory.

Alex rolled with it. "So, this Mystery Rosebush Man would have died in the house—if he's haunting it, right?"

"Correct. And then Jérémie Marsan comes in, and then..." Tom grappled with what came next. "The ghost recognizes him?"

"Marsan killed Rosebush Guy?"

"Or maybe he was related to the killer," Elenora offered.

"And the ghost settled the score," Tom added.

Alex snickered. "Yeah, I can totally picture that. And since Marsan worked in construction, I bet it's Mafia-related. The ghost of a don did this."

Tom laughed. "Now we're getting somewhere!"

CHAPTER SEVEN

Montréal, 1972

"Hurry up, man! My nads are crawling up my throat." Wheezer Tremblay bounced from foot to foot to ward off the chilly, bone-seeping October air. He was a skinny guy with slicked-back hair held in place from lack of washing.

"You're so baked I'm surprised you can feel anything," Jean-Luc Rivard retorted, battling the rusty lock on the front door of the Maple Street house he'd just inherited from his asshole snake of a father.

He suspected the rest of the house would be consistent with the ornery lock. His dad had bought the run-down mammoth dwelling several years earlier and done diddly squat with it. Jean-Luc guessed he must have tried to use it for something shady, and the city had shut him down, forcing him to move on to his next scam. Typical of him.

Robert Nicolas Rivard had left the real estate piece of shit to his useless son in his will. Jean-Luc saw the gesture as his father's last *fuck you* to him, but he was determined to not let the joke be on him. He had big, devious plans for the creepy property. It would propel his acting career and notoriety to great heights, and nothing less.

Fuck you, too, Dad. Until I have time to go piss on your grave.

"It's just a manner of speaking," Wheezer slurred. "My balls are still where they should be. Just so you know."

Jean-Luc snorted and rolled his eyes. "My bad. I shouldn't have taken you literally."

The lock gave, and he rose back to his full height before rolling his head and shoulders. The porch's rotting planks whined under his weight. Jean-Luc Rivard was tall and well-built. He also had sinfully good looks and charisma to match.

He pushed on the door, expecting a loud and ominous creak, but it opened without protest. A throat-grabbing smell escaped from inside. In the faint light filtering in through the front door and the grime-coated windows, he could see particles of dust and surely something biohazardous saturating the air from floor to ceiling.

"After you." Jean-Luc invited Wheezer to go in.

His friend went inside without question, and Jean-Luc followed.

A massive staircase met them in the foyer. A parlor lay to the right, a corridor next to the stairs led to the back of the house, and a ballroom-sized room stood to the left.

"Man, it's dark in here," Wheezer complained.

Jean-Luc yanked a pair of sunglasses off his friend's face and shoved them against his chest.

The stoner grabbed the glasses, his vaporous gaze

squinting before sluggishly landing on the staircase. "Oh, look! There's another floor."

Jean-Luc rolled his eyes again and wondered why he'd bothered dragging his friend with him when he was higher than a kite on quaaludes. Wheezer was a lot of fun, but it took patience to remain chill with him when one was sober.

Marching into the ballroom, Jean-Luc took in a massive old-fashioned chandelier hanging in the middle of the ceiling. Its gaudy opulence clashed with the horrid wallpaper peeling off the walls. At the end of the room, a grand fireplace added another majestic touch. The house had dramatic flair. *A marriage of fancy and sinister*, Jean-Luc thought. It was perfect.

"How did the old bat croak?" Wheezer asked from behind him.

"Violently," Jean-Luc lied.

He knew the house's previous elderly owner had passed away peacefully in her sleep, which was a bummer. That made the odds of her haunting the house very slim. But no one had to know the truth, and Jean-Luc was intent on propagating the lie of a sensational death.

"Oh." Wheezer sobered up a notch.

Jean-Luc resumed checking out the place with his plans in mind. As a budding actor craving fame and fortune, he was frustrated that his career had not taken off despite his obscene handsomeness. With much time on his hands between rare theater and low-budget-film gigs, he was always looking for ways to get noticed and make things happen. What could he do to get some tabloid love? He needed a scandal to gain exposure.

A string of so-called satanic controversies had recently

rocked the music world and caught his attention. The public didn't seem to get enough of those sordid stories. Flirting with satanic worship seemed like a perfect answer. After all, it was all about theatrics, and he was pretty good at that.

Before long, Jean-Luc had gotten himself a copy of *The Satanic Bible* and *The Satanic Rituals* and appointed himself a high priest in the Church of Satan. He'd started performing black masses in his seedy apartment to a surprisingly large following that had kept on growing, even after he upped the cover charge. He'd had to add a second mass on Saturday nights. Business was booming. And the best perk of all: sex-starved female groupies lined up around the block to throw themselves at him. It was the beginning of his best life. He could feel it.

Soon, the rumors about his dark nature and dealings would spread around the right places. The phone would start ringing, and he would be in high demand for film work—at least for horror ones. He would become a cult figure.

And now that he owned a wonderfully macabre old house, he could make it all happen faster. No loser landlord could limit his ambitions anymore.

He and Wheezer entered a kitchen straight out of a time capsule.

"That doesn't creep you out?" Wheezer's uncomfortable gaze swept the room.

"What? The décor?"

"No. The old lady croaking in here."

"Why the hell would that creep me out?"

Wheezer's brittle attention went from dead little old ladies to the odd-looking fridge. "Whoa! You think this dinosaur still works?" He opened the door, stuck his head inside, and jerked back just as fast. "Jesus," he muttered, slamming the door. "This thing must have been used in a morgue."

Jean-Luc made a mental note to hunt down used appliances through the classifieds while Wheezer was busy inspecting the burners on the antique stove.

"I guess beers would be okay in there."

"In the oven?" Jean-Luc asked.

Wheezer dragged a confused gaze to Jean-Luc. "Hmm? What's in the oven?" He pulled the heavy appliance door down and stuck his head inside.

"Never mind." Jean-Luc absently turned on the cold-water tap. The gurgling banshee wail that shook the faucet made him reverse course quickly.

"You think we'll see her?" Wheezer asked.

"Who?"

"The old lady."

"I'm counting on it."

"Yeah, okay. But that's creepy, right?"

"Creepy's great."

Creepy attracts. Creepy sells. He'd been thinking of renting a few of the bedrooms to friends. But maybe he ought to keep some as nightly rentals and charge even more. Sell a full macabre experience to gullible rich kids who would pay good money for the thrill of spending the night in a haunted house right after worshiping the devil. Maybe he could franchise the concept.

He was so done being a starving artist.

A second doorway in the kitchen led them back to the main hallway. Jean-Luc noticed a set of stairs going down to the basement. He knew the house didn't have power, and he'd come prepared. He fished a flashlight out of his back-pack, flicked it on, and headed down with his friend on his heels.

As expected, the basement was pitch dark. The flash-light's round beam highlighted the stone walls, giving the place a dungeon-like feel. *Jackpot!*

Jean-Luc felt a shiver of excitement as he walked into the main room. He could picture it all—candles spread on the floor around the room, the gothic atmosphere, him and his disciples wearing hooded robes, their chants echoing against the walls to a chilling effect.

He pointed his flashlight at the floor. He would draw a pentacle right there. He could already hear the gasps.

A genius idea hit him. He would rig a pouch of fake blood inside his sleeve, pretend to cut his wrist, and pour the blood over the sign as if offering himself to Satan. The crowd would be floored.

"This room is beyond perfect," Jean-Luc said with awe.

"Yeah, man. A TV over there, beanbag chairs over here, and we're all set for hockey."

CHAPTER EIGHT

"Where's Céleste?" Elenora asked Pierre as she set up the stroller on the sidewalk. He rarely went anywhere without his faithful German shepherd sidekick.

Pierre jerked his head toward the crime scene house. "Doing some recon for you," he said tongue in cheek before whistling.

The dog emerged from the tall grass of the unkempt front lawn and trotted his way. While Pierre was joking, Céleste was a decorated retired K9 who had also assisted him in paranormal investigations.

"You guys go ahead. I've got this," he said and went to retrieve Aubrey from her car seat.

She greeted him with a squeal of delight.

Elenora tapped her daughter gently on the nose. "You behave, missy."

Noticing Céleste, Aubrey ignored her mother and squealed again.

"Thank you, Pierre."

"Always a pleasure."

Elenora joined Tom and Alex, and the three of them waded through an assortment of weeds to the property's backyard. She took in the faded majesty of the battered house. Its stunning architecture featured a wraparound porch and two turrets. Gables and dormers broke up its steep roofline. The place must have looked magnificent back in the day.

Through the backyard's overgrown vegetation, it took Elenora a moment to locate the yellow tape cordoning off a row of thick and unruly rosebushes. She recognized the fatal spot where Jérémie Marsan had landed. A cluster of crushed branches at the top made it even more obvious.

Elenora put on a pair of gloves, looking forward to testing a new mental trick Yukiko had given her to "suck" info through latex and read surfaces despite the challenging presence of the gloves. The technique was similar to the radio receiver one: focus on the feel of the latex against her hand and mentally dial it down.

She laid her right palm on top of the damaged rosebush, closed her eyes, and implemented the trick. An image of Jérémie Marsan's lifeless body draped over the shrub appeared before her. *Yes! It worked!*

The young man's appearance and position matched those in her premonition. She focused on the current vision, trying to perceive any feeling or additional information, but she learned nothing new.

She looked down in front of the bush, and the mysterious extra set of arms from the premonition came into view. They lay over the ground and stuck out from under the rosebush at its base. The mystery victim was several feet under Jérémie Marsan, not right below the young construction worker, as

Elenora had initially thought. The arms were covered in long once-white sleeves in a fashion that was not recent. The hands were large and masculine. The victim was likely a man from a distant past.

If the two victims were from different times, she must have been having two separate visions at once. One on top of the other. That was a first.

Elenora kneeled to further study the unknown victim and reached for the closest arm to get a read, but her hand went right through it. She felt around on the ground under the two limbs, but nothing came to her.

Hmm.

Her gaze followed the arms toward the rosebush. Lowering herself and craning her neck, she saw the top of a headful of dark curls. She moved a few branches aside for a better view.

"Ow!" A jolt of pain made her yank her hand away from the bush. The hasty movement caused even more pain. Her eyes flew open, and she took in the pricks and scratches on her hand.

"What happened?" Tom barked with concern. Ever since Elenora's near-fatal visionary close calls with Barlow, he was quick to assume the worst. "Is it the vision?"

"Just a bunch of thorns. I love roses, but holy fudge..." The scratches on her hand bled inside the glove. Splotches of crimson bloomed under the latex. Elenora looked away. She was getting better at handling the sight of blood, but it still made her uncomfortable and potentially queasy.

"I'll go get my first aid kit." Alex headed to his car.

"Thanks, Alex!"

"Did you see Marsan?" Tom asked, and Elenora told him

what she saw.

"Maybe the mystery guy's buried under the bushes," he said.

Elenora nodded. That could make sense.

She crouched again, laying her uninjured hand over the ground, mindful not to touch anything prickly. Shutting her eyes, she made herself see past the glove again. She then willed herself to see underneath the grass. She even visualized a shovel digging a grave, but no image or clue came to her.

"We'll need a shovel if we want answers." She reopened her eyes and stood.

Alex was back, and his big fingers fiddled with the tiny plastic latches on the first aid kit.

"'Kay. Gimme your hand," Tom told Elenora.

She looked away when he peeled off the blood-soaked glove.

Alex planted himself in front of her. "What do you need a shovel for?"

"Tom thinks maybe our mystery victim is buried under the bushes." Elenora felt a cool sting and winced as Tom swept a cleaning wipe over her wounds.

"I'll ask Renaud to send Krenz and Houde." Alex whipped out his cell.

"You think he and Marsan died the same way?" Tom asked Elenora.

Another sting made her grimace. "You want my opinion for real, or are you just trying to distract me?"

Tom chuckled. "Both?"

Another sting. She looked up at the opening in the attic's exterior wall. The plastic sheet covering it flapped in the light breeze. She studied the trajectory between the hole and the rosebushes in search of an answer, but her gut was silent.

"You can look now." Tom let go of her hand and offered her a clean glove. She carefully slid it on over the bandages.

"The two bodies are so close to one another that they could have been pushed the same way from the attic," Elenora said. "But the deaths seemed to have occurred at vastly different moments in time. So, what are the odds?"

"You think it's a stretch that one killer pulled the same maneuver twice?" Done texting, Alex analyzed the trajectory from attic to rosebush as well.

"I couldn't get a good look at the guy under the bushes, but judging from his clothing, I'd say he's been dead a long time," she replied.

"A few years? Decades?" Tom asked.

"At least decades. A century, maybe."

"Great. Here we go again with historical creeps," Alex grumbled. "Any chance the first guy jumped?"

"A suicide?" she asked.

"Yeah. Or just fell—an accident. Maybe this is just a very weird coincidence."

"Is that what your gut's telling you, Alex?"

Alex might not have had psychic powers, but like Tom, he had sharp instincts. He let out a long sigh. "Not really. I just..."

"You just wished this was a straightforward murder," Tom quipped.

"How d'you know?" Alex asked dryly.

"A murder that didn't require bringing in a witch or two as consultants," Tom added.

Alex groaned. "Not if we can help it."

CHAPTER NINE

"Now, *that's* a man cave." Alex whistled as he took in the basement's main room.

The stylish sconces adorning the stone walls had just flicked to life, shedding elegant lighting on the empty yet rich-looking space. The beautiful hardwood floor was...desecrated by a giant pentacle carved in the middle of it, as if someone had used a wood-burning kit. The smooth grooves were stained deep red.

"Oh, hell! I take it back." Alex recoiled after spotting the occult symbol in which Jean-Luc Rivard, the satanic cult leader, had been found dead decades earlier.

The trio stared at the pentacle in baffled silence.

Alex shook his head, a pained scowl on his face. "Okay, one word: why?"

He loved to work with his hands and do woodwork. It bothered Elenora to see an exquisite wood floor trashed that way, but it must have stung Alex even more.

"I agree," Tom commiserated.

Elenora pushed herself to move past her outrage and

focus on the task at hand. They had decided to comb the house from basement to attic, and when they'd come in from the side entrance a moment earlier, a strange sensation had greeted her. The air had seemed muffled, as if thick with humidity while remaining dry. This contradiction had muddled her brain, and she'd tried to shake off the bizarre impression. But it had lingered. Then, when she'd entered the room with the pentacle, the sensation had intensified.

"According to the file, this is where the original owner of the house had his infamous postmortem photography studio," Tom said.

Elenora glanced around the room, still trying to make sense of the persisting heavy atmosphere. The space was empty, and yet it felt full. Death had permeated the basement in two distinct eras—first, when the departed clients were photographed, and then when Rivard died—but those events had occurred a long time ago. Even so, had the essence of death been lingering since, making the air peculiar?

Or a spirit?

Elenora watched for any warm chill or other sensation, but the air's thickness was the only noticeable thing. She remembered Yukiko telling her that sometimes, elements from the past left traces behind, and as Elenora gained more control over her abilities and sensed nuances better, she might pick up on those vestiges. Maybe that was all it was.

Or maybe the basement needed a good dehumidifier.

She took careful steps toward the pentacle.

"You're gonna try to read it?" Tom looked ambivalent.

"Yeah."

"You sure?"

"Yup."

She crouched by the imposing symbol, and Tom came to stand near her, alert. Alex put his hand on his gun.

Bracing herself for horrific images, Elenora touched the floor inside the pentacle. A muted vision appeared in her mind, offering her a series of hard-to-make-out eclectic tableaux. People in dark hooded cloaks, she guessed. A rubber goat's head? Candles scattered around the room, orange flames flickering in the dark. People passing a bong around—maybe. A young man laughing hysterically next to another guy eating noodles with chopsticks from a takeout container—weirdly, *that* image was clear. But the background was vague and looked like a mountain of flesh and intertwined limbs rocking.

The images were jarring and veiled. Elenora struggled to get clearer pictures, concentrating harder on seeing past the latex barrier of the glove. But that was all the clarity she got. It seemed as if someone had dumped a gallon of bleach over her brain to wash out what she was attempting to see. This interference reminded her of how Barlow's spirit had clouded her visions—not quite the same, but similar.

The images ceased, leaving Elenora with her mental depiction of the pentacle. She realized she hadn't seen Jean-Luc Rivard's dead body. Keeping her eyes closed, she shifted to the center of the pentacle and placed her palms against the floor.

A faint gory image of the lifeless young man surged in her mind, matching the picture she'd had the displeasure of seeing in his file. He lay dead, his facial expression frozen in a mask of fear, his naked torso streaked with blood underneath his hooded cloak that flapped open.

Eager to rid her mind of the gruesome depiction, Elenora

moved her hand around to swap it with a different insight but ended up with another dual vision. Like a double exposure, the fuzzy image of a mustached man in dapper clothes came into sight over Rivard's bloodied corpse. He stood next to a vintage camera perched on a wooden tripod with a black cloth at the back.

The photographer?

The superimposed images vanished, and Elenora crawled around the pentacle, searching for more. But that was it. She told Tom and Alex what she'd just seen. "Most of the images were clouded and hectic. I wonder if something or someone is interfering with my mind. Hopefully, Serena will make sense of the disjointed flashes."

Serena possessed a particular form of transmission magic. She could capture visions straight out of Elenora's mind and translate them into playable video files. This unusual psychic collaboration between the two women made them a formidable duo.

"Did you see Rivard committing a crime in the name of Satan among those flashes?" Tom scribbled in his notepad.

"No. And except for seeing him dead, I can't say I got a good look at him in the other flashes. It was hard to identify any of the figures. Though he may have been one of them."

"What about the photographer?" Alex asked. "Was it Joseph Gill? Or one of Rivard's cult weirdos taking pictures of their...whatever you'd call their shit?"

"I think it was more likely Joseph Gill. His clothes were refined and old-fashioned, and the photography equipment was the furthest you can get from a Polaroid camera."

"And you saw him appear behind Rivard, you said?" Tom raised a perplexed eyebrow.

"No. I mean, I saw him overlaid with Rivard. Those were two separate flashes from different timelines. Like the ones of Jérémie Marsan and the rosebush man."

"Right." He nodded thoughtfully.

Alex surveyed the room suspiciously and cleared his throat. "Did you feel any kind of spiritual presence?"

"No, I didn't sense a presence—not that I'm an expert," Elenora replied.

Alex's question reminded her of the air's peculiarity. It still felt oddly heavy.

"Hold on." She closed her eyes to focus on the atmosphere. Stretching her arms in front of herself to avoid walking into a wall, she went around the room with her senses wide open, ready to welcome other visions or just about anything.

As she walked along the back wall, she got another flash of the photographer behind the same camera a few feet away from her. The vision lingered, giving Elenora time to explore it. She noticed a plushness underneath her sandals and glanced down to see a tasteful rug covering a large area of the floor.

Looking around, she saw a row of narrow wooden chairs lined against a back wall across the room. Closer to her was an elegant brocade armchair, and a painted backdrop hung behind it. She turned back toward the photographer, but he and the camera had vanished. She found herself back in the room with Tom and Alex.

"I'm pretty sure the photographer is Joseph Gill."

"You saw him again?"

"Yes. And his studio. He had a fancy chair right over here. And a lavish backdrop. The room looked swanky. But that's all I got."

Tom gave her arm a little squeeze. "Thanks. You're doing great. How do you feel?"

"I'm good."

Alex disappeared into an adjoining room, and they followed him. The good-sized windowless room had sinks and work surfaces, damask wallpaper, wood shelves, and spider webs.

Something must have caught Alex's eye, for he quickly crossed to a wall lined with shelves, a giant frown creasing his face. He skimmed a hand over a minute straight line that somehow blended in with the intricate wallpaper pattern. Taking his key chain out, he sank the tip of a key into the tiny crack and pulled—a hidden door swung open. Behind it, a small cavity contained a portable safe with a combination lock.

Elenora gasped in surprise. "How did you know about this?"

"Dumb luck. Wallpaper's a bitch to put up. I was just admiring the seamless craftsmanship when I noticed the fissure." Grinning with satisfaction, Alex retrieved the little black safe.

"Awesome catch, man," Tom said with a matching grin.

Alex put the safe down on the nearest surface, tried to open it, and soon blew out a breath of frustration. "Of course it's locked. Why did I even bother thinking today might not suck after all? Is Bacon back from vacation?"

François Bacon was a colleague at the precinct with a street past and creative techniques. The safe would be putty in his talented hands.

"If not, I'm sure Serena would be happy to help," Tom teased.

Alex groaned.

"Let me see if I can get anything from it." Elenora touched the safe and felt a jolt of pride, followed by a sense of familiarity with the receptacle, even though she couldn't possibly have seen the century-old model before. Still, her fingers itched to turn the dial. As if muscle memory had kicked in, she entered a combination, and the lock clicked open. "Okaaaaay..." she said, bewildered.

Alex gave her a freaked-out look and stepped back.

"I'm not possessed," Elenora insisted, wondering if she should add *anymore*. Because seriously, what the hell was that? Had she channeled the owner of the safe?

"How about we worry later?" Tom suggested, opening the safe's door.

Delicately, he retrieved its contents: a collection of artistic black-and-white pictures, some in daguerreotype form, others on photo paper. There were families and single subjects, from infants to seniors. The grandiose brocade chair Elenora had seen appeared in all the pictures. And there was another constant: everyone looked solemn.

The antithesis of the modern selfie.

"Man, people were uptight back then. Or creepy. Or both." Alex was looking over Tom's shoulder at the photos.

"Didn't they have to pose for a long time? It's easier to hold a blank look than a smile," Tom replied.

"Sure, but it's still creepy. I mean, look at her."

Alex pointed at a young brunette with a sophisticated hairdo and a haunting look. She was sitting in the brocade chair and flanked by a handful of men who seemed related to her. Her eyes held an intense uneasiness.

"If this picture was taken today, I'd tell you someone in that room is abusing her."

Elenora could only agree with Alex's observation. The young woman lived in an era where abuse must have happened just the same as it did these days, except maybe behind a thicker veneer of politeness. What had happened to her? Elenora empathized with the woman in the photo, but her concerns about the stranger's well-being were a century too late. Still, Elenora couldn't help feeling for her and wondering about her story.

"May I?" She held out her hand for the picture, and Tom gave it to her.

Upon contact with the photograph, a muted sense of distress—*grief?*—echoed through Elenora. But no clue emerged about the brunette. She tried to push deeper into the vision but came up empty. She gave the picture back to Tom.

Alex rubbed his chin. "I thought Gill took pictures of dead people. These folks all look normal to me. Maybe these are exceptions?"

"Not this one." Tom pointed at the portrait of a baby propped against a cascading dark velvet drape. A barely noticeable pair of hands in dark gloves stuck out of folds in the fabric and held the little one in place. "Someone's holding the baby from behind."

"Huh. Imagine that."

"And the baby's staring at the camera," Tom added. "I don't think anyone could instruct a living infant to stare at a lens for a long time and remain still. I bet it was touched up."

Alex shook his head. "What a bunch of weirdos."

Tom put the pictures back in the safe, and Alex tucked it under his arm. While the pictures might not be evidence of either Jérémie Marsan's death or Jean-Luc Rivard's, they shouldn't remain forgotten in a musty basement. Once the investigation was over, the owner of the house could decide their fate. Elenora hoped the owner would be open to donating them to a museum.

They headed up the stairs to investigate the main floor, where most rooms were also bare, save for the odd stepladder and construction equipment and supplies scattered around. Several walls were covered with floral, damask, or other elaborately patterned wallpapers that seemed original to the house. Other walls were sloppily painted with eye-gouging color schemes, a tribute to people's questionable taste in the seventies.

The kitchen took the cake with its mismatched avocado, pea-soup, and rust-colored appliances and its beer-barf-friendly linoleum floor tiles that lifted and curled in a few places. The walls fought back with more wallpaper in a purple-and-pink palette and the occasional spot of grease. The picture of a sad clown painted on a velvet canvas was the only thing missing.

"Why didn't they start the demo in this room?" Alex's expression of disdainful horror said he wasn't entirely joking.

"They're masochists?" Tom tried, amused.

Alex turned to Elenora and made a sweeping motion with his hand. "Are you getting anything from this? Other than nausea?"

Elenora roamed her gloved hands over key surfaces in the kitchen then shook her head. "Nothing. Except the air feels less thick now." It was easier to breathe, and she liked that.

After checking a severely outdated powder room and two uneventful bedrooms on the main floor, they headed up the stairs to the second floor, where they inspected a master bedroom with an en suite, four other bedrooms, and two bathrooms.

They went up another floor. Elenora recognized the attic from her vision and got a dreadful feeling of déjà vu. She kept a safe distance from the plastic sheet dancing over the missing window's opening.

Alex headed straight for the wall where Jérémie Marsan had swung his sledgehammer right before his death. Tom joined him, and Elenora approached carefully.

"Marsan hit the wall here?" Alex pointed at a spiderweb of cracks in the plaster.

She nodded.

He frowned. "Are you sure he gave it a full swing? That's barely a scratch."

"It looked like he did."

Elenora shut her eyes and ran her fingers over the slightly caved-in point of impact. Blurry, dark elements flashed in her mind. She tried to bring the cryptic images into focus, but they refused to sharpen. Suddenly, she felt light, like she was floating, and a strong breeze licked her bare skin.

"Elenora!"

Tom's strangled scream jolted her back to reality. He and Alex towered over her, both holding her by the wrists. It took a moment for Elenora's brain to register what had happened. A chill ran through her as she realized she was dangling outside from the gaping hole in the attic.

And the two men were the only thing preventing her from falling.

CHAPTER TEN

Elenora had faced several fears and close calls in the past year, but few could rival the stomach-dropping feeling of being a hair away from free-falling to one's doom.

Fortunately, before she had a chance to hyperventilate, Tom and Alex got a better grasp on her arms and pulled her back inside the house. To safety. Assuming whatever fresh hell had just happened wouldn't happen again.

As her feet landed on the attic floor, Elenora's fight-or-flight instinct kicked in. Her body attempted to flee from the invisible threat, but her legs went limp, and she stumbled. Tom slid an arm around her in a grip that suggested he would never let go and slung her arm around his neck. Alex did the same, and they led her to the staircase.

"What happened? What's going on?" she asked, her voice unsteady, as they lumbered down the stairs. Her legs started working again, and her mind revved to make sense of what had occurred while she was lost in that latest vision. She had been mostly unaware of the world outside of it.

"We're calling in the witches, and you're going home." Tom's breathing was ragged, and he was beside himself.

By the time they reached the second-floor landing, Alex had recovered enough to give her an explanation. "It was fucking freaky. Kinda like what you said happened to the construction kid. You touched the wall, then you got thrown across the room—like the wall gave you an epic shove but without it moving. It doesn't even make sense." He threw a guarded look over his shoulder, as if expecting their mystery attacker to have overheard him and come after them.

They picked up speed and went down the rest of the stairs in silence. On the last flight, they heard a baby fussing through the front door.

Aubrey?

Footsteps stomped on the front porch, and the protest grew louder. Elenora's heart skipped a beat. Her daughter shouldn't be near this place. She dislodged herself from Tom and Alex's hold and flew down the remaining stairs. She couldn't let Aubrey enter the house.

"She's just hungry, love!" Tom yelled after her. "Slow down!"

The front door creaked open, and a cold chill passed through Elenora as she landed on the last step. Pierre peeked his head inside.

"Don't come in!" she shrieked.

Calmly, Pierre stepped back onto the porch. Elenora followed him outside, scooped Aubrey out of his arms, and fled until she reached the sidewalk. Only then did she allow herself to breathe.

The sudden sprint had quieted Aubrey, who was now staring at her mother with wide eyes. Elenora let out a sob and a chuckle that further confused the baby. She held her daughter closer and swayed from side to side to reassure them both and keep her daughter from seeing her nervous tears.

"Mommy missed you. Did you have an awesome stroll with Grandpapa?" she asked into the baby's hair, using a falsely chirpy voice.

Pierre's comforting hand stroked her back.

She freed one hand to wipe her tears before handing Aubrey to Tom. "Here, go see Daddy."

Tom took Aubrey, and while he wasn't crying, he still looked white-knuckled. He, too, forced himself to put up a happy front for his daughter.

Alex ran a hand through his hair, mussing it. "I guess that solves how Jérémie Marsan died." His tone was a mix of sarcasm and dread.

"I gather you had a special kind of fun in there?" Pierre asked, at once sympathetic and eager to know more.

Céleste sat at his feet, alert, her eyes intent on the house.

"This place ought to be burned to the ground, bombed, excavated, filled with a fuckton of concrete, and have a fifty-foot-high wall built around it. Then, the whole neighborhood should be exorcised for good measure," Alex spat. He soccer-kicked a pebble, sending it flying an impressive distance down the sidewalk.

"We need surveillance on this place. We can't risk anyone wandering in there for whatever reason." Tom had regained parts of his usual calm and wits.

Alex reached for his cell. "On it. I'll also warn Krenz and Houde to stick to the backyard."

"Guys, you're killing me. What happened?" Pierre asked.

"Who the fuck really knows," Alex mumbled while texting.

Tom told Pierre about the freak incident in the attic. Pierre's face darkened, and his hand landed on Elenora's back again.

"Thank God for Alex's quick reflexes," Tom said grimly. "He caught Elenora's arm the second she flew away from the wall."

"Yeah, but I let go." Alex sounded guilty. Leave it to him to feel bad even when he saved the world.

"She *slipped* from your grasp. You slowed her down and dove for her before I even realized what the hell was going on." Tom choked on his words. "Thanks to you, we got a good grip on her and prevented her from..."

Instead of finishing his sentence, he moved Aubrey to his hip and pulled Alex into a one-armed hug, which his partner returned awkwardly. Tom's shoulders shook with a few sobs. Alex patted his friend's back as he struggled to keep a hold on his own emotions.

"How dreadful. How are you feeling?" Pierre asked Elenora quietly.

She had rarely seen such concern in his eyes. "I'm still in a daze, but I was immersed in a vision when it happened, so I wasn't even aware. I felt like I was floating, and the next thing I knew, I was dangling over thin air. It happened so fast—I didn't even have time to freak out."

It suited her just fine that she hadn't consciously experienced her near fall, but she realized that losing track of reality had made her body vulnerable. That was a new kind of scary. She would have to keep her safety in mind whenever she provoked a vision, especially in treacherous locations.

A cocktail of emotions overwhelmed her, and she sat down on the curb. She had to remind herself to stay calm, if only for Aubrey's sake. After all, as scary as the close call had been, she hadn't fallen to her death, just like she hadn't been hit by a bus. She couldn't dwell on what could have happened—that was unhealthy. Though, to be fair, normal people rarely had to worry about being thrown out of a giant hole in an attic by...what? A possessed wall? An angry ghost?

"Would you say a ghost did this?" Elenora asked Pierre.

He had experienced an array of paranormal events during his off-the-books collaborations with the OPO.

"It sounds like it could be a poltergeist. You were physically assaulted, and something similar happened to the construction worker."

"A poltergeist? You mean like the movie?" Alex asked.

"Yeah, kinda like the movie."

Tom looked thoughtful. "Could a poltergeist have possessed the coworker?"

"I don't think so, but I could be wrong. If I've learned anything while dealing with the paranormal, it's to never assume that anything is clear-cut. But if you're considering a possession theory for the coworker..." Pierre's gaze skated between Tom and Alex. "Then, logically, one of you would have pushed Ele, no?"

Tom and Alex looked at one another before they both said, "He didn't do it."

"That might answer the question, then." Pierre sat down next to Elenora. "Was there anyone else in the house? Did you feel a presence?"

"I didn't sense anyone." Elenora filled him in about the

oddly thick air, the visions she'd had in the basement, and the photographs they'd found.

Alex suddenly dashed to his car and retrieved a tire iron from the trunk. He stalked back toward the house purposefully. Céleste followed him, keeping up with the detective's brisk pace.

"You're not going back in there, are you?" Tom called after him.

Alex shook his head and held up a hold-on-a-minute finger. His shoulders were tense—it was obvious he would rather be doing anything else, but the man was highly driven by his sense of duty.

Elenora, Tom, and Pierre watched him with curiosity as he opened the front door with caution, crouched, and slid the tire iron inside the house. Sticking close to him, Céleste assumed a defensive stance, ready to defend him.

"What the hell is he doing?" Pierre asked.

Realization dawned on Tom's face. "He's retrieving the safe. He left it by the door when we went upstairs."

Tom had guessed right. Alex soon came back, scowling and carrying the safe at arm's length like it was radioactive. He put it in his trunk and slammed the lid shut, as if that would add a layer of protection.

"On top of your security patrol, maybe someone from the OPO should secure the hole in the attic with plywood and magic," Pierre suggested to Tom. "I can give 'em a call."

"That'd be awesome, Pierre. Thank you. We also need to bring them on the case. I'm gonna ask the chief once my heart attack's over."

"I'll talk to Serena." Pierre got on the phone.

Aubrey started fussing. Elenora absently pulled the

diaper bag from the storage net under the stroller and took out a bottle of breast milk she'd pumped earlier. The baby tracked her movements and flailed her arms to speed up the delivery. When things didn't move fast enough for her taste, she squirmed in Tom's arms, trying to launch herself out of his grasp.

"Hey, girl! Cool your tiny jets!" Tom grabbed the bottle Elenora offered him and plugged it into the voracious little face. "Every. Single. Time. You'd think the world was ending. I wish I had that much passion."

Elenora cracked up. Aubrey's hilariously dramatic antics were a welcome relief to the stress they had just experienced.

"Jérémie Marsan's colleague will be at the precinct in about an hour to speak with us," Alex announced, looking up from his phone.

"Are you gonna try to read him?" Pierre asked as Elenora zipped the diaper bag shut.

"Why should I try to read him?" she replied, curious. "The only living person I've ever successfully read was Rolland when he was possessed. You think a poltergeist might have possessed the coworker, after all?" Her gut twisted. She couldn't deal with another Barlow.

Pierre shook his head. "No. I was just thinking that since the colleague was also in the attic when it happened, maybe his subconscious picked up on something before Marsan got attacked—or during the attack itself. Something he couldn't articulate to Tom and Alex. I assume he's traumatized and trying to make heads or tails of what he witnessed. Maybe you can *see* what he experienced."

"Call me dense, but didn't Ele just say she can't read regular people?" Alex looked genuinely puzzled.

A slow smile appeared on Pierre's face. "I know. But one, her abilities are evolving, and two, at worst, she can read objects, right?"

"Right..."

"The guy's forearm might have nothing to tell, but what if his watch has something to say? Even if it's a long shot."

"Better a long shot than no shot at all," Tom mused.

Hmm. Pierre had an interesting point. Maybe it was worth a try. Anything that could get them a clue and prevent more attacks was worth a try.

But how weird and unprofessional would it look for her to touch a stranger who didn't know about her powers, especially in an environment of authority? A stranger would probably consider her a fraud if he found out what she was doing. And how would this even work without telling him she was psychic?

"You've just had a huge shock. No one will think less of you if you'd rather sit this one out and go home," Tom said, giving her an out.

Going home sounded tempting, and Elenora's near-death experience had left her shaken, so maybe she couldn't think straight. Maybe Tom was right to encourage her to go home. But if she went home, she would replay the close call in her head and torture herself with wondering if her special kind of help could have made a difference with the witness. She would regret not trying.

"What would I tell the witness?"

They'd pondered the question before and had found no good answer. Tom, Pierre, and Alex all scrambled for a reply.

"Do you *want* to meet with the witness, Ele?" Alex asked.

"I think so."

"Then screw it. Just tell him the truth if you have to. What's he gonna do? Refuse to comply in a police station? Report you?"

"Nora, most people wouldn't believe that you're psychic, anyway," Pierre added. "At worst, they'd think you have a few screws loose. Can you live with that?"

Other than coming across as professional, Elenora didn't usually care much about what other people thought of her. But she wasn't keen on looking like an impostor at her workplace. She would have to pray the witness wouldn't report her.

Tom read her mind. "If you're worried about the witness complaining, it would be his word against mine and Alex's. And the chief already knows. So, we're talking colleagues here, and they think too highly of you to let a weird rumor affect their opinions of you."

"Yeah, it would take a lot more than a crazy accusation from a witness to hurt your credibility or destroy your reputation. People love you. If anything, he'd be the one looking like a loon," Alex added.

But it would be awkward, she wanted to argue but realized how absurd she was being. Yes, it would be uncomfortable and embarrassing to reveal herself to a stranger. But no one had ever died from awkwardness. Whereas someone else could die if they didn't put an end to the murderous threat in the old house, pronto.

"All right. Let's get this show on the road," Elenora declared before collapsing the stroller.

CHAPTER ELEVEN

In one of the precinct interrogation rooms, Elenora sat next to Tom and Alex, across from Harold Sanschagrin, Jérémie Marsan's coworker who had witnessed the baffling attack. He was a big man in his fifties and quietly nervous. Elenora knew a police environment often put people on edge, even witnesses with nothing to hide—or psychics on the verge of revealing their deepest secret.

"Were you wearing this watch on the day of the accident?" she asked him.

"Yeah. Only got the one."

"May I touch it?" Her words made her cringe. She sounded like a fortune teller at a fair.

"Sure?" He gave her a wary look and began to unfasten his watch.

"No, please keep it on."

He stopped and shot her another wary look. At least he was cooperating.

Elenora took a deep breath and tried to ignore the embarrassment burning her cheeks. Tom gave her an encouraging smile, and Alex, a you-got-this nod.

Come on. Get a grip.

Under Mr. Sanschagrin's scrutinizing gaze, she hovered her hand over his watch and stretched her fingers so she would touch both the watch and his wrist, hesitant to lower her hand. The man's breath hitched. Her eyes flew to his face, and she saw him flinch—she was freaking him out. The poor man was already traumatized enough, and she was making things worse. It was unfair of her. She took her hand away. She had to reassure him, and that meant telling him what she was doing. There was no way around it.

Dammit... Okay, here goes nothing.

"Mr. Sanschagrin, let me explain what I'm doing. I assure you I'm not gonna hurt you. You see, I... I'm sensitive to the paranormal," she confessed. "By touching your watch—and your arm—I'm hoping to get an insight into what happened to Mr. Marsan. This could help solve his case and prevent another tragedy."

There. She'd said it. Out loud.

Did she feel any better? The jury was still out.

Did she feel any worse? Not really, come to think of it.

She waited for Mr. Sanschagrin to laugh in her face or recoil in disdain or express outrage at such a blatant fraud taking place in a police precinct. Instead, his eyes became glassy, and his bottom lip quivered.

"The paranormal..." he whispered. "You mean, you don't think I'm insane?"

"I don't think you're insane."

"The first cops I talked to sure thought I was. They're sure

I did it. They didn't believe a word I told them and said I needed to see a shrink. But I swear, I told them the truth. I just can't explain what happened. What I saw was...not possible."

Elenora nodded. "I understand. I saw what you saw."

"You *what?*" His eyes bugged in disbelief.

"I had a premonition about what happened."

He blinked at her for a moment before becoming hopeful. "So, it really *was* some paranormal shit?"

"What happened is very hard to explain, indeed." Elenora weighed her words carefully. "We are not ruling anything out yet, including a paranormal event."

"I'm not crazy?"

She shook her head. "You're not crazy."

A smile of extreme relief broke over his anxious face.

He might not be crazy, but he's gonna be scarred for life.

His relief would be temporary. How would he ever get over the trauma of what he'd seen and of knowing he'd had a brush with the paranormal? What therapist would believe his tall tale and truly help him? Give him proper therapy? Elenora imagined most would placate him and medicate the crap out of him.

The man faced an impossible problem. And leaving him to fend for himself wasn't right. But how could she help him?

What does the OPO do with civilians who witness paranormal activity?

Elenora resolved to ask Serena and find a solution.

"If it's okay, I'm going to touch your watch and your arm now," she said to Mr. Sanschagrin, returning to what she could do for the moment.

He eagerly slid his arm closer to her. She smiled at him and placed her hand over his watch and wrist. Closing her eyes, she made herself receptive, searching for images, memories, and feelings. For signs of evil or negativity too. But she only sensed the man's trepidation, mostly from the vibrations of his fidgeting leg.

"Mr. Sanschagrin, please tell me about Jérémie," she said, keeping her eyes closed.

She heard him shift in his seat and recognized the grief in his gravelly voice.

"He was a good kid despite his past. Didn't have it easy. He worked hard and loved to make people laugh. It's—" His voice broke, and he coughed. "It's such a shame, what happened to him." He didn't go on.

Elenora opened her eyes. His gaze bored into hers expectantly, but she had nothing. Damn, she wished she had something.

What if she refreshed his memory? Could it stir a vision?

"Now, please close your eyes, and tell me what you saw," she requested gently.

Mr. Sanschagrin nodded and did as asked. He recounted what he'd seen, and Elenora willed her mind to stand in his shoes and see the facts from his perspective. She resorted to every mental trick she had learned so far, but none yielded results.

Ultimately, the only impressions she got came from her good ol' empathetic intuition. The man was truly baffled by his colleague's freak accident and grieving Jérémie's sudden departure. She was convinced that as they had suspected, he was telling the truth and uninvolved in the young man's demise. The tragedy had deeply affected him, and he needed help.

She removed her hand. "You may open your eyes now, Mr. Sanschagrin. Thank you so much for trusting me."

He grunted. His eyes opened, and once again, his hopeful stare snapped to hers. "What did you see?"

Elenora held back a sigh. "I'm afraid I saw nothing. But I believe you. *We*"—she made a sweeping gesture to include Tom and Alex—"believe you. You are not crazy."

His smile didn't quite conceal a hint of disappointment, but he was still grateful. "That means a lot to me. Thank you."

She squeezed his hand. "We will work hard to understand what happened."

"Given the peculiar nature of this case, we hope you'll understand if we ask you to please remain discreet about what was said in this room," Tom said.

"Of course."

Elenora slipped Mr. Sanschagrin her card. "What you went through was exceptional and no doubt traumatic. Please contact me if you need to talk." At the very least, she could lend him a sympathetic, nonjudgmental ear.

He took the card. "Appreciate it."

She stood. "Detective Madigan, may I have a quick word?"

Tom got up and followed her out to the hallway.

"You got nothing, huh?" Tom asked in a low voice once the door clicked shut behind them.

"Nothing paranormal, but I'm convinced he's innocent and as traumatized as you and Alex were when you saw what happened to me earlier. I suspect he doesn't know anything more about the manifestation than either of you do."

Tom winced. "Sorry you came here and revealed yourself for nothing."

"It wasn't for nothing."

Revealing herself had yielded a surprising outcome. Harold Sanschagrin's reaction had reassured her, and his singular plight had confirmed she was in a unique position to help—to make a difference.

Tom playfully searched her face for clues. "Jeez, that wasn't cryptic at all. What did I miss?"

She chuckled. "Nothing affecting the case. I'll tell you later."

"'Kay. Let me finish in there before you guys leave." Tom moved to slip back into the interrogation room.

"Oh, hey." Elenora stopped him as something occurred to her. "He mentioned a shrink. Did they recommend a psych eval?"

"Yeah, but we're calling the shots now. I'm not sure an eval will be necessary."

"Good. 'Cause I don't think it's a good idea for someone to see him just yet. You know I love Julie, and she's great, but I can imagine what she'd think of him. I don't think we want to go there. Maybe the OPO is better equipped."

"I agree. Let's keep that option on the back burner for now." Tom jerked his head toward the door. "I better go back in."

"Go. I'll stick around."

Elenora looked for Pierre. She found him sitting on a bench down the hall with Aubrey on his lap and Céleste at his feet. He was chatting with Detective David Demontigny, who was a nice guy but a bit of a barnacle. The detective spotted her and waved. She waved back.

"Elenora! So good to see you!" he called as she approached.

"Good to see you, too, David." She plastered a smile on her face. If he saw her coming out of the interrogation room, he would no doubt ask her what she was doing in there. *Gah!* What was she going to tell him?

"I knew you couldn't stay away for long," Demontigny teased her.

"How have you been?" she deflected.

"Oh, you know. Same old, same old."

"I was just telling him you volunteered to help with a victim's traumatized coworker." Pierre winked at her.

She smiled at him, grateful for his preemptive thinking.

"Feeling a little cooped up at home with the baby, eh?" The detective chuckled. "My wife couldn't wait to go back to work. The twins drove her crazy. They still do, mind you."

"Twins. I can't imagine," Elenora said as Aubrey started whining, further saving her bacon.

Demontigny made a face. "Well, it's been a pleasure. Don't be a stranger," he said, leaving.

She picked up Aubrey.

"So?" Pierre asked eagerly once the detective was out of earshot.

"I got nothing from the witness, but it was worth a shot. I'm glad I did it." She told him what happened and her thoughts about Mr. Sanschagrin's unenviable situation.

"What's next? Serena's place for a download?" he asked once she was done.

It made sense to go and see Serena so she could capture the images Elenora had seen in her mind since the night before. But Elenora needed to do something else first. She had mulled over the unpleasant idea on the drive to the precinct and hadn't told anyone in case she changed her mind. It repulsed the hell out of her, but she couldn't resist the pull inside her—knowing how much she stood to gain. And it was the right thing to do.

She grimaced. "I'd like to drop by the morgue first."

CHAPTER TWELVE

Would visiting the morgue ever get easier? And would she have the misfortune of asking herself this question again?

Elenora stared at the white sheet covering Jérémie Marsan's lifeless body, hesitant to proceed with her second covert cadaver reading in the precinct morgue.

Her first experience had been with one of Barlow's victims, a murdered plastic surgeon named Réginald Haché. In her line of work, Elenora had seen several dead bodies at crime scenes. She'd even seen people die before her eyes. But she'd otherwise been shielded from physical contact with the dead.

Being in such proximity to death made her queasy. The prospect of touching a corpse had been daunting the first time, especially since she hadn't known what to expect. This time, she had less time to mull over the imminent dreadful contact, but she was apprehensive just the same. Knowing what awaited her didn't help.

And then there were the victims themselves. The plastic

surgeon had been an unlikeable man with no family and to whom Elenora had felt an emotional distance. Jérémie Marsan was the opposite. Elenora had worked with a lot of street kids and understood the type of damaged youth he had been. She admired him for turning his life around and felt a connection with him.

The menthol she'd smeared above her upper lip to lessen the smell of death stung her nostrils. She approached the sheet-covered body at a snail's pace, her heart aching. Her sense of empathy warred with a growing feeling of revulsion. She didn't want to gag or even shudder in the presence of the departed young man.

Taking a deep breath wasn't a good idea, so she reminded herself why she was there instead. The best thing she could do to honor Jérémie's memory was to gather as much intel as possible to help solve his case and bring closure to his loved ones. That was her part to play.

Come on, you got this.

"Do you wanna try just touching his arm first? You may get answers without having to see him," Tom suggested.

Thank God he was by her side. And he was right—maybe she didn't have to see the deceased to read him.

She blew out a breath of relief. "That'd be so great."

"I thought you might like the idea." His eyes crinkled as he smiled at her. "Ready?"

"Ready."

Tom lifted the sheet just enough to expose Jérémie's right arm. Elenora knew the limb would be cold and stiff, and touching it would unsettle her.

Don't psych yourself out. Just get it over with.

Elenora brought her fingers to the young man's arm and

got down to business. She pushed her mind through the glove and met a blank canvas. She visualized the attic in the old house and opened her senses.

After a moment, her memory of the space morphed into a vision similar to the premonitory dream she'd had, except now she saw the attic through the young construction worker's eyes. She recognized Harold Sanschagrin, who lifted a floorboard with his crowbar in one corner of the room.

Elenora felt and saw her hands pick up the sledgehammer and swing it toward the hazardous wall. She willed the vision to slow down, and it did. As the massive tool hit the wall, an invisible force pushed her, sending her flying backward.

She further dialed down the speed of the vision as she floated across the room in a surreal fashion. She caught Harold Sanschagrin's dumbfounded gaze on her. And the sheet of plastic briefly resisted against her back as she went through the hole and fell, the clear sky above filling her view.

Pain shot through her back and neck when she landed. The wind got knocked out of her lungs. Elenora gasped, and her struggle for air pulled her from the vision.

"Are you all right? What happened?" Tom whispered in her ear.

Breathing better, she saw him peering over his shoulder for a sign of Carl. Fortunately, it looked like the morgue technician was still on his break. Though he was known to move around quietly—as silent as his clients, his colleagues liked to tease—so one never knew when he would come out of nowhere.

"I confirm that Jérémie was pushed the same way I was

and, again, that Harold Sanschagrin had nothing to do with his death."

Tom nodded, looking at her expectantly.

"That's all," she said, disappointed.

"Wanna leave?"

Yes?

No?

"How much longer do I have?"

Tom glanced at his watch. "About five minutes."

Hmm. Maybe she could find out more. She needed to try again. "Squeeze my shoulder if he returns."

"You got it."

Elenora put her gloved hand back on the young man's arm, closed her eyes, and called out to him in her mind. *Jérémie, I'm Elenora. I want to help you. Please let me in. Did anyone want to harm you?*

She listened intently for anything. And when nothing came, she pictured herself changing the station on her mind's radio, trying various frequencies.

She waited patiently, but to no avail.

Then she remembered that when she'd read Réginald Haché's corpse, she'd gotten images by brushing bare fingers over his mangled jaw, whereas she'd only touched Jérémie's arm. Maybe a little exploring would produce results. Since the clock was ticking, she yanked her glove off for skin-on-skin contact, hoping to heighten the connection. Thankfully, the autopsy hadn't begun, and the body was intact—she wouldn't stumble upon an open chest cavity.

Elenora roamed her hand over the young man's six-pack underneath the sheet, feeling like a creep trying to sneak a feel. She forced any thoughts of indecency from her mind.

There was no time to feel icky or self-conscious. She brushed her fingers over his heart, and a carousel of images and emotions flashed in her mind.

Heavy prison doors opening in front of Jérémie, who stood elated to taste his newfound freedom.

Jérémie reunited with loved ones—his girlfriend, his mother, and his sister—shedding tears of joy and hugging.

The young man, on one knee, proposing with a modest but beautiful ring for which he'd earned every penny, and his girl saying yes.

Overwhelming feelings of love, bliss, and pride accompanied the memories. Elenora's heart both soared and broke at once.

She felt a squeeze on her shoulder, and her arm linking her to the victim got pulled back.

"Yes, we're good," Tom said behind her as her mind readjusted to reality. "Thank you so much, Carl."

Tom reached around her to adjust the sheet over Jérémie's body and whispered, "Let's wash that hand, shall we?"

Alex and Pierre waited for them with Aubrey and Céleste in the hallway outside. It was empty, so Elenora told them about her findings. Or lack thereof.

"Jérémie Marsan seemed pretty serene before his death," she concluded. "He had a fresh start and was grateful for it. Unfortunately, I didn't get any clues as to the identity of his attacker."

"Damn. I was hoping your bravery would be rewarded. How are you feeling?" Alex asked.

"Like I need a shower, but other than that, this time was slightly easier to stomach than the first. Emphasis on *slightly*."

Tom discreetly raised a hand to hush everyone. Their colleague Renaud was heading for them. He was a svelte kid in his mid-twenties, who had immigrated from France a few years earlier—a sharp-minded, high-energy, and eager-to-please darling with perpetually disheveled brown hair and mischievous eyes.

He greeted everyone before zeroing in on Aubrey, cradled in Pierre's arms. He crouched in front of her, an enthusiastic grin on his face. His fingers curled over one of her fists, and he shook it until he got a drooly smile out of her.

"Aubrey, my dear, I found an old roommate of the satanic weirdo, and she works three blocks from here. Can you believe that?"

CHAPTER THIRTEEN

Elenora briefly debated whether to head straight to Serena's place while Aubrey was being an angel or play baby roulette and tag along with Tom and Alex to chat with Micheline Lamirande, who had lived with Jean-Luc Rivard in the old house.

She felt raw from reading Jérémie Marsan, but her desire to right the wrong of his unfair and premature death had grown exponentially since she'd left the morgue. It had also eclipsed her remaining jitters from her attack at the house. It was crystal clear to her now that she could have been the next victim, and her initial fear was turning into anger. The malevolent paranormal threat on Maple Street had to be stopped before it caused any more damage.

Thankfully, the witches and the OPO were coming on board. Hopefully, they would kick its ass. And Elenora itched to kick its ass too. She didn't want to sit and watch from the sidelines. She wanted to bring her psychic A-game to the investigation and help the good guys win.

Tom's invitation to talk with an ex-satanist enticed her.

The woman had known Jean-Luc Rivard, had lived at the Maple Street house, and had experienced firsthand the man's satanic rituals. However, Aubrey's nap time was around the corner. Pierre was willing to keep hanging out with the baby, but Elenora had to consider the potential mega crankiness and tiny wrath that could be unleashed. Surely Pierre could only take so much abuse from a pint-sized tyrant.

"Are you certain you fully understand what you're signing up for?" Elenora asked him.

Pierre chuckled. "She's being very good, and if she tires of the stroller, I'll drive her around until you're done. I'll text you if there's a problem. How's that?" He grinned. "I've dealt with slightly worse, you know."

Pierre had become Aubrey's unofficial manny soon after her birth and was blooming and glowing in his new role—if the words *blooming* and *glowing* could apply to a rugged, retired detective who used to eat bad guys for breakfast. He could handle Aubrey in his sleep. It was also a pleasant day, and the baby was engrossed in the sights and sounds of the busy downtown. Still, Elenora didn't want to take advantage of him.

"Okay. But I'll owe you one. *Another* one. Not sure how I'll ever repay you," she said before calling to Tom, "Coming in a sec!"

"A full report will do nicely. Go do your thing, Mommy." He pushed the stroller toward Sainte-Catherine Street. "We might as well walk you there."

Céleste heeled next to the stroller, watchful and businesslike, as if she was on Aubrey's protection detail. The sight cracked Elenora up—the still-buff, not-to-be-messed-with ex-detective and the badass canine guarding her daughter. Her eight-month-old had an entourage worthy of the Secret Service.

Elenora's amusement came to a grinding halt when her eyes met the mocking gaze of a little blond boy smirking at her while his mother tied his shoe. She did a double take—the kid rang a bell...

The boy at the bottom of the river?

Following the accident that had claimed her father's life, Elenora had had her very first vision—that of a young boy at the bottom of a river. She'd lived most of her life with no recollection of the sight until she became pregnant with Aubrey and her psychic abilities awoke. Throughout her pregnancy, the little twerp had frequently plagued her dreams with eerie taunts, and she could never figure out what his problem was. She and Serena had tried to download him from her mind more than once but had always failed to capture him.

It dawned on Elenora that she hadn't seen him in a while.

She turned for another look at the boy, to see if he was a ringer for the little bullying jerk from her dreams. The kid was no longer staring at her, and his appearance didn't match that of the child in her head. Her tired subconscious must have been playing a trick on her.

"Here we are," Tom announced, stopping in front of Taverne Chez Miche.

Renaud hadn't been kidding when he'd said they would find Micheline Lamirande within spitting distance of the station. The dive bar she owned occupied the first floor of a run-down building that seemed to be held in place with rubber bands. No doubt the entire block would soon be torn down to make room for a condo tower.

Elenora followed Tom and Alex inside, and her eyes adjusted to the dim light. The scuzzy interior matched the exterior. A burly worker intercepted them, his in-your-face body language suggesting he thrived on provocation.

"We're looking for Micheline Lamirande," Alex said curtly, flashing his badge at the worker and sizing him up.

The other man did the same. Of similar stature, Alex was in great shape and had impressive combat skills, but judging by the worker's steely confidence, he would be a worthy opponent in a brawl.

"Miche?" the man asked.

"Yes."

"You with the kid who called earlier?"

"Yeah."

The man pivoted and jerked his head for them to follow him.

They made their way across the room around well-worn tables. On them stood mismatched but equally uncomfortable-looking wooden chairs. A whiff of cleaner implied the floor had been cleaned recently, but the soles of Elenora's sandals still found a handful of sticky patches.

Micheline Lamirande's office sat at the back, past two questionable bathrooms. A pungent smell gripped Elenora by the throat when they entered the minuscule windowless room. It was sparse, unexpectedly tidy, and had a plain desk in the middle. The woman sitting behind it had to be in her seventies and gave the impression that they would wheel her dead body out of her business before she even considered retirement.

"You want to know about Jean-Luc Rivard?" Her hoarse voice held a hint of amusement, and a matching glimmer danced in her eye.

Tom nodded and whipped out his notepad. "I'm Detective Tom Madigan, and these are my colleagues, Detective Alex Bélanger and Elenora Bello. There's been a death at 34 Maple."

"The young guy? Yeah, I read about it. That's sad. Though I can't say I'm all that surprised." She shook her head. Then a slow smirk appeared. "Man, that place was fucked up. But it was all bullshit, you know."

"What was all bullshit, ma'am?" Tom's tone was warm and inviting.

"Rivard, for starters."

"What about him?"

The woman sucked in a long breath as if preparing for a thorough trip down memory lane. "First, to understand, you have to know what he was like. He was a brash asshole. Gorgeous. Charismatic. An attention-starved, lying piece of shit. Great in the sack. Fuck, was he ever great in the sack..." She reached for a pack of cigarettes in the top drawer of her desk. She lit one and took her sweet time with the first puff.

Tom prompted her, "That was the bullshit?"

She exhaled, shaking her head. "The whole cult crap was bullshit. It was all an act for him to get attention. And money, drugs, and pussy." She shrugged again. "All bullshit. All an act."

"The black masses, they were just a rumor?"

"You mean his *party trick*?" She snorted. "Nah, those were real. But again, just an excuse to attract attention to himself. He thrived on that shit. He thought he'd become Hollywood's next big thing. We all know how well that worked out for him."

"What happened during a black mass?"

"We'd go to the basement, which looked like a medieval dungeon, with candles scattered around. We wore those hooded black robes. Our self-proclaimed high priest put on a fake goat's head and read some shit in Latin in his deep, dramatic voice."

Micheline took another puff and savored the memory before she added, "And we'd chant his words back at him. No idea what we said, but I'll admit it was creepy as hell—I have goosebumps just thinking about it. And before you think I'm a first-class idiot, you have to understand we were all high back then and fascinated with the occult. That really helped compound the effect. As they say, you had to be there."

Elenora knew what she meant—she had kind of *been there* herself. The woman's account of what had gone on in the mansion's basement fit with what she'd seen. Micheline Lamirande was speaking the truth.

"I can only imagine," Tom replied.

"We felt like we were a part of something much bigger than ourselves, you know? And it was a great way to rebel against conservative parents." She snickered, took a long drag, and stared into space.

"But in the end, it was just a party trick?" Tom asked.

She nodded. "Rivard was damn good, though. Convincing. He was an actor, you know, and had a flair for theatrics. I had to give it to him. Some of his tricks felt so real. Like the time he set the pentacle on fire with his blood. It was...mind-blowing. I couldn't tell you how he pulled that one off. But then, other bits were just lame. I think he became desperate to outdo himself."

"Like what?"

"Like he started obsessing about the house being haunted, and he was on a mission to convince everyone. So, he'd move your stuff while you slept. Or he'd slam the kitchen cabinets in the middle of the night and pretend it wasn't him. Real mature," she scoffed. "He should have stuck to his Satan schtick."

"Did he ever claim to have interacted with a ghost?" Elenora asked then coughed. Her throat and eyes stung from the smoke. She hadn't been exposed to a cigarette in a long time.

"Oh, yeah! He said it was the old lady who lived there before us. She warned him the house was dangerous and wanted us to leave." She chuckled. "The ghost of a grandmother was telling us to get out. Right. Can you say shit like that while sober? Damn drugs. Anyway, he kept rambling on and on about her. He couldn't figure out if God had sent her or if she worked for the devil, who wanted to trick him... Good times."

"So, she spoke to him? He saw her?" Alex asked.

"No. She told him about our impending doom via a fucking Ouija board." She rolled her eyes. "Not convenient at all. But then again, he could afford some potent drugs. Or he might have been schizophrenic." She shook her head. "Tell me. If a house was haunted, why would the ghost warn you to get out? They're supposed to scare the shit out of you and make you get the fuck out. Not give you a gentle reminder that maybe you should consider packing."

"Hard to disagree with that," Alex concurred.

"Right?" Micheline seemed delighted to get Alex's approval. She gave him an appreciative once-over.

"Did you ever witness anything disturbing in the house?" Tom asked.

"Aside from Rivard?" she deadpanned.

Tom bit his lips to stifle a smile. "Yes, aside from Rivard."

"Never anything firsthand."

"No odd feelings?" Elenora asked.

Micheline mulled over the question. "No…"

"An impression of being watched, maybe?" Elenora helped.

The woman laughed. "When you live with a bunch of pervs, it's hard not to get the impression you're being watched."

Elenora smiled. "I meant more like a ghost or anything supernatural."

"For real? I don't think so, no."

"What about the devil? You think he ever showed up during a mass or at any other time?" Tom asked.

Micheline Lamirande cocked an eyebrow at him. "You're seriously asking me this?"

"Please humor us."

She snorted. "All right. If the devil ever showed up, it was only in spirit. And I don't mean a ghost. I mean just pure depravity and selfishness."

"Do you remember Rivard's death?" Tom flipped to a new page in his notepad.

"Yeah. It was freaky, wasn't it? I was gone by then, but I read about it. It was all over the papers." She took one last puff of her cigarette before stubbing it out against the bottom of a glass ashtray. "He finally got the damn exposure he wanted."

"You think the devil or a ghost might have had anything to do with his death?"

She gave Tom a blank look that said she wondered if she was being punked. "Am I still humoring you?"

"Please."

"Honestly, I wouldn't put it past him to have hired a special effects guy to help him stage a spectacular suicide."

A knock made them all turn. The beefy worker from before filled the doorway. "Chucky's having issues with the new supplier."

"Be there soon." Micheline turned an inquiring look on Tom. "Anything else?"

"I think we're good." He dropped a business card on her desk. "Thank you for your time, Ms. Lamirande. Please call if you think of anything."

"Ah, the good old days..." Alex quipped as the trio exited the bar.

Pierre sat on a nearby bench with Aubrey in his lap, the two of them people-watching. He turned his head upon hearing Alex and stood.

"The extent to which some people will go just to get attention never ceases to amaze me." Tom collected his daughter and changed his voice to address her. "Were you good? Did you see lots of people?"

"It'd be ironic if Rivard was the one haunting the house right now," Alex said. "You think he had anything to do with Marsan's death? This whole satanic actor thing is giving me a headache. As if regular murders aren't complicated enough to solve."

"Yeah, I dunno. Ele, what's your take? Got any impressions from Ms. Lamirande?" Tom asked.

"Nothing new. Her recollections match," Elenora replied. "But I agree that Rivard's unusual life isn't helping. Maybe it's muddling the big picture."

"What a clusterf—*fluff*." Alex caught himself as his eyes landed on Aubrey. "Can you say *clusterfluff*, Aubrey?"

Elenora slapped his arm playfully. "Don't encourage her!"

He chuckled.

"I'm taking notes. Watch out when you have kids," she teased.

He kept grinning.

"Alex is right. This is a clusterfluff, and we've barely started." Tom put Aubrey in the stroller.

"So, what d'you get from the ex-roommate?" Pierre asked.

Elenora told him about their chat with the bar owner. "What do you think?"

"It sounds like Rivard was all smoke and mirrors. Maybe you should overlook the satanism—for now, anyway. It doesn't sound like demons were involved, which they often are when the devil has a direct hand in a situation—in my experience. Plus, I don't think the devil takes satanism very seriously."

Alex snickered. "Satan doesn't endorse satanism?"

"Why would he? I'm sure it strokes his ego and he finds it amusing, but beyond that... Unless a satanist actually kills another human being, what does having an orgy or substituting urine for holy water at a black mass—or even sacrificing a goat—do for the devil?"

"So, you think we should dismiss Rivard's satanic theatrics and concentrate on his claim of seeing a ghost?" Tom asked.

"And on his bizarre death? For now, yeah."

They walked to the soundtrack of the stroller's wheels grinding against the sidewalk for half a block.

"The bar owner said the ghost was the previous owner?" Pierre asked.

"Yes. Angéline de Montbleu," Tom answered.

"You think she might be your poltergeist? And the reason for Rivard's death?"

"If that's the case, he should have gotten off her lawn when she told him to," Alex said dryly.

"She would have killed him because she wanted him out of her house?" Tom asked.

"Why not?" Alex shrugged. "I can't imagine an old lady being keen on having a bunch of partying potheads and assholes trashing her sophisticated home. Maybe she'd had enough. She warned Rivard, but nothing changed. That would piss me off."

"But she didn't warn Jérémie Marsan, as far as we know," Tom pointed out.

"Maybe she didn't bother with the warning this time and went straight to killing him. Have him serve as a warning to the crew or something."

"Even though none of the construction workers lived in the house?" Elenora asked.

"Maybe she wanted to make sure no one ever moved back in," Alex said. "Who knows what goes on in the head of an elderly ghost—maybe she was senile. Maybe she thought the construction crew was destroying her home like the other yahoos."

"I can't wait to see what Serena makes of all this," Pierre said cheerfully.

CHAPTER FOURTEEN

"So, *this* is the infamous Carrie," Pierre said as Serena approached with a sizable black-and-white rabbit in her arms.

She'd been wanting a pet but didn't have time to walk a dog. And she'd thought a cat would be cliché in her case. So, after some research, she'd rescued a Dutch rabbit.

"Yup. And she's a real gem. Especially when she's not chewing my charging cables." The witch's gaze dropped to Céleste, obediently sitting next to Pierre. "She's used to dogs, and Céleste's great, but should I keep them apart?"

As if to address Serena's concerns, Céleste lowered herself to a lying position and rested her head on her front paws, making herself as unthreatening as possible.

"Good girl." Pierre patted her.

Serena crouched in front of Aubrey and brought Carrie close. The baby looked at the rabbit with fascination, and her hand shot straight to the nearest velvet ear. Elenora intercepted the hand in time and held the miniature starfish fingers wide open to prevent them from gripping.

"Gentle, Aubrey. Pet the bunny gently. Like Willem. You don't want to scare her."

Aubrey voiced her delight at touching the impossibly soft fur.

"So, how does that free-roaming thing work?" Pierre asked with interest.

"A bit like a cat. She has a litter box with recycled newspaper bedding and hay in it. They like to munch and do their business at the same time. Rabbits are weird. I never thought I'd have a bale of hay in a plastic bin in my condo's living room. But here I am, taking urban farming to a new level."

Pierre laughed. "I'm getting you a pair of overalls for Christmas."

"I'd like to see you try," she teased back.

"She's free to go around?" Elenora took in the pretty ball of fluff.

"Yup. As long as she has no access to electrical wires, it's all good."

"They like wires?"

"They think wires are roots and chew them to get rid of them as they would in a den. They think they're helping."

Serena bent and released Carrie. The rabbit hopped away, flicking her back feet at them.

"Oh good. I pissed her off. You wouldn't believe how susceptible they are. Everything's an offense. Such divas." She sat on the sofa next to Elenora.

"Speaking of divas," Pierre said. "Since you've never met a satanist you didn't like, Serena..." A teasing grin grew on his face.

The witch groaned. "What now?"

Elenora brought her up to speed on their latest findings,

adding to what Pierre and Tom had already told her about the case.

"So, let me get this straight," Serena said. "We've got a dead construction worker, possibly the ghost of an elderly female aristocrat moonlighting as an asshole poltergeist, and a fake wannabe disciple of the devil, who might have had a paranormal ass-kicking and died in a baffling way." She pinched the bridge of her nose. "Maybe we should investigate a different case."

She reached for her tablet on the coffee table while Elenora handed Aubrey to Pierre. The baby's eyelids looked heavy, and her head bobbled. She'd had a quick nap in the car on their way over, but maybe a second nap was in the cards. Elenora crossed her fingers.

Pierre also read Aubrey's signs of drowsiness. He cradled her in his arms and stood to walk her around and lull her to sleep.

"Ready?" Serena asked Elenora.

"Ready." Elenora gave her hand to Serena and closed her eyes, eager to know what her friend would think of the insights. So much had happened since the night before.

"Let's see what we've got."

Soon, the familiar ant-like sensation crept up Elenora's arm, signaling that the witch was about to access her visions. She recalled the premonitory dream that had started it all. Her mind then wandered through the day's events chronologically, first imagining herself in the backyard of the old house, then inside the home, going from the basement to the attic—grabbing every insight along the way. Finally, she revisited the poignant flashes from Jérémie Marsan's body at the morgue. A pang of sadness echoed against the blank backdrop that followed the last memory.

"I understand," Serena murmured and squeezed Elenora's hand before letting go, breaking the connection.

Elenora opened her eyes, and her gaze fell on Carrie, who suddenly flopped onto her side on the floor near Céleste. The rabbit looked boneless and alarmingly not alive. "Is she okay?"

Serena chuckled. "Yeah, that's normal. She nearly gave me a heart attack the first time I saw her do that. I thought I'd killed my pet within hours of bringing her home. Turns out, it just means she's very relaxed and happy. And likes messing with people."

Elenora laughed. Willem had quirks too. So far, he seemed to love staring at walls, licking his reflection in the mirror, and flushing the toilet. That last one had spooked the crap out of her until she caught him in flagrante delicto, solving the mystery of the disturbing random flushes.

Serena clicked around on her tablet before lifting her head, looking for Pierre. He stood by the floor-to-ceiling living room window, admiring Mount Royal from the condo's killer fourteenth-floor view of the mountain and neighboring skyscrapers. Aubrey was as floppy as Serena's rabbit in his arms, deeply asleep.

"Yo, Pierre," Serena called softly. "Wanna see what we got?"

He turned and keenly joined them on the sofa, mindful not to wake the baby.

The witch started the clip of Elenora's ominous premonitory dream about Jérémie Marsan's demise. Elenora leaned over the tablet to see, once again, the chilling images from her mind. She tried to watch with objective hindsight.

Then came the double vision of Jérémie and the mystery limbs sticking out of the rosebushes. Both sets of images appeared clearly on video, as if an editor had overlaid new footage on top of an existing one.

Serena frowned. "Crap. I screwed up, Ele. We're gonna have to recapture these two feeds."

"You didn't screw up. That's what I saw."

"You saw this? Like, two visions at once?"

"I did."

"What are you, under-challenged?" Serena teased before turning serious. "What do you think they are? Two visions linked to a common spot?"

"That's my guess."

Pierre leaned closer for a better look at the screen. "Fascinating."

"It's happened twice so far," Elenora said. "You'll see another double vision later."

"Huh." Serena stroked her chin. After a thoughtful moment, she added, "I'll try to split them apart later. See if it can be done and if they contain more info on their own." She shook her head. "Gee whiz, Ele, you're a national treasure."

Elenora scoffed. Being a national treasure was low on her list of wants and priorities. She was gradually accepting her new fate but still mourned her old life as a plain Jane.

Serena played the next clip, which took place indoors. She paused it. "You didn't pick up anything more on the accidental gardeners?"

"Not really. But there are memories from reading Jérémie Marsan coming up. And a crew is digging for bones in the backyard as we speak. Maybe we can identify the owner of the mystery limbs the old-fashioned way."

"Noted. I'll tell Claire-Lune to race you." Serena gave her a mischievous grin.

Claire-Lune, Serena's twin sister, was a witch with outstanding communication abilities. As a skillful ethereal librarian and researcher, she rivaled the best search engines on the internet. She had a knack for unearthing information out of thin air, and if a document of any kind ever existed throughout history, she would likely find it, or at least traces of it. If any information could be coaxed from a clip on Serena's tablet, she would be the one to draw it out.

Elenora laughed. "She's got magic. We've got shovels. I can see how that'd be completely fair."

"Who said anything about fair?" Serena resumed playing the clip, which showed the jumbled, washed-out flashes of dark-cloaked figures celebrating a black mass.

"Morons." Serena snorted. "The things I could show those whippersnappers. They'd wet themselves and run for the hills."

Her friend wasn't wrong. Thinking of all the mind-blowing darkness she'd seen in the past year, Elenora wondered how those civilians would have fared had they faced the real deal. Then again, she wouldn't wish any of what she'd experienced on a human oblivious of the paranormal. Ignorance truly was bliss.

Serena viewed the rest of the images with a cynical scowl and paused when she came upon the clashing double vision of Jean-Luc Rivard's lifeless body and the photographer.

"So, I'm guessing dead satanic head twit here. And the photography dude?"

"Correct. Joseph Gill, postmortem photographer extraordinaire," Pierre said.

"You can tell he was the life of the party," she quipped, scrutinizing the photographer's image. "What a pompous, stuffy-looking prick... Anyway. What do we have next?"

"This is where it gets hairy," Elenora said.

The next clip revealed her vision during her dreadful assault in the attic. She hoped the images would hold clues about the attacker. But how could they? She'd only seen a blur of dark colors impossible to decipher.

"The shove that could have killed you?" Serena's eyes filled with anger.

"Yeah."

"I'm gonna banish that fucker so fast when I get the chance," she fumed before hitting play.

Sure enough, the brief clip only showed blurry, moving spots, most of them dark—as they had appeared in Elenora's mind. That was it. Nothing new seemed to emerge from the recording.

Serena squinted, holding the tablet a few inches from her face, and played the clip again. "Did I miss something?"

"Nope. That's all I saw. I was hoping you could somehow extract more information from it."

The witch grunted. "Let me see what I can do, but it doesn't look good. I'll send it to Claire-Lune too. I'll give her all the clips."

Pierre studied the last frame. There was a flesh-colored blob in the middle of the image. "Maybe this is a hand?"

Serena reviewed the clip frame by frame. The fuzzy, skin-toned mass moved from the bottom to the center of the image, revealing very little. But it could indeed be a hand.

They moved on to the last sequence resulting from reading Jérémie Marsan's body at the morgue.

"The poor fiancée. What a goddamn kick in the teeth," Serena said as she witnessed the young man's last bittersweet moments.

Elenora's heart squeezed too. "Yeah. I feel bad for her."

"That was the last set?"

"Yes."

Elenora's phone rang, and she put the call on speakerphone. "Hey, Tom. What's up?"

"Renaud found more on the house. Joseph Gill had it built in 1899. He and his wife, Jane, lived there for eight years before selling it in 1907 to a rich businessman named Albert de Montbleu, who owned several estates. It's unclear whether de Montbleu ever lived in the house, but in 1922, its ownership was transferred to his daughter Angéline, who owned it until her death in 1962."

A string of coughs erupted from the phone. "Excuse me. Then the house sat on the market for seven years and was bought in 1969 by Robert Nicolas Rivard, Jean-Luc Rivard's father. The kid inherited the house three years later in 1972. That's all we have so far. Also, the dig in the backyard yielded nothing."

"No bones? No bits of fabric? Nothing?" Elenora asked.

"Not a thing."

"I hope I didn't imagine this." She was already kicking herself for potentially wasting her colleagues' time with an unnecessary dig.

"You didn't. We got it on file." Serena gestured toward her tablet.

Oh. Right.

"How did the capture go?" Tom asked.

"Smoothly, as always. Though I still can't wrap my mind around how Serena does it." Elenora gave her friend an appreciative glance.

"Likewise, sister. You're the one doing most of the work," the witch replied.

"Got any thoughts on this whole thing, Serena?" Tom asked.

"I think you guys are right to suspect a poltergeist."

"Okay. What should we do next?"

"I think we should all go to the house, do a séance to draw the asshole out, and banish it. It's the only viable long-term solution I see."

Thoughtful silence filled the room.

"Banishing sounds very final," Tom said eventually. "Could we question the perpetrator before you proceed? It'd be a shame to get no answers."

Serena rolled her eyes. "If you insist, Tom. But just so you know, you're turning into Pierre."

Pierre chuckled. "Hey! I might've cramped your style, but you have to admit it's satisfying to confront them and make them squirm before sending them on their unmerry way."

She smirked. "You're not entirely wrong."

"Okay, let's go for a visit. When would be a good time for you?" Tom asked.

"I'm available tonight," Serena said.

"Tonight should be good. I'll check with Alex."

"Great. I'll ask Yukiko and see who else is available. I'll twist Claire-Lune's arm, and hopefully, Wren and Juniper can join us too."

"Juniper?" Elenora asked, perplexed.

Juniper was a medic—a healing witch, maybe—at the OPO. The reserved, petite woman had helped save Rolland's life and seemed very competent in the medical field.

But why would her presence be sought for a séance? Were injuries expected?

"You think the poltergeist might harm someone again?"

Serena's eyes narrowed at Elenora's question. "I assume the spirit's an ass, and it might take its best shot at us, but... Why are you asking this?"

"Because you want Juniper at the séance. Why?"

"Oh. She's telekinetic. That makes her handy with poltergeists."

Elenora had heard the word *telekinetic* before but was unfamiliar with the ability's details.

"Juniper can move things with her mind," Pierre explained. "When push comes to shove, she can intercept the shove and shove back tenfold. She's very attuned to movement, and sometimes, she can even anticipate it before it occurs."

Elenora pieced things together. "So, if a poltergeist tries to throw someone across the room, she could nip the attack in the bud?"

"Not guaranteed, but she might have a chance, yes." Serena sounded proud of her colleague.

"So, she has both healing and telekinetic powers?" Elenora was getting used to having her mind blown, and yet, the witches' abilities never ceased to amaze her.

"Kind of. She mainly has telekinetic powers that have helped heighten her medical knowledge and aptitudes. Her primary ability is why she's such a great healer. She can move elements inside a body down to the atomic level," Serena said.

"For instance, she can stop internal bleeding by squeezing things," Pierre added with enthusiastic admiration.

"*Squeezing things?* Is that a recognized medical procedure?" Elenora ribbed Pierre.

He let out a good-natured laugh. "Probably was at one time, when using leeches was all the rage."

Serena shuddered. "Oh, God. Don't remind me."

"The way she took care of Rolland was amazing." Elenora remembered how Juniper's quick intervention might have saved her friend when he was fighting for his life.

"She has limitations, of course, as we all do. But I'd stay on her good side."

Serena was being humorous, but it made Elenora realize that a power such as Juniper's could have devastating effects in the wrong hands. The thought was terrifying.

"You're wondering if there are douchebags out there with evil plans and powers like Junie's?" Serena guessed.

"Are there?"

The witch shrugged. "Maybe. But unless they manifest themselves, there's no way to know. However, that's why the OPO exists, and we do a lot of preventive work. A lot of scanning to catch them and foil their plans as early as possible." She patted Elenora's knee. "Hey. You have enough on your plate. Don't start fretting over imaginary threats."

"Yeah, one thing at a time," Pierre said.

"That's right. What the wise old geezer just said." Serena smirked, and she got a playful kick from Pierre's foot.

CHAPTER FIFTEEN

Elenora's power nap was short but restful enough. She reached for her phone on the nightstand—five new texts.

Yukiko Daigo: I'm so happy you're coming tonight. It will be an awesome learning experience. :)

Elenora chuckled. Yukiko saw opportunities to learn and grow in the most dreadful situations. But the upbeat medium wasn't wrong. How often would she get to face a murderous poltergeist?

Hopefully, only this once.

While she looked forward to witnessing the banishment of the supernatural attacker, she had no desire for an encore.

Serena: Yo, dude, stop fretting.

Elenora chuckled again.

Serena: This is just routine bullshit.

Serena: Maybe not completely routine, but bullshit for sure. We'll all have each other's backs.

Serena: Aaaargh! I hope I'm not freaking you out by trying to reassure you. Forget I said anything.

Elenora smiled at her friend's well-intended words. A séance with a murderous spirit should indeed freak her out. But once again, she was nowhere near panicking as much as she ought to be—or rather, would have in the past.

She did feel some apprehension about the night's plans—and the inevitable guilt of leaving the house without Aubrey. But once more, a light buzz of anger drowned most of her jitters. Jérémie Marsan's life got cut short unfairly, just as it was finally getting good.

And she could have been killed too.

Anger as a motivating force was foreign to Elenora, and a little scary. She rarely let vengeance drive her. Going out for blood went against her values and would also be a dangerous state of mind in her line of work. But in this case, she was willing to make an exception.

The thought made her feel guilty. She sat on the edge of the bed and reread the texts from Yukiko and Serena to get out of her head.

Just make sure you're doing this for the right reasons.

She sent a quick reply to Serena.

Elenora: It's all good. Looking forward to it. :)

She sprang from the bed and left the room. As she went down the stairs, she heard Tom's voice. He was home from the precinct. She found him with Pierre on a video call in the dining room.

Pierre had stuck around after their visit to Serena's and had insisted on staying with Aubrey while Elenora and Tom went to the old house on Maple. She'd offered to hire a sitter to give him a break, but he had argued, tongue in cheek, that he'd promised the baby they would watch the new CSI series together.

When Elenora still hesitated, he'd added, "I've also been itching to read that new cardboard book you got her. Surely you wouldn't dare deny me the pleasure?"

She'd given in.

Elenora made her way around the dining room table. Tom glanced up from his laptop screen and smiled at her. Aubrey was sitting in his lap, the head of a rubber giraffe engulfed in her mouth.

"It could very well be her," said a female voice from the laptop.

Elenora recognized the speaker as Claire-Lune. While the witch's voice sounded the same as her identical twin's, her cadence was calmer than Serena's.

The differences between the two sisters didn't end there. For one big thing, Serena liked to wear a glamour that made her appear a good twenty years younger than Claire-Lune. They looked like the same person but at different stages of life and often passed for a mother-daughter duo—an energetic young woman and her poised, middle-aged mom. They were both naturally much older than Claire-Lune even looked. The hint of vampire blood they'd inherited made them age way slower than normal human beings.

Elenora peered at the screen to see if she'd guessed correctly. It was indeed Claire-Lune speaking, and Alex was there too.

"Hey, Claire-Lune. Alex."

They both greeted her.

"Get this," Tom said to his wife. "Angéline de Montbleu

was a medium. Claire-Lune found an ad in a spiritualism journal advertising her services."

"She might really be our poltergeist?" Elenora found the notion of a little old lady attacking her and killing Jérémie Marsan disconcerting.

"She might be," Claire-Lune answered. "Since she died of a heart attack in her sleep, it's more of a stretch, but we can't rule her out. That said, there's no point in wasting time confirming it's her. We should simply confront whoever shows up at the séance."

"And get answers from them," Tom insisted.

That sounded like a good plan.

"So, I'll see you all tonight?" Claire-Lune asked to wrap up the call.

"Yes. But before you go, I have a question for you," Tom said. "Was it normal for a postmortem photographer to have his dead clients come to a studio? Didn't those guys go to homes to accommodate the grieving families, not the other way around?"

Like her sister and some of her colleagues at the OPO, Claire-Lune had lived through the nineteenth century and had firsthand experience with the bizarre customs of that era.

"I do remember them going around despite their bulky equipment. I agree that Joseph Gill's approach wasn't the norm. Maybe the studio was his gimmick. In an article I read, he claimed he could take even better pictures in his own environment. 'More lifelike,' I think he said."

Alex hummed. "Could one of the dead people brought to the house have stayed behind? Maybe in retaliation? I can't imagine they were happy to be ferried around to have their picture taken."

"It's possible but unlikely. Most souls don't remain here or cling to their bodies unless they died under violent or unusual circumstances. I doubt a well-off family would have brought a dearly departed with a highly traumatized corpse to get pictures. However, I guess it's not impossible that a troubled soul made it into the house, fell in love with the woodwork, and decided to stay."

"A spirit can make such a decision?" Elenora asked, intrigued.

"Rarely, but under special circumstances, sure. It's probably not the case here, but who knows?"

"And to think I could have been an accountant," Alex deadpanned.

Claire-Lune laughed. "With all due respect, Alex, I don't see tax forms ever giving you enough adrenaline."

Alex chuckled. "Clearly, you haven't seen my brother-in-law's returns. I get white-knuckled just thinking about them."

Aubrey squawked as if in agreement, making them all laugh.

"Thanks for everything, Claire-Lune. See you at the house," Tom said.

"You know I look forward to it." The witch's eyes glimmered with excitement.

"Who else is coming?" Elenora hoped that many of her colleagues could make it.

"Serena, of course. Wren, Juniper, and Yukiko. Your mentor is quite intrigued by the possibility of channeling a former medium, if Miss de Montbleu turns out to be our *poltergal*. I'm quite curious too."

CHAPTER SIXTEEN

By the time Elenora and Tom arrived at the old house, the sky had darkened with heavy rain clouds, making it feel later in the evening than it truly was.

Parked across the street, Alex waited in his car for them to arrive—and possibly to avoid Serena, who was sprawled on the front steps of the house, twirling a lock of hair while absorbed in her phone.

Claire-Lune, Wren, and Juniper appeared from the backyard. Seconds later, Yukiko showed up on an old, nearly silent chopper motorcycle—she'd had it converted to electric —and was clad in vegan leather riding gear. The look was striking compared to her usual billowing skirts, but the medium still radiated harmony and gentleness—just of the badass variety.

Once they'd all exchanged greetings and some hugs and introduced Alex to Yukiko, Tom untacked one end of the yellow Police Line Do Not Cross crime-scene tape hung over the front steps, moved the ribbon to one side, and unlocked the front door. He stepped aside to let Juniper assess the potential threats within.

"Drumroll," the witch said before opening the door with caution. All ears, she waited a moment before entering the house. She disappeared from view and soon called, "Seems good!"

Wren started to follow but stopped over the threshold. Serena bumped into her and backed up. Wren also took a step back and moved her arm up and down through the doorway. "Hmm. What do we have here?" she muttered to herself. "Junie, please come back here a minute!"

Juniper came back. "What's up?"

Wren and the other witches were now gathered around the doorway.

"I feel a spell." Wren stuck her arm through the entrance again but kept it still this time. She nodded. "It's discreet, but I feel it."

"A tripwire?" Serena asked.

Wren shook her head. "This feels like overkill for a simple tripwire. It feels intricate...and potent."

"A protection spell, then?" Claire-Lune said.

"Maybe. Do you guys feel anything?"

The three other witches slid their arms over the threshold.

"Nothing," Serena declared while Claire-Lune and Juniper shook their heads.

"What does this mean?" Tom's vigilant gaze scanned around the door and the porch.

"It could be a protection spell to keep people away," Wren said. "But who and why? It didn't prevent the construction crew from entering and working in the house."

"Or us," Tom added.

"Or you," Wren concurred before losing herself in thought. "Hmm. Maybe someone with witchcraft abilities found out about the poltergeist and—" She frowned. "No, scratch that. Doesn't make sense. I'm sorry."

She waved a hand like she wished everyone would forget she'd spoken. Maybe she even wanted to disappear underneath the floorboards of the porch. Elenora had noticed that about Wren. The reserved, brilliant spell maker liked to err on the side of caution to a ridiculous extent—quite the opposite of Serena's trademark impulsivity—and it included voicing theories. Was she afraid to mislead people? Or look like a fool? Maybe both?

"Please don't be afraid to speak your mind, Wren. We're experts at throwing spaghetti theories at the wall," Tom said kindly, sweeping a pointer finger between himself, Alex, and Elenora. "Any other thoughts on this mysterious spell?"

Wren hesitated but finally said, "Maybe someone put a magical barrier around the house to contain the poltergeist inside. But I don't see the point of doing that."

"But that could explain why the spirit is lashing out. If it's trapped," Serena replied.

"It could. But if someone can put up a complex magical barrier, then why not just deal with the poltergeist and be done with it instead of containing it?" Wren countered.

"Maybe the spirit knows something but won't talk, so they need to keep it around?" Claire-Lune offered.

"But why the need for containment? If it's haunting this place, isn't it stuck here?" Alex asked from the bottom of the steps, keeping a safe distance.

"Probably," Claire-Lune confirmed. "But there are ways

to move a lingering soul to a different place. Like if, say, another party wanted to kidnap it for whatever reason."

Alex cocked a concerned brow at her.

"Whoever this spirit is, they're becoming more intriguing by the minute. Shall we go in and make contact?" Tom suggested. "Assuming it's safe for us to go in, of course."

Wren moved her hands over the threshold one last time before standing back, miffed. "I'm not entirely positive." She turned to Serena, Claire-Lune, and Juniper. "What do you guys think?"

"We think you're probably overcautious, as always," Serena said, impatient. "I'm with Tom. Let's just go in and figure out what we're up against."

Without protest, Wren carefully entered the house with Juniper trailing after her.

Elenora, Tom, and Alex waited for the others to go inside before following. Everyone gathered in the large room with the chandelier and the gigantic fireplace.

This could have been a ballroom, Elenora thought, now that she had a moment to take in the impressive space.

Juniper stalked around while Alex assumed a defensive stance, prepared for an invisible attack. Serena put a hand on his shoulder, making him jump.

"Easy. No sudden movement. Just relax, okay?" she said in a low voice. She seemed just as tense as he was.

He glared back at her.

"Just sayin'." She raised her hands in surrender.

Despite the knife-cutting tension in the room, Yukiko remained chill. Eyes closed, she soaked up the vibes. Her eyes flew open, and she asked Elenora, "Do you feel it? The air?"

Elenora tuned in to the room. As she had noticed on her first visit, the air was oddly thick. She said so to Yukiko.

"The air is weird for sure," Juniper agreed, her attentive gaze still sweeping the room.

Alex's hand reached for his gun, catching Serena's attention.

Her eyes widened. She shook her head in alarm and hissed in a hushed tone, "It could be used against us. Chuck it!"

His features darkened with understanding. He and Tom both quickly released the magazines from their respective guns. Serena proffered her hands to take the ammunition, and they complied.

"Are you gonna put a spell on those or something?" Alex asked, intrigued.

"Or something." She rushed to the front door and threw the magazines outside. "Don't worry, I know where they landed."

Yukiko unzipped her backpack in the middle of the room and took out five tall white candles, which she positioned in a circle on the floor. She sat cross-legged, and the witches joined her, forming a bigger circle around the candles.

Tom whispered to Elenora, "Why are they in a circle? When you and Yukiko summoned Mary Gallagher, wasn't it just the two of you?"

"A circle of people helps but isn't mandatory," she whispered back.

Reminded of Mary's séance, Elenora wondered if she would be able to see the poltergeist by herself before a witch cast a revealing spell.

Yukiko brought an elegant silver stick lighter to a wick to

light it, but all the candles flew away in opposite directions, taking everyone by surprise. Juniper stopped the candles in mid-flight, and they hung in the air.

"What, no foreplay?" she called to the air. Her splayed hands wobbled. She seemed to struggle to rein in the candles. The candles also wobbled, resisting for a while, until they obeyed and floated back to the floor, where Yukiko had placed them.

Wren mumbled a spell at them. "I don't know if that'll hold. I don't feel at the top of my game tonight."

Yukiko reached for her lighter again, but Claire-Lune jumped in. "Allow us," the witch said, lighting the candle closest to her with a snap of fingers next to the wick. The other witches followed suit, and five flames burned bright in the blink of an eye.

"I never get tired of that trick," Yukiko said with a huge smile.

Elenora was impressed too.

Even Alex deigned to show appreciation. "I bet that came in handy back when everyone used to smoke."

Claire-Lune let out a frank laugh. "Had it not been for that pesky secrecy thing, we sure would have been popular back then."

A breeze blew out of nowhere, snuffing out the flames. The witches stiffened, and their suspicious gazes traveled around the room.

"I don't suppose someone left a window open in the house," Tom said, unconvinced.

"The draft came from the back of the room." Juniper stood and headed in that direction to investigate.

Alex and Serena went with her.

"Do you know if someone from the OPO had the chance to patch the hole in the attic?" Tom asked Claire-Lune.

"They did. They nailed a sheet of plywood from the outside and threw a bunch of spells over it. I don't think they found anything odd, if that's what you're wondering. Then again, they didn't set foot in the house."

Juniper, Alex, and Serena came back from their recon mission, shaking their heads. The two witches sat back down in the circle.

"Shall we try again?" Claire-Lune bent to relight a candle, and the other witches did the same.

Every flame promptly reignited. Only to die just as fast again.

Serena blew out a frustrated breath. "He's fucking with us."

"How d'you know it's a *he* and not the witch who used to live here?" Alex asked.

"First, she was a medium, not a witch—get your terminology straight. Second, only a man can get under my skin like that." She pivoted, scrutinizing the room. "Are you man enough to show yourself?" she asked the air.

They braced themselves for a reaction and kept still.

The wail of an ambulance in the distance briefly cut through the heavy silence.

"Flying candles is all you got? Really?" Serena called provocatively.

Claire-Lune gripped her arm and mouthed, *Not helping*.

Serena shrugged. "He started it."

"We come in peace. We'd just like to talk," Yukiko tried.

They waited some more, but nothing happened.

Claire-Lune jerked her chin at the candles. "Should we try a continuous flame?"

The other witches nodded in agreement. Their synergy fascinated Elenora. These women had been working and growing together for years, and it was beautiful to see. Their bond existed beyond friendship and affinities, and they completed each other in a natural, powerful way. They were a true sisterhood, and Elenora caught herself wishing she could be a part of something like that.

"Ready when you are," Yukiko said.

"On my mark," Serena said, and the witches hovered their hands over the candles. "Go."

With fingers fluttering, they fed the wicks with a steady flame.

"Spirit in this house, I respectfully summon you. Please show yourself," Yukiko said with a gentle yet commanding voice.

Elenora felt the air in the room further thickening, raising the hair on the back of her neck. The flames flickered wildly but kept burning. A rush of air swirled around the room, quickly becoming brisker. The room shook, and the massive chandelier above the witches began to swing.

Juniper struggled to her feet, fighting to rein in the violent wind while her stubborn colleagues fought to keep the flames alive.

"Show yourself, spirit!" Yukiko shouted to be heard over the deafening whistling of the wind.

A shrill gust blasted through the room as if in riposte, and the whirling wind grew even fiercer. Elenora, Tom, and Alex clung to one another to weather the freak indoor disturbance, fighting to remain standing.

An empty can of paint made a ruckus over the din as it rolled across the room like a possessed tumbleweed. A stepladder in one corner rattled until it tipped and fell to the floor in a metallic clatter.

The chandelier ceiling medallion creaked and moaned, loosening. Bits of plaster rained down. The fixture dropped an inch.

"Watch out!" Alex screamed as the enormous light fixture came straight down at Serena.

CHAPTER SEVENTEEN

Elenora gasped as her eyes tracked the falling chandelier.

Alex dove on Serena and knocked her out of the way as the mammoth light fixture came crashing down where she'd just been, in a mess of twisted metal and sharp bits of pulverized crystal. The bulk of it barely missed the detective's legs.

Once the crystalline sound of broken glass quieted, the room fell into another deafening silence. The air stood still, the flames on the candles were gone, and everyone in the room was stunned.

Serena raised an arm, declaring herself safe. "I'm okay!" she croaked. But her bewildered state betrayed how slowly she was grasping what had happened.

Alex moved away from her and stumbled to his feet.

"Maybe we should call it a night," Wren suggested, her voice shaking.

"The voice of reason, ladies and gentlemen." Claire-Lune gave her colleague a weak smile.

"Works for me." Alex attempted to brush himself off, but

his dust-covered, crystal-embedded clothes were a lost cause and twinkled like a piece of Swarovski jewelry.

Serena stared at him with wide eyes. He offered her a hand to help her stand, and she took it.

"Thanks," she mumbled.

"Don't mention it."

She looked around, noticing that everyone was looking at her. "Are you guys okay?"

"Yes. Are you?" Claire-Lune asked, concerned.

"I'll recover." Serena raised her eyes to the ceiling, where ripped electrical wires dangled from the chandelier's broken, ornate plaster base. She then contemplated what was left of the mangled fixture on the floor. "On the bright side, that'll shave some time off the demo."

Juniper chuckled and hooked her arm around Serena's. "Let's get out of here before the jackass gets even more creative. You okay to walk?" She guided her fellow witch toward the front door, assessing her gait as they went.

Putting a hand over the small of Elenora's back, Tom led her away from the heap of metal and broken glass and out of the room.

As Elenora reached the foyer, a warm chill grazed her left arm and spread around her, wrapping her like a hug. She stopped dead in her tracks. The chill lingered and tugged at her, beckoning her toward the parlor.

"What is it?" Tom whispered.

"Hold on."

Shimmering coming from the parlor caught her attention. It grew into a glow that materialized into a dim spectral form. Elenora moved closer into the small room, closer to the translucent white silhouette of an elderly woman wearing a housecoat from the sixties. The apparition's intensity oscillated between getting clearer and brighter and vanishing.

A bad transmission?

The odd thought crossed Elenora's mind, then she asked, "Miss de Montbleu?"

She felt Tom stiffen next to her. She squeezed his hand to let him know it was okay. Her gut told her not to fear the elderly spirit.

The ghost's eyes widened in surprise, as if she hadn't expected to be addressed. She nodded eagerly, and a big, friendly grin spread across her face. She mouthed words at Elenora.

Elenora strained her ears, but she could only see the woman, not hear her. How frustrating. "I'm so sorry. I can't hear you."

The old lady frowned before speaking some more. Again, no sound came from her mouth. Elenora focused on the specter's lips, trying to decipher her words, but her view got obscured by Serena stepping in front of her protectively to face the ghost.

"Don't engage, Ele. It's probably a trap." The witch flapped her arm at Elenora behind her back, attempting to shoo her out of the room.

"Wait," Elenora told her friend and craned her neck to assess the departed woman, who watched them with interest. She seemed truly harmless. And hopeful. "I don't think it's a trap."

"Always assume it's a trap."

"And always assume Serena's being cynical," Claire-Lune jumped in.

Serena snorted. "How could I not be?"

"Trust your instincts, Elenora." Yukiko squinted intently at where Elenora had been looking.

"Can you see her?" Elenora asked.

"No, but... Tell her you welcome her."

The witches assumed offensive positions, ready to strike.

"Angéline de Montbleu, I welcome you."

As the words departed Elenora's lips, the colors in the room drained a little, and the spectral form became opaquer as it gained color, to the point where it almost looked like a living person. As if "the other side" had borrowed from Elenora's side of reality to make the departed woman more concrete. She looked to be straddling two worlds.

"Can you hear me now, dear?" Miss de Montbleu's voice was audible at last.

Elenora nodded and couldn't help smiling, making the old woman ecstatic.

"By golly! It's working! I can't believe it's working! You can truly hear me?"

"Yes, ma'am. I can both see *and* hear you."

The specter looked bowled over. "You have no idea how many times I've tried to connect with people in this house."

She floated closer to Elenora and reached for her hands.

It's probably a trap. Serena's warning echoed in Elenora's mind, and she almost recoiled but caught herself—she wanted to act in good faith. Give Miss de Montbleu a chance. *Innocent until proven guilty.*

The ghost's hands went right through hers.

"Oh!" Miss de Montbleu let out a small chuckle of surprise. "Of course. What was I thinking? But you look so real."

"You look very real to me too."

The specter's smile reached her eyes. "It's so nice to make your acquaintance."

"It's very nice to meet you, too, Miss de Montbleu," Elenora said to be polite but also for her colleagues' benefit as she remembered that no one else could see the ghost.

They all seemed on pins and needles, waiting to find out where this strange interaction would lead. No doubt thinking that she was talking with the poltergeist.

"I'm Elenora."

"Elenora. Please call me Angéline."

"Okay, Angéline. You were a medium. Is that correct?"

"Yes...though maybe I still am. It looks like I summoned you." She was still giddy.

"You summoned me?" Elenora asked, amazed.

Yukiko had guessed right—warm chills meant a spirit was calling for her.

"Well, maybe not in the traditional way." Angéline pointed at Yukiko's backpack. "Not having access to the right material like you young ladies do certainly doesn't make it easy."

"I can imagine. So how did you do it?"

Elenora's question made the woman ponder.

"I... I'm not certain. I saw you lovely folks, and I tried to get someone's attention, not expecting anything, but then you were looking at me. So I focused my efforts on you."

"Try cutting to the chase," Tom whispered behind Elenora.

Right. As much as she wanted to know more about her own abilities, they needed answers to more pressing questions. But how could she ask this gentle ghost if she was a destructive poltergeist without insulting her? Without setting her off if she turned out to be it?

"Ask her if she's the poltergeist," Alex said bluntly, making her cringe. You could always count on him to get right to the point.

"Hmm?" Angéline tilted her head in confusion.

"My friend Alex would like to know if you made the strong winds in the other room," Elenora said. That phrasing sounded more diplomatic than asking her point-blank if she'd committed murder.

Angéline glided to the edge of the ballroom and took in the paint can and the upended stepladder. She also couldn't miss the impressive mess of the chandelier's remains.

"Oh dear, what happened in there?" She put a hand to her chest. Her surprise seemed real. "I did hear a disturbance earlier..."

"You didn't move these objects?"

"I wish. The only thing I've ever been able to move is the pointer of a Ouija board—*if* I put all my might into it. And even then..."

"Did you talk to Jean-Luc Rivard with a Ouija board?"

"Is that the young man with...questionable activities who lived here after I passed?"

"Yes."

"Indeed."

"May I ask what you told him?"

"I warned him about the dark influence this place was having on him."

"The satanism?"

"The satanism?" She tilted her head again. "Do you

mean his misguided attempts to communicate with the devil?"

"Yes."

"No. I wasn't too worried about that. Nothing serious could have come of his silly method. I meant the darkness that was channeling through him. The poor chap was in over his head and falling in with the wrong crowd, if you ask me."

"What kind of darkness?"

Angéline released a long sigh. "I've tried to figure that out for a long time, my dear. I wish I knew." She started to fade.

"Miss de Montbleu, please stay with me," Elenora pleaded.

The connection was breaking. The specter's lips moved, but her voice was no longer audible, and her form waned even more. The colors in the room returned to normal. A breeze picked up around Elenora and pushed her toward the foyer. Taking the hint, she didn't fight it and walked of her own volition.

"The party's over?" Tom asked.

"I'm guessing the asshole's crashing it," Serena muttered.

A forceful gust of wind assailed them, pushing everyone toward the front door.

"Calm down, loser! We got the memo!" she screeched.

As Elenora reached the door, she chanced one last look at the spot where Angéline had been in the parlor. But the ghost had vanished completely.

CHAPTER EIGHTEEN

Once safely on the front lawn, which was squishy from earlier rain, Elenora found herself bombarded with questions.

"Are you okay?" Tom's anxious eyes searched hers.

"What happened in there, Ele?" Alex asked, his brows knitting together.

"You saw Angéline de Montbleu? Like you saw Mary Gallagher?" Yukiko's voice dripped with awe.

"How did it happen?" Wren asked over Claire-Lune's "What did you do?"

"Jesus, let her speak!" Serena's plea quieted everyone. She bent over the grass, scooped up the gun magazines she'd tossed earlier, and gave them back to Tom and Alex.

"Yes, I'm okay," Elenora said. "Yes, it was Angéline de Montbleu, and no, I don't think she's the poltergeist. What happened was, when we were heading out the door, I felt a warm chill—much stronger than Mary's chill. In fact, it tugged me toward a shimmering in the parlor, which transformed into a full ghost. As far as I know, I did nothing special to make her appear. At least not consciously. Actually, Miss de Montbleu thinks *she* summoned *me*."

Elenora glanced back at the house for signs of the specter in the parlor's window but didn't see her.

"She summoned you as a medium..." Yukiko mused, wide-eyed. "Amazing. Just amazing. Who knew that was even possible?"

Serena pulled Elenora into a side hug. "You, my lovely friend, are a magnet for the darndest things. Color me impressed."

Elenora laughed. "A magnet, yes. Things *happen* to me. I can't take any credit."

"It's the result that counts."

"So, what did Miss de Montbleu say?" Tom asked.

Elenora recounted the conversation she'd had with the departed medium's spirit.

"You're convinced Miss de Montbleu isn't the poltergeist?" Alex asked her once she finished.

"Not unless she's a very good actress."

"Could two spirits be in the house, then?" he asked the witches. "Miss de Montbleu and the poltergeist, whoever it is?"

"Could be," Claire-Lune said.

"What do we do now?" Tom asked.

"I'd say we try to find out more about this *darkness* Miss de Montbleu mentioned—my money's on it being related to the poltergeist. Then we come up with another plan to have a chat with the cranky jerk," Claire-Lune said matter-of-factly.

For the witches, the night's events were business as usual.

Tom nodded, liking the plan. "On our end, we'll study

what we have so far and dig deeper into the house's past residents."

"I'll dig too," Claire-Lune replied. "And let's brainstorm some more. I have faith we'll be back here in no time for a rematch."

Wren's gaze traveled to the front door. "If only I understood the dang spell over the threshold. It might hold useful information."

"Don't kick yourself, Wren," Serena said. "You've been working way too hard lately."

"Yeah. Give yourself a break. I'll help you figure it out," Claire-Lune concurred before addressing everyone. "In the meantime, let's put a protection spell around the house to make sure no one breaks in." She gave Tom and Alex a good-natured grin. "No offense to your security patrol and your pretty yellow tape."

Tom laughed and went to lock the door.

Serena snorted. "Yeah, the tape really keeps me out of crime scenes."

Alex glared at her. "It's protocol and a powerful symbol of authority."

"I'm sure it thoroughly deters thugs, demons, and evil spirits."

He huffed. "Not everyone has magic fingers."

Elenora felt a gaze on her and searched for the source: Wren. Deeply lost in thought, the mild-mannered witch must not have realized she was staring at Elenora.

"What is it, Wren?"

"Hmm?" The witch snapped out of her thoughts. "Oh, just a very wild idea. Don't mind me."

"May I help with something?" Elenora grew curious.

"I don't know. It's quite far-fetched." Wren's eyes skated to the front door.

"Girl, spit it out," Serena said.

Wren hesitated then shook her head, giving in. "Tom, would you please unlock the door again?"

"Sure."

Tom headed to the porch with Wren and Elenora in tow. He unlocked the door and moved out of the way. The witch ran her hand over the door. She then opened it and, once again, moved a hand over the threshold. Looking satisfied, she turned to Elenora.

"Would you mind touching the doorframe and seeing if you can get anything from it?" She waved Serena over. "Reena, would you please try to capture whatever Elenora senses?"

"Ohhh!" Yukiko exclaimed, catching on. "Since Ele can pick up airwaves, you think she might pick up a spell? Is that where you're going with this?"

"I know it sounds eccentric, but yes. Maybe she'll see or feel something about the spell or hear an incantation. Anything she grasps might help."

"You guys are mad geniuses." Serena's eyes filled with admiration and excitement.

"Or just plain mad," Wren said self-deprecatingly. "Elenora, what do you think?"

"I think your faith in my abilities is scary. But sure. What's the harm in trying?" Elenora found Wren's supposition intriguing. Could she seriously sense a spell?

Serena inspected the threshold, as if searching for a threat.

"You think the polterjerk might try shutting the door on

you, Serena?" Alex called from the lawn, once again keeping a healthy distance.

"I wouldn't put it past it," she answered.

"Then, allow me." He came up the steps, moved past the two women over the threshold, and leaned against the open door to keep it from closing. "Now you can concentrate on Ele."

Juniper followed his lead and parked her five-foot-nothing frame next to him in front of the door. Despite Alex's bulk, her magic might come in handy. He gave her an appreciative nod.

"You guys are awesome." Serena reached for Elenora's left hand. "Whenever you're ready, Ele."

"Do I only touch the doorframe? Or feel around the space as well? What am I looking for?"

"Your guess is as good as ours. I'd say just allow yourself to feel. Follow your gut." Wren cast an expectant look at her.

No pressure.

Elenora laid a hand on the right-side jamb, closed her eyes, and made her mind go blank. She waited for images to appear. It took her a moment to notice a tingling in her fingertips. The tingling evolved into a hum. Short, discordant pulses punctuated longer vibrations. She studied them closely. They seemed to repeat themselves in a pattern, like a chant.

An incantation?

The vibrations intensified, and a slight burning sensation appeared briefly on her fingertips. Elenora heard shouts and found herself in the middle of a commotion, in Tom's arms, a few feet away from the door.

"What's going on?" She blinked and caught on to reality.

Alex rammed his shoulder into the closed door. The poltergeist must have struck again.

"Serena's inside." Tom's voice was calm, but she could feel his quiet agitation. "She was...sucked in, and Alex got shoved outside. The door closed on him. It all happened so fast—"

Light flashed around the door, and it flew open. Alex tumbled inside the house headfirst, and Serena caught his fall.

She guided him outside, yelling, "Fuck you!" over her shoulder.

The door slammed shut right behind them.

Serena froze and paled. Elenora followed her line of sight to see the cause of her dismay. Doubled over on the lawn, Juniper breathed hard. Claire-Lune and Wren rubbed their hands up and down her back, murmuring a spell. Serena rushed to them and joined in.

"Is Juniper all right?" Elenora asked Tom. "What happened to her?"

"She suddenly jumped on you as you were reading the doorframe and started to glow like she was absorbing some kind of energy from you. That's the best way I can put it."

Juniper raised her hand in the air like Serena had done earlier. "Thank you, ladies. I'll be fine," she rasped.

"I didn't mean to put anyone in danger." Wren wiped away a tear rolling down her cheek.

"As if you even need to say that," Claire-Lune told her soothingly.

"Okay, what the hell was all that?" Alex rubbed his shoulder.

The witches exchanged grave looks.

"The spell might be dark magic," Juniper explained with a sour expression, a hand over her stomach. "I only figured something wasn't right when Elenora's fingers started heating. I tried to absorb the magic." Her gaze swept over Elenora. "Are you okay?"

Dark magic?

Her fingers heating?

The slight burning sensation...

"I think so. I did feel my fingers getting warm very briefly. You felt that?" Elenora searched her fingers for signs of burns but found no trace of injury.

"She did. And so did I. Listen to me, Ele." Serena planted herself in front of Elenora with a grim expression and clutched her shoulders. Her eyes drilled into her friend's, demanding her undivided attention. "If you ever feel that heat again, you drop everything and run. Okay?"

The witch didn't ease her disturbing stare until Elenora agreed that she would take any such manifestation of heat very seriously.

"Did Elenora absorb the spell? Will this affect her?" Tom asked in a thick voice.

"No. Unless the spell was created to be absorbed—which I doubt is the case here—she wouldn't have absorbed it. And her fingers would be tingling right now." Claire-Lune's confident words seemed to reassure him.

"What does dark magic mean for us?" Alex asked.

"As its name suggests, dark magic is mostly rooted in evil," Claire-Lune replied. "It's dangerous to practice and pushes the boundaries of what is morally acceptable. It goes beyond regular magic, and it's a vile means of achieving a goal, regardless of consequences."

"It's reckless and selfish," Serena added.

Claire-Lune shuddered. She wasn't the type to shudder.

Alex narrowed his eyes at her. "Please tell me you're cold."

Claire-Lune turned her olive-green eyes on him. "Dear Alex, I wish I could say yes, but I'd be lying."

"So, it's really bad?"

"Being dramatic won't help." She gave his arm a little pat before asking her sister, "Did you get anything on the spell from Elenora?"

"Lemme see." Serena searched for her tablet. Juniper found it on the porch, its screen cracked.

"He's gonna pay for this," Serena muttered when she saw the damage.

Fortunately, the tablet still came to life. They all huddled to view clusters of dots dancing around like snowy static from an old television set. A matching white-noise soundtrack played with occasional whooshes, crackles, and screeches.

"Dammit. It didn't work," Elenora said, bummed. Juniper had gotten hurt for nothing.

"Quite the contrary!" Wren barely contained her enthusiasm.

"But this is not what I sensed," Elenora replied.

"I don't doubt that. And I didn't expect it to be. Or for it to make sense—most spells are abstract. Yet you managed to capture some of its essence. With analysis, we might get insights into it. This is a mighty great start!"

Wren's smile was the largest and the most excited Elenora had seen on her.

"This is truly awesome. Great work, girls!" Claire-Lune

said before she turned her attention to the house and became pensive.

Night had fallen, and it made the place look even more sinister.

"Wren, do you think the dark spell might influence what's happening inside?"

Claire-Lune's question made Wren's smile falter. "I think it likely weakens our magic and gives the poltergeist a leg up."

"I was afraid you'd say that."

CHAPTER NINETEEN

"Remember the two overlaid visions I had this morning?" Elenora asked Tom before letting out a heartfelt groan. "Oh, that bit's sensitive." Sunk into the coziest armchair they had at home, she was getting a foot massage.

Tom sat on an ottoman in front of his wife, her feet in his lap. He had a knack for finding tight muscles and kneading the tension away.

At a little past ten o'clock, the house was quiet. Aubrey slept, and Pierre and Céleste had gone home. Elenora basked in the peacefulness, recovering from the day's roller coasters and parade of perplexing events. Her brain had turned to mush, and her body seemed just as spent and useless.

"You mean like seeing Marsan's body in the bushes over someone else's limbs?"

"Yeah."

"What about those?"

"It kind of happened again when I saw Miss de Mont-bleu, but instead of it being two visions, it was like... It's hard to explain. Like her spiritual plane had appeared over our reality. Like an overlay. As if both planes merged and borrowed from each other."

Tom stopped the massage and looked up.

"When Angéline solidified," Elenora went on, "the colors in the room faded and appeared to pump themselves into her. A bit like when Serena helped me see Delphine's departing spirit last year. The colors had faded then, too, though they hadn't colored her spirit."

"But in Delphine's case, it was a vision, not a live spirit," Tom pointed out.

"You're right." Elenora yawned. "I need to tell Yukiko about the colors. I can't believe I forgot. I'll talk to her tomorrow. After some rest. I need to be objective."

"You think you'll be able to sleep tonight? I'm still revved up."

"I hope so."

Tom ran his thumb along the sensitive arch of her foot. Shooting pain made her grunt and jerk her foot away from his grasp. Both the pain and what she was about to say made her grimace.

"Do you think the overlays are a sign that my *abilities* are expanding?" She was always tempted to make air quotes whenever she said *abilities*. It felt arrogant to admit she had special powers out loud. Self-derision seemed like a more appropriate and humbler response.

"Like Dr. Brent said might happen?"

"Yeah."

"That sounds plausible. But you've also been learning and practicing a lot with Yukiko. It makes sense that your abilities would evolve in one way or another."

"Many people change careers when they hit middle age. I wonder how many go for a change this drastic," she quipped. "When did our lives become so complicated?"

Tom leaned in, his knees sinking into the plush chair cushion on either side of her. "A little complicated, maybe. But I'm not bored. That's for sure. Are you?" He kissed her before she could answer and leaned closer, crowding her.

"You're squishing me, dear," she mumbled against his lips.

"Maybe that's the plan?" he replied playfully, not budging.

"Mmph."

Tom chuckled and kissed her neck before backing up. He sat on the ottoman, and she brandished her other foot at him.

"Don't forget this one." She smirked.

"Oh, is that how it is? No squishing, but—"

"Squish my foot." She giggled. "But not too much!" Her giggle morphed into a yawn that threatened to unhook her jaw. A wave of drowsiness made her sink farther into the chair. Maybe she could sleep here tonight.

Tom rubbed her other foot for a moment. Soon, his eyes lost focus. "Something dark came after Rivard, and he died atrociously in the house—supposedly, the best condition for a haunting. What are the odds this guy's our winner?"

Uh-oh. Tom's mind was back on the case, and he was in the mood for spitballing. If she let him drag her down that rabbit hole at this hour, she wouldn't be in bed before midnight.

"Maybe that's what the cunning Miss de Montbleu wants us to believe," she teased him, reclaiming her foot and shimmying to extract herself from the chair's deep and comfortable embrace.

Too deep in thought, Tom missed her teasing tone and took her at face value. "You think *she's* the poltergeist and behaved sweetly to mislead us?"

"Yes. Because evil's number one job is to be evil, and no one ever suspects the sweet little old lady." She grinned widely.

He looked at her and realized she was pulling his leg. He chuckled. "Okay, then. That settles it. I'm gonna go back to the house right now and book her."

Elenora thought she would fall asleep like a ton of bricks the moment she hit the sack, but she still lay awake over an hour later. Her mental hamster kept its wheel spinning at breakneck speed, rehashing the day.

She relished replaying her short but thrilling conversation with Angéline de Montbleu and hoped they could talk again. She'd never thought she would ever wish to interact with a ghost. But it had been a very special encounter with a kind soul from the past, and she felt truly privileged.

The dark spell over the front door also filled her thoughts. Especially the witches' concerns over it. They seemed unsettled.

Her mind bounced between these memories and those of Harold Sanschagrin's horrible predicament, the poltergeist's failed attempt to throw her out of the hole in the attic, the chandelier assault, and Juniper's pain after saving her from the dark spell. Those moments were kind of hard to forget.

The whole day was hard to forget and should have made her cower in fear. She should want to stay away. Yet, once again, she was more jittery than horrified. And a shred of anger still burned within her.

The poltergeist's actions had been chillingly tangible. The windy havoc it had wreaked on Elenora and her group in the ballroom and the falling chandelier could have been fatal, just like the assault in the attic. She was certainly still disturbed by her near fall and the dark spell that had crept up on her when she'd prodded it. But she was *disturbed* not *scared out of her mind.*

Was she adapting and conditioning herself to be less reactive? To be less alarmed by these unnatural events in her life, like she'd done with the nightmarish visions at night?

The idea of conversing with a spirit used to terrify her. Now she was stoked to have encountered Angéline and wished their connection hadn't been severed. She yearned to know more about the departed medium and the warm chills —not so she could learn to muffle them, but so she could explore the possibilities. Willingly explore her strengths. She wanted answers. She was done being a victim of her circumstances and wanted to be an active participant instead. And she very much liked that shift in mindset.

It sure beat being scared shitless.

The baby miraculously let her sleep in on this glorious Saturday morning. Elenora savored the lack of chaos as she leisurely got out of bed and headed to the kitchen. Tom was drinking coffee and reading the paper. He didn't appear to be champing at the bit to resume working on the case—a rare sight. He must not have heard from the witches.

The absence of news from them disappointed Elenora.

"Morning," she said.

"Morning."

"Mama," Aubrey cooed from her high chair.

"Hey, sweetie." Elenora kissed her daughter on the forehead, dodging sticky fingers. "Thank you for letting Mommy sleep. That was so nice of you."

Aubrey smiled broadly, showing off a new tooth poking out of her lower gum.

"You're getting a new pearly white! My, my, you've been busy."

Uninterested in dental talk, the baby went back to fishing cereal loops from a plastic bowl on her high chair tray.

"I agree. Totally boring." Elenora chuckled as she headed to the coffee machine to make herself a latte. "I gather there's no news?" she asked Tom over her shoulder.

"You gather correctly."

"D'you think it's too early for me to call Yukiko?"

Tom gave her an amused look. "Whoa, Nellie! It's Saturday morning. How about letting the poor woman have a break?"

Elenora chuckled at her impatient enthusiasm. What was up with her? Her mentor certainly deserved a break, especially since what Elenora wanted to discuss wasn't a matter of life or death.

She sat next to Tom with her latte and reached for the top section of the newspaper. She usually read the news on her tablet but insisted on having a paper copy of her favorite newspaper delivered on the weekends. The smell of ink paired with a fresh cup of coffee first thing on a day off made her nostalgic—and told her stubborn brain to relax.

She leafed through the section, her attention flighty. Was she too wound up to decompress?

"Maybe we should go see Muriel while we have a break and Aubrey's manageable," Tom suggested, looking up from the Living section.

Elenora withheld a sigh. Spending a quiet day at home with him and the baby would be so nice, but it indeed seemed like a good time for a visit.

"Sure. Let's head there after breakfast." *And get it out of the way.* A pang of guilt followed that uncharitable thought. She hated feeling like a terrible daughter.

Maybe today will be different.

The hairs on her arms stood up straight.

CHAPTER TWENTY

Why could Elenora converse with a woman who had been dead for decades but couldn't reach the woman before her, who was technically alive?

How cruel was that?

And would she ever stop thinking about how painful her mother's situation was? Would the perpetual crippling gut punch ever go away? Would she ever stop feeling some odd, misplaced guilt despite not being responsible for Muriel's grim fate?

These questions consumed Elenora as she waited for time to pass in her mother's room. The space was small and tidy. Decorative touches made it inviting: old and new family photos, flowering plants, and a collection of porcelain figurines prized by Muriel back when she had been lucid. However, the woman's ghastly presence negated the room's warm vibe. She sat in a recliner, as still as a statue, her gaze empty. Aside from her soft breathing, not a muscle had moved since her visitors' arrival.

As with most visits, Elenora and Tom had started with

the usual one-sided pleasantries, asking Muriel how she'd been, how the food was lately. They'd heard the center had hired a new nurse...

"We're doing well," they then said, followed by a recap of what had recently happened with Aubrey, her milestones, life at work and in general.

This was the usual script. All in the hope that some news, a word, anything might trigger a reaction in Muriel. Then, when they ran out of topics, their conversation often turned to a case and what they should get at the grocery store on their way back home.

Tom sat at the edge of Muriel's bed with Aubrey asleep in his arms. He leaned closer to the recliner's hollow occupant to catch her attention. The gesture signaled their imminent departure. One last try to connect with Muriel before hitting the road. As always, he got no reaction. His gaze traveled to Elenora's, silently asking, *Ready to go?*

As Elenora picked up her purse to leave, a new, fresh-out-of-school nurse made a chirpy entrance.

"Hello, there, sir. Ma'am. Little one. I'm Nurse Bessett."

They introduced themselves, and then the nurse said the most baffling thing.

"Muriel must love holding the baby."

Elenora and Tom exchanged a stunned look while the young woman crouched in front of the resident.

"Don't you, Muriel?" She squeezed the woman's hands before turning to Elenora and Tom, expecting them to agree with her.

Elenora was stumped. Was the young nurse being sarcastic? She seemed the opposite of sarcastic, all cheerful puppies and rainbows. Maybe it was her inexperience talking, being too new to understand the full extent of Muriel's situation. Elenora decided to cut her some slack and chalked up her misplaced enthusiasm to youthful ignorance.

"Well, we did put Aubrey in her arms a few times when she was a newborn, but my mother didn't respond to her."

The nurse seemed surprised, disappointed even. "And you never tried again?" *Such a shame,* she seemed to think.

As well-intentioned as she might be, her remark and attitude stung Elenora and made her feel even more awful—as if she'd been depriving her mother of the baby's affection on purpose. Anger crept up inside of her.

"Her arms are as limp as noodles," she blurted out defensively, "and she hasn't responded to an outside stimulus in decades. She's not even aware of the baby. So, no, we never tried again." Hearing the brusqueness in her tone, she winced. Even if it was a sore subject and she was tired, there was no need to be curt with the well-meaning caretaker. "I apologize. That came out wrong."

"Since Muriel is so frail," Tom added diplomatically, "we thought it best not to burden her with a squirming baby."

"I understand." Nurse Bessett recovered her smile. She became thoughtful and seemed to debate whether to voice something on her mind. "I don't want to overstep, but maybe it's worth another try? I mean, even without a physical reaction to tell us something matters to her, it might still make her happy to hold her granddaughter. With some help, of course."

The nurse had a point. The medical team had never found proof that Muriel's mind was entirely gone, and maybe she still appreciated some things in life without being able to manifest appreciation.

A truckload of guilt fell on Elenora. Why had she not understood this before and persevered? Why had she deprived her mother of contact with Aubrey? Could she possibly feel any worse?

"I guess that wouldn't hurt." Her strangled words betrayed her emotions once more. At least this time, they didn't come out as an unfair verbal assault.

Tom got up to bring Aubrey to Muriel, but Nurse Bessett intercepted him.

"May I?" She held out her arms to take the baby.

"Of course."

The transfer woke Aubrey up, but before she could protest being in a stranger's arms, the nurse cradled her and cooed, all smiles.

"Hello there, little cutie. Did you have a big nap?"

Aubrey's frown vanished, and a smile appeared around her pacifier. Elenora thanked the stars for giving her such an easygoing little girl.

"Let's go say hello to Grandmama, shall we?" The nurse bent toward Elenora's mother. "Muriel, I'm putting your granddaughter down on your lap, okay? I will hold her the whole time, so you don't have to worry about dropping her or anything."

She crouched in front of the resident and gently put the baby on her lap, remaining in front with her arms caging in the little one. Aubrey chewed on her pacifier as if her life depended on it, drool leaking down the sides, and raised a fascinated gaze to her grandmother's face.

Despite knowing that nothing would come of it, Elenora held her breath and searched for a reaction from her mother's dysfunctional body acknowledging the little one's presence—

a glimmer in her vacant eyes, the beginning of a smile, a twitch. Anything. But as expected, no reaction came.

The young nurse persevered with unkillable ardor. "Isn't she the most beautiful little girl you've ever seen, Muriel? Isn't she precious?"

Elenora had to give Nurse Bessett some credit for trying. She also resolved to provide regular physical contact between Aubrey and her mother from now on. Even if it didn't make a difference.

On the off chance that it did.

One of Aubrey's hands reached for her grandmother's face, and everyone sucked in a breath of anticipation. But Muriel remained still, her dead gaze lost ahead of her while tiny fingers roamed underneath her jawline.

Aubrey pushed the pacifier out of her mouth with her tongue. "Mamama?"

Was she trying to say *grandmama*? Elenora's heart melted a little. At least her daughter recognized Muriel and would grow to know her even if their connection was one-sided.

After a moment, the nurse declared, "Now, Muriel, I will take back little Aubrey."

She shifted to lift the baby, but Muriel's arms wrapped around the baby, shocking everyone in the room. She brought Aubrey against her chest greedily, as if ready to ward off anyone who would dare take her granddaughter away from her. Then she rocked gently, her eyes staring into the distance with an intensity never seen before.

Joy briefly sparked inside Elenora. They'd finally had a breakthrough with her mother, no matter how weird it seemed. But dread took over just as fast as she absorbed the unnerving fervor in her mother's eyes and her uncompromising hold on Aubrey. The most frightening thought entered Elenora's mind: was her mother possessed?

With Tom next to her and ready to intervene, the nurse tried to coax Muriel into relaxing her grip and letting go, but to no avail. She tried to lift the woman's fingers one at a time, but her clutch on the baby remained too strong.

"Nurse Bessett, please give us a moment?" Tom asked calmly.

The nurse was unsure of his request at first but then agreed to leave. "I'll be outside if you need me."

"Thank you. And please close the door behind you." Tom took the nurse's place in front of Muriel to catch Aubrey, should she decide to release her suddenly.

The nurse's footsteps receded behind them, followed by the soft click of the door closing.

Tom whispered to Elenora, "Touch her to see if we have company."

He had reached the same conclusion as Elenora. It freaked her out to search for evil inside her mother, but it made sense to do so. She crouched next to Tom and gently put a hand on her mother's arm, preparing herself for any kind of reaction—physical, mental, or emotional. She closed her eyes and waited.

Utter darkness greeted her. She encountered no thought, memory, emotion, or dark force.

She opened her eyes and shook her head. "I'm getting nothing."

"So, nothing *evil*?" Tom mouthed the word *evil*.

"No, but maybe I'm being fooled."

He nodded thoughtfully before placing a hand on

Muriel's knee. "Muriel..." He sounded steady and sweet. "I'm so glad that you love Aubrey. Your granddaughter. She's such a sweet baby, isn't she?"

Elenora stared at her mother's eyes, hoping her husband's words would get Muriel's attention and get through to her. But the older woman's gaze remained intensely distant and her grip tight.

"Muriel, Elenora needs to feed Aubrey. May we take her back?" Tom slowly slid his hand underneath his daughter. "We don't want her to fuss or go hungry, do we? You can hold her again after she's done eating."

Miraculously, Muriel's hold softened, and Tom lifted the baby unhurriedly, no doubt to avoid a knee-jerk reaction.

As Aubrey neared her father's chest, Muriel's hand shot out and seized Tom's forearm.

"She's not *his*," the woman grunted with great effort.

Tom stilled and calmly studied his mother-in-law. "What do you mean, Muriel?" he asked evenly.

Muriel's hand became flaccid and slid off him. Her arm fell onto her lap in a muffled slap. Her eyes were dull again.

With Aubrey safe, Elenora and Tom exchanged horrified glances. *What the hell just happened?*

"Nurse?" he called, cautiously moving away from Muriel's reach.

The door opened, and Nurse Bessett poked her perky face in. "How can I help? Oh, you got the little one back. Excellent."

"Would you please fetch Dr. Graham?"

"He appeared thoroughly baffled, but I don't think demonic possession would ever cross his mind," Elenora said to Serena via speakerphone in the car. "He mumbled something about a thought disorder to his staff. But we're not supposed to know that. Tom can read lips."

Elenora had told her friend about her mother's cryptic message, the other creepy bits, and Dr. Graham's impression.

Serena's snort echoed in the car. "But how does the good doctor explain a miraculous—and insanely brief—recovery from a mental coma after decades? I mean, don't blink, right?"

"He doesn't. They're gonna do tests, monitor her, and try to get her to react again. There's not much else to do."

"Except worry yourself sick?"

Of course, Elenora would find time to do exactly that.

"Could the poltergeist have attached itself to me or Tom and followed us to my mother's?" she asked.

"You mean, like, to mess with you?"

"Yeah. Or whatever else a vindictive dead entity might do. Claire-Lune mentioned that a spirit could move to another location or something."

"Well... Usually, a medium needs to bind the spirit to an object to move them, and poltergeists don't typically possess people. Subtlety isn't their thing... And you felt nothing odd when you touched your mom, right?"

"Right. And the air in the room was normal, now that I think of it."

"Good. Maybe the doctor's onto something after all. I mean, what your mom did and said is creepy as fuck. But I also know firsthand how we see boogeymen everywhere once we've seen one. Our imagination can easily run rampant and assume the worst. But sometimes, a pipe is just a pipe."

"You mean, maybe what happened with Muriel really is a small miracle?" Tom asked.

"Maybe. But at any rate, worrying won't help. Right, Ele?"

"I hear you." Despite herself, Elenora added her mother to her mental list of worries.

After a shared silence, Serena said, "Oh! This might cheer you up. Wren may have found a way to screw with the dark spell."

CHAPTER TWENTY-ONE

Wren had concocted a spell to subdue the dark magic over the threshold of the Maple Street house. It should help the witches wrangle the poltergeist and prevent it from "going apeshit on their ass"—Serena's words. They proposed to strike again the next morning.

Elenora looked forward to the new attempt. She was eager to see the malevolent spirit brought down and curious to know if Angéline de Montbleu would show up again. The visit would also be a welcome distraction to hopefully give her mind a break from rehashing her mother's haunting words.

She's not his, Muriel had rasped accusingly. Who was the *she* in question? Aubrey? If so, who was the male to whom she didn't belong? Muriel had hissed those words at Tom, so he wasn't the male in question, or she would have said *yours.*

Logically.

But was logic even involved?

Maybe her mother had meant to insinuate Aubrey wasn't Tom's, but her blank stare hadn't recognized her interlocutor... But Tom *was* Aubrey's father—Elenora knew without the shadow of a doubt. So, if Muriel was trying to dispute his paternity, her reasoning was bizarre and incomprehensible.

Of all the first words she chose to utter after decades of silence...

Maybe it is a thought disorder.

If Dr. Graham was correct, did it mean that if Muriel spoke again, they should expect more cryptic words? That if her mind woke up for good, it would be in no state for her to rejoin the world of the living?

The thought hurt. All those years, a sliver of hope that her mother might miraculously come back to life had remained buried deep inside of Elenora.

Maybe it was time to let go of that hope.

Elenora called Pierre, and an hour after they spoke, he showed up with Céleste and a pan of lasagna from an Italian bakery to be helpful and to further commiserate about her mother's mind-boggling manifestation. He spent the night, too, so she and Tom could head out to the old house in the morning without worrying about Aubrey. Once again, she counted her blessings to have Pierre in her life.

On the way to Maple Street, Elenora wondered if her father would be as keen and present in Aubrey's life as Pierre if he were still around. She had few but warm memories of him and knew in her heart that he would have been awesome. Since the baby's birth, she had often wondered how different things would be if he were alive. Would her mother still have had a mental breakdown if tragedy hadn't struck their family?

There was no point in dwelling on what could have been. Elenora redirected her thoughts toward gratitude to ward off sadness. Pierre wouldn't be in her life if the accident hadn't happened.

And neither would Serena and the witches.

The thought was scary. How lost and alone would she be without their wisdom, support, and friendship? How could she possibly have dealt with her freak abilities?

"Looks like we're the first to arrive," Tom declared as they neared the old house, saving Elenora from her spiraling thoughts.

Exiting the car, her sundress clung to the back of her thighs from the heat—she pulled the fabric away from her legs. The weather forecast predicted a hot and humid day. The sun hid behind gray clouds, and the air was heavy. Elenora glanced at the once-majestic home. While rain wasn't expected, the atmosphere and lack of light cast a veil of gloom on the house. It would be even darker inside.

Did every single one of their visits have to feel so dang ominous? Couldn't they, just once, come over and have blinding sunshine blasting through the windows, making the place well-lit and airy instead of giving a serial-killer-hidden-in-the-pantry vibe? The summer had been very sunny so far. So what was up with the horror cliché timing? Elenora chuckled.

Her attention turned to the sound and movement of the nearly simultaneous arrivals of Alex's car, Juniper's Jeep full of witches, and Yukiko's motorcycle. Soon they were all gathered on the sidewalk at the junction of the weathered stone walkway leading to the house.

"So, what have we got?" Alex asked.

"Wren came up with a spell that should temper the dark magic on the house—" Claire-Lune started.

"Though it won't nullify or eradicate the spell, like I was hoping," Wren seemed to feel the need to specify.

Serena put a hand on her shoulder. "Hey, it's a great start, and we're delighted to work with that. Crippling the bastard might be enough for us to get the upper hand."

"And we've tweaked our approach for keeping it in check now that we know what to expect. These calibrations should also make a difference." Claire-Lune looked confident and eager to get started. Her gaze swept their little crowd. "Are we ready to roll?"

Alex gestured toward the path. "After you."

Claire-Lune led the way to the front porch. As she walked, with a swift motion of her wrist, she took down the spell she'd put on the house to keep anyone from entering.

Serena emitted a low whistle. "Getting efficient there, sis. Soon you'll be able to cast spells *and* chew gum at the same time."

Claire-Lune blew on her fingernails, playfully rubbing them on her shirt, then untacked the police tape once she reached the steps.

"My turn will take a little longer, I'm afraid." Wren carefully laid her hands on the front door.

Elenora wondered if she was as hard on herself as Wren seemed to be. The remarkably talented witch surely had no need to be so self-critical and plagued with doubt—especially when a little self-love could go a long way. Something for Elenora to keep in mind and put into practice more often. But old habits died hard.

Wren's fingers skated over the door in an intricate pattern. They glowed on and off, and she muttered strings of foreign-sounding words. She lost herself in her task and seemed to relax, or at least get some satisfaction out of the process.

Near her, Juniper held a splayed hand at the door, her head cocked in focused attention, ready to react.

Wren's magic made a light whooshing sound, and she took a step back. "Tom, would you please unlock the door?"

Once Tom was done wrestling with the rusty lock, Wren moved her fingers over the door one last time before opening it. She swept her hand over the threshold and seemed pleased with what she found. "The new spell seems to have dampened the dark one. However, I don't know how stable it will remain or for how long. So we shouldn't dawdle. And let's hope the dark spell won't fix itself in the meantime."

"It could fix itself?" Alex asked, at once surprised, concerned, and fascinated.

"It could contain a healing element allowing it to self-repair. Or if the poltergeist is controlling the magic to keep people out of the house—"

"The poltergeist might be doing this?" Alex's jaw hit the porch floor.

The witches nodded. Tom's brows furrowed at the prospect.

"It dawned on us while studying the dark spell that it might be the case," Serena said.

"If the poltergeist is controlling the dark spell to keep people out," Tom said, "would that make it a witch?"

"A witch or a warlock, yes," Wren answered.

"A *dead* witch or warlock... She or he could still practice magic?" Tom's brows furrowed even more.

"Let's hope not—it's just a theory. But we've seen stranger things."

Alex peered inside the house, looking like he was considering a major change of plans.

Serena slapped him on the back. "It's too early to freak out, big guy. We don't know enough yet."

"At any rate, let's take advantage of the wrench we just threw in the dark spell and get cracking." Claire-Lune walked past them and into the house.

At Alex's hesitant look, Serena's expression softened. "You can wait outside if you'd rather. No shame in that." Her tone held no snark.

But her lenient words spurred him instead. "So you guys can get attacked by another light fixture or a flying toilet? I don't think so."

Serena considered him for a moment before going inside. Elenora could swear her two fiery friends were finally starting to warm up to each other. In their own rough and peculiar way. Not that either of them would ever admit it.

"Ready to go in?" Tom asked Elenora. He seemed antsy to get things done.

"Let's blow this popsicle stand."

CHAPTER TWENTY-TWO

Elenora entered the ballroom and found the witches crouched around the chandelier, studying its mangled carcass of twisted metal and shards of crystal while Alex hovered protectively nearby.

"If our perp acts up again, this thing could be worse than a nail bomb," Tom whispered to them.

"My thoughts exactly," Claire-Lune whispered back. She considered the pile of debris for a moment before moving a hand over it in a clockwise motion. "This should slow down any funny business."

"How's the air?" Wren asked Juniper before turning an inquisitive gaze on Yukiko and Elenora.

"Seems normal to me," Juniper answered.

"Same," Yukiko agreed.

Elenora assessed the air pressure and detected no suspicious thickness. "It feels fine to me too."

"Perfect. Let's get rid of this thing, then," Claire-Lune declared about the chandelier.

Alex grabbed the chain, endeavoring to drag the whole

thing out of the house by himself. Tom jumped in to help, and within seconds, Juniper moved her hands, providing an invisible push and lift to the broken light fixture with the countless sharp edges, helping them move it without cutting themselves.

They hauled it out the door, and Elenora watched their progress from the front window once they got outside. In no time, the formerly dazzling chandelier decorated the front lawn. Juniper considered it, hands on her hips.

"I'll help you guys throw it in the construction dumpster at the side of the house. But we'll have to make transport look inconspicuous," she told Tom and Alex. While the residential street was quiet, it was daytime on a Sunday, and people were home.

Wren joined them. "I'll throw a cloaking spell over it. Then, Junie, you can take it from there."

Elenora heard activity in the room behind her and turned. Yukiko had returned with a broom and a garbage bag.

Claire-Lune waved her hand dismissively. "Never mind the broom. Just hold the bag open."

Elenora helped with the bag, and in less than a minute, the twins magically gathered all the shards, dust, and fragments left on the floor and sent them flying into the bag. This nifty—and highly practical—trick amazed Elenora. She hated cleaning with a passion and wished she could trade her psychic abilities for that one.

Serena chuckled. "I know what you're thinking. We're just taking a shortcut 'cause the clock is ticking. But when we're at home, we still have to clean with elbow grease. Trust me."

"Why?"

"Because this spell takes a lot of effort and concentration. To do it on a larger scale would be like running a marathon— as in *sweating buckets*. Ugh! No thanks. It's more efficient to do things the old-fashioned way." She made a face. "That said, I still hope someone will soon come up with better and easier cleaning spells." She arched a brow at Wren coming back into the room and gave her a pleading look. "Right, Wren?"

"Don't look at me!" Wren laughed.

"If it were up to Serena," Claire-Lune said to Elenora, "the OPO's entire R&D department would focus their efforts on making her life easier, starting with making food appear on her plate without cooking and having her favorite shows ready to watch before they're even written."

"Oh, come on! I'm not that bad! And it's called having priorities." Serena chuckled.

Tom, Alex, and Juniper returned and surveyed the room. "I don't see any other potential hazards. Do you, guys?" Tom asked.

"I think we're good to start," Claire-Lune said.

Yukiko unpacked her summoning gear. Once again, she arranged the candles in the middle of the room. The other witches joined her in a circle while maintaining a vigilant eye.

Trying to make herself useful, Elenora monitored the air pressure. With the candles out, she expected the air to thicken, but it didn't. In fact, it struck her that the air was suspiciously light and pure, especially considering the humidity outside.

How odd.

The old house didn't have air conditioning, and with the

windows closed, the air should have been stuffy at the very least.

"What's up?" Serena asked her—not much got past her.

Elenora told her how the current state of the air confused her.

Abandoning her candles, Yukiko straightened, closed her eyes, and gauged the air attentively. "I see what you mean."

"What does that mean?" Tom asked.

"Sometimes, a supernatural element can mess with the laws of physics—a spell or a presence." Claire-Lune's eyes roamed around the room as she explained. "In either case, we're prepared."

Yukiko calmly lit the candles one by one while everyone remained on high alert, expecting an assault. The medium's eyes scrutinized the flames.

"Spirit in this room, I respectfully summon you. Please show yourself."

Unlike before, the flames remained alive. But they also didn't flicker. They burned brightly while eerily still.

Yukiko repeated her request for the spirit to show. Once. Twice. Three times. She blew out a breath. "Dammit, it's resisting."

"It's fighting back?" Juniper raised her arms in a defensive stance.

"Not so much fighting back as...artfully dodging me."

"It knows what it's doing, and it's got the means to do it." Claire-Lune sighed.

"If it's avoiding us, then is it safe to assume it's not gonna throw shit at us this time?" Alex's eyes scanned the room.

"Probably. But it won't show its face either," Yukiko replied, her voice defeated.

"It's just a different type of *fuck you*." Serena threw her head back in frustration. "I just knew *he* would make it impossible. Ugh!"

"A knowledgeable medium like Miss de Montbleu might know how to evade a summons..." Elenora mused, not liking her words one bit. She wanted to believe her encounter with the elderly spirit had been truthful. Without deceit. Instead, it looked like she *had* fallen for the sweet-granny routine. Ironically. She still had a lot to learn about dealing with spirits—and judging people's character, apparently. "It's not like I've never been fooled before," she mumbled, mostly to express her disappointment.

Tom slipped an arm around her shoulders.

"I shouldn't have joked about her last night." She made a face.

He gave her a squeeze and a smile. "Don't worry. Maybe there's something we don't know. We'll do our due diligence before we banish anyone."

"I trust your gut, Ele. And I still think it's a guy," Serena said.

"But we know for a fact that Miss de Montbleu is here. And she was an accomplished medium. How could it not be her?" Elenora asked painfully.

Yukiko smiled empathetically. "It's true that it doesn't look good. But at least she was kind to you when you saw her."

And slightly less kind when the ghost tried to dispatch Elenora.

"Maybe we are dealing with Miss de Montbleu. Or maybe there *is* a second spirit who's magic savvy," Claire-Lune said softly.

Yukiko looked up at Tom. "There's a pentacle downstairs, correct?"

"Unless the poltergeist magically erased it since we saw it, then yes, there should be a pentacle downstairs. Why?"

Yukiko picked up a candle in each hand, keeping them lit, and stood. Juniper and Serena gave her a hand with the rest.

"Since it's refusing to be summoned in this room, we might get better traction over the pentacle."

⁕

Being back in the basement after everything that had happened since her first visit allowed Elenora to view the main room with fresh eyes. She pushed aside her unpleasant thoughts about Angéline de Montbleu and opened her senses, ready to catch anything new or that she might have missed.

While Yukiko, Serena, and Juniper set the candles on the pentagram's five tips, Elenora noticed Alex standing in the doorway, his back glued to the frame. He looked ready to split.

Serena sat cross-legged next to Juniper on the edge of the pentacle. She, too, noticed Alex's uptight stance by the door. "What's up, Alex? You look more freaked out than usual."

"You think it's wise to summon a powerful, evil magical guy over a satanic symbol? Isn't that asking for trouble?" He shuddered.

"You mean the pentacle?" Serena replied while Claire-Lune and Wren sat, completing a circle around the symbol.

"Yeah. What else?"

"The pentacle is not a satanic symbol per se, nor a sign of

inherent evil. In fact, in witchcraft, it's usually positive. A bunch of wackos popularized a corrupted version of it and bent its meaning."

Alex jutted his chin at the pentacle. "You mean *that* is not a sign of evil?"

"*That* is a sign of misuse and disrespect. Yes, this one was meant to worship evil. But it was also created by some attention-seeking, clueless twit. I wouldn't lose sleep over it." Her voice held an edge.

Alex took in the witch's passionate resentment, and his face softened. "Sorry, I didn't mean to offend."

"Yeah, okay. Thanks. Didn't mean to sound bitchy. It's just that the popular misconception really gets my goat."

"I get it." He nodded sympathetically.

A small smile appeared on her face.

Yukiko finished fussing over the position of one candle. "Would you guys mind joining us?" she asked Elenora and Tom. "I'm only asking because the spirit is resisting, and your presence in the circle might help." Her kind gaze traveled to Alex. "But you don't have to. No pressure."

Tom took Elenora's hand—his keen curiosity palpable—and the two of them joined the circle.

Alex's jaw tightened as he hesitated by the door, uncomfortable again. "Fine," he soon mumbled, his neck reddening.

As he dragged himself to the circle, Serena scooted aside to make room for him. With his eyes intent on the lines of the pentacle, Alex sat awkwardly between her and Wren, looking like he was trying to avoid the sign.

"As a kid, you lifted your feet when the car crossed a train track, didn't you?" Serena elbowed him teasingly.

He pursed his lips in response.

"Would someone please kill the lights?" Yukiko asked.

Four witchy hands raised in unison, and a simultaneous flick of four wrists aimed at the switch flipped it off from a distance, bringing darkness to the room. With the candles casting an orange glow and sharp shadows off everyone's features, the space took on an ominous vibe.

"Spirit in this room, I respectfully summon you. Please show yourself," Yukiko said, and Elenora opened her senses once more.

The flames moved ever slightly but mostly remained still. The room was bathed in silence. The medium repeated the summons. Her unanswered words lingered in the room along with a collective sense of frustration.

"Crap," Serena muttered.

Yukiko took a cleansing breath and invited the spirit to show itself yet again. With a similar absence of results. She tried a different approach. "Angéline de Montbleu, I respectfully summon you. Please show yourself."

Would calling Angéline by name convince her to reveal herself? Elenora held her breath with mixed anticipation. A part of her didn't want the kind elderly spirit to be the murderous poltergeist and get banished. The other part still yearned to see her again.

The wait for a response seemed to take forever.

Elenora stared at one flame and repeated Yukiko's words in her mind in case it helped. *Angéline de Montbleu, I respectfully summon you. Please show yourself.* She closed her eyes and tried to will Angéline to show. *I welcome you...*

"Well. That was a big fat nothing."

Serena's annoyed voice brought Elenora's attention back to the candlelit room. And then a realization came: Miss de

Montbleu was avoiding them because she knew they were on to her.

Bummer.

Elenora shifted position, her hands landing on the floor on either side of her. As her palms connected with the wood, flashes she'd already seen of Jean-Luc Rivard and his followers appeared before her—superimposed with reality—and surprised the crap out of her. The images seemed much clearer than before. She closed her eyes to get rid of the distracting lights of the candles. This time, she was able to recognize both Jean-Luc Rivard and Micheline Lamirande among the figures.

A new vision of Rivard followed. He wore his dark, hooded robe and stood over the pentacle in front of his disciples. His bearing was solemn and lordly. He produced a dagger and held it high so everyone could have a good look. Dramatically, he brought the blade to his forearm, pushing the tip up his sleeve.

He's gonna cut himself. Elenora tensed, not keen to see blood. *Relax. It's just a vision.*

But what followed made her heart quicken even more. Jean-Luc Rivard's steely composure morphed into shock as the weapon seemed to take on a life of its own. The young man appeared to battle for control of the blade as it inched toward his wrist. Queasiness shot through Elenora's stomach.

Jean-Luc Rivard looked on in horror as the knife sliced through his skin and drew blood. A line of crimson trickled down and landed on a pentagram line, igniting a flame that traveled along every groove of the pentacle in a matter of seconds, setting the entire symbol ablaze.

Wearing a horrified *wtf* look, the fake cult leader stepped back from the flames right in time to avoid catching his robe on fire. His grip loosened on the dagger, and it dropped to the floor.

The vision disappeared, and Elenora opened her eyes. Everyone was staring at her.

"I saw Jean-Luc Rivard cut himself and set the pentacle on fire with his blood," she blurted out. "I don't think he could control any of it."

"You think someone or something made him do it?" Claire-Lune asked.

Elenora nodded and described what she'd seen.

"Should we try to summon Rivard?" Tom asked.

"If his spirit was in this house—whether or not he's the poltergeist—technically, he should have answered my general summons," Yukiko explained.

"Oh. Okay."

"Unless the dark spell or our screwing with it is preventing him or any other spirit from answering," Claire-Lune said.

Could this be why Angéline hadn't answered?

"Let me try," Yukiko said before summoning the cult leader. Three times. Her efforts yielded no results. She called it a day, and with Wren's help, she packed her candles.

Tom stood and started pacing the room, brushing a knuckle over his lips. "So, we have at least one spirit—maybe two. A poltergeist wreaking havoc despite a dark spell on the house, who might have magical abilities." He stopped. "And who could have cast the dark spell, correct?"

"It's possible, yes," Claire-Lune answered.

Tom nodded and resumed pacing. "Elenora met Angé-line de Montbleu's spirit—so we know she's around and likely avoiding us. Unless something is preventing her from appearing today—maybe because we tweaked the dark spell. Is any of this incorrect or implausible?"

"No," Claire-Lune confirmed.

"And Ele just got a new vision confirming that Jean-Luc Rivard set the pentacle on fire with his blood, an event Micheline Lamirande described to us. She thought it was bogus, but apparently not. An unidentified force—most likely supernatural—seemed to have made him do it."

"The darkness Miss de Montbleu thought was influencing him," Elenora said.

"Or so she claimed..." Alex jumped in. "Maybe that's what she wants us to believe. Maybe *she's* the darkness and wants to redirect our attention."

Elenora groaned inwardly. Of course, if Angéline de Montbleu was the poltergeist and lying to them, she could have been responsible for Jean-Luc Rivard's torment and atrocious demise. Still, it was hard to believe that a mild-mannered elderly woman could be capable of such evil manipulation and violence. But not an impossibility. And in Elenora's new normal, nothing seemed impossible. She had to remember that and stop being so naïve.

Always assume it's a trap. Serena's words bounced around in her head.

And always assume I'll give the worst criminal the benefit of the doubt, Elenora retorted to herself.

Satan included, probably. Not that she wanted to test that supposition.

But she believed in people being innocent until proven guilty. She'd seen the truth prevail in improbable scenarios often enough to know not to trust appearances or hasty verdicts of culpability.

Something didn't feel right about Angéline de Montbleu being guilty. While Elenora understood she might be their perp, her gut refused to get on board.

"So, we're back to Miss de Montbleu..." Juniper said.

"Miss de Montbleu or not, we're back to square one." Serena crossed her arms over her chest, and her eyes narrowed as something dawned on her. "Hey, if that Rivard creep got possessed, maybe the darkness corrupted him, and now he's got a chip on his shoulder. We know he died here violently, so he could still be in the house—but not showing up for whatever reason. He loved spectacle. To me, he sounds like an excellent candidate to be our haunting asshole in residence. I vote for him over the medium."

"Okay, well, speculations are fine, but you know what's even better?" A wide grin spread over Claire-Lune's face. "If it's avoiding us, whoever it is, now's a great time to peek at the attic."

CHAPTER TWENTY-THREE

Taking a page out of Alex's playbook, Elenora observed the activity in the attic from near the stairs to allow for a quick exit. She eyed the sheet of plywood the OPO had secured over the opening in the exterior wall. It looked sturdy. But returning to the dangerous space had given her a sobering reminder of her brush with death and shaken her courageous resolve to take down the poltergeist.

Recovering from trauma can take years. Give yourself a break.

"How are you?" Serena appeared at her side.

"I believe I'll be fine, but I definitely need a moment."

"I might hide it well, but I often need a moment too. We deal with some crazy shit. And even with magic, we still get reminded that most of us are not immortal."

She sounded sincere. Elenora never would have guessed that her audacious and impetuous friend could feel that way.

Serena unzipped a backpack, from which she took out rock-climbing gear.

Elenora looked at it with curiosity. "What's this for?"

"It's to avoid teasing death again." The witch showed her a safety harness. "Here. Put this on."

Elenora moved the puzzling equipment around to figure out how it worked.

"Allow me." Serena gave her a hand putting it on. "I will tether you to me *and* the banister. With Juniper's magic on top, if you get shoved again, you won't go very far."

Elenora's gaze traveled to Tom and Alex, who were testing the stability of the plywood covering the gigantic hole to the outside. They seemed satisfied. She felt her nerves ease.

Serena finished putting on her own harness and clipped a rope to it. She chuckled. "I know this looks silly and like overkill, but I'd rather look like a wiener than take a chance with your life. I'll even add a tethering spell to bond you to me *and* Juniper. How's that?"

"Okay, wow. Thanks." Elenora laughed. The level of caution did seem ridiculous. But so what? "I appreciate the trouble. When I probe the cracked wall again, I'll be able to focus on it instead of panicking."

"Awesome."

With the dark spell subdued and the poltergeist hiding from them, the witches were hopeful Elenora might get answers from reading the wall Jérémie Marsan had hit. She hoped they were right. She couldn't wait to get answers. The fact that she'd just had a new vision in the basement boded well.

Serena clipped a second rope to Elenora's harness and secured the other end to the banister.

Elenora surveyed the room. Yukiko, Wren, and Claire-Lune seemed to assess the space with their eyes closed while

Juniper, Tom, and Alex gathered the construction tools and supplies scattered around the room—including Marsan's sledgehammer.

"Should we put these in one of the bedrooms?" Tom asked Juniper as they headed down the stairs.

Elenora didn't catch the witch's reply, but she suspected they would soon return, and then it would be showtime. She wandered to her target to the sound of her harness clanking.

You've got this.

As she got closer, the air thickened, and her stomach dropped. The change was subtle, but she perceived it nonetheless. She turned to search for Yukiko. The medium must have felt the change as well—her concerned gaze snapped to Elenora's.

Claire-Lune caught their silent interaction. "What is it?"

"The air," Elenora and Yukiko answered together as Tom, Alex, and Juniper returned.

"Oh! Now that we don't want him in the way, he's showing up. Figures," Serena grumbled before raising her voice. "Don't you have something better to do, asshole?"

"Would you like us to abort?" Tom asked Elenora.

"It's up to you, but we've got your back," Claire-Lune said.

"We do. However, we must keep in mind that, while the dark spell is lessened, it is still in effect and could always surge or come back fully," Wren added.

Juniper took a step forward and assumed a defiant posture. "I had a good night of sleep."

Alex moved to stand in front of the sheet of plywood, arms akimbo. "I'm pretty good at catching."

Serena jiggled the rope tethering Elenora to her to remind the psychic she wasn't going anywhere.

Elenora turned back to the wall and pondered the risk. If the same thing as before were to happen, several mechanisms were in place to slow her down and catch her before anything too hairy occurred. At worst, she would get a few bruises. At best, they would gain valuable information. "Let's do this."

Wren appeared at her side. "If you encounter resistance or anything weird, don't fight it. Just disengage, okay?"

"Got it."

Tom and Juniper went to flank Alex, forming a human barrier in front of the plywood.

Elenora's gaze swept the room to make sure everyone was ready for her to proceed. After they all nodded, she brought her right hand to the wall and closed her eyes when her fingers touched the lightly cracked plaster.

The blurry flash she'd seen before appeared, but in focus this time, and showed a man's hand laying a black-and-white photograph on a bed of burgundy velvet. The picture featured a fair-haired woman holding a baby in a blanket against a fancy backdrop. She was stunning, impeccably dressed, and looking distressed.

A suffocating weight crushed Elenora, blasting her back to reality. She found herself pinned to the floor, with the harness digging into her side. It took her a few seconds to figure out that Tom was draped protectively over her.

What the hell happened now?

The floor shook. She twisted her head to peek around Tom's forearm and saw Juniper, arms outstretched and moving sluggishly, like she was fighting to keep an invisible force at bay. The other witches seemed to be helping her to the best of their individual abilities. Alex's piercing eyes darted around, as if trying to assess an invisible enemy.

"Take a chill pill, man! She's no longer a threat!" Juniper bellowed, her small stature clearly no reflection of her might.

As if responding to the witch's command, the floor stopped moving, and the air in the room lightened. Juniper lowered her arms, bent forward, and grabbed her thighs in a recuperating stance.

"The air is stable. I think it's gone," Yukiko said.

Tom finally relaxed his grip on Elenora and moved aside, freeing her and allowing her to breathe better.

"What happened?" she asked him as Serena and Alex asked her, "What the hell did you see?" with matching looks of bewilderment.

"The poltergeist acted up again," Tom explained. He looked as stunned as everyone else in the room. "While you were reading the wall, another tornado waltzed in. It felt like the whole house was about to blow, and the damn sledge-hammer we brought downstairs actually made its way back up." He shook his head in disbelief.

"It was deliberate," Alex muttered, casting an accusatory glare at the offending sledgehammer trapped under his foot, as if he expected it to move again.

"Totally deliberate," Serena agreed.

"How did it get back in here?" Elenora tried to understand.

Tom gave a bewildered shrug. "It flew up the staircase and went straight at us. Thank God Juniper saw it coming and stopped it in time."

"And then you were thrown back from the wall again, and Tom caught you," Serena said. "That pretty much sums it up. Now, what the hell did you see to piss it off this much?"

"I saw the blurry flash again, but clearly this time," Elenora answered.

"The one Pierre thinks has a hand in it?" Serena asked.

"Yes, and he was right—it's a hand holding a photo of a woman and a baby."

"May I grab the flash?"

Elenora stuck her arm out to Serena. They proceeded with the capture, and before long, the brief clip played on the witch's new tablet.

"That's Jane Gill, the photographer's wife. And their daughter, Clementine." Claire-Lune fiddled with her phone before showing them a picture of Joseph Gill, his wife, and their child.

Everyone's gazes moved between her cell and the tablet, comparing the two images. It was indeed Jane Gill with her daughter.

"Hmm... Okay. So how does this picture relate to the wall?" Tom asked, pensive.

Claire-Lune pointed at her sister's tablet. "This looks like a postmortem photo of the little one."

That would explain the devastation on Jane Gill's face. Elenora looked at the baby, who was staring at the camera. If she was indeed dead, her eyes must have been touched up. *What a weird thing.* Elenora would never get used to that eerie aspect of postmortem photography. Or of postmortem photography itself, for that matter.

Claire-Lune frowned and hummed. "I don't recall reading anything about their daughter passing. As far as I know, the papers never reported it. In fact, when Joseph Gill sold the house, he made a big show of telling the world that he and his family were setting off on a trip around the world. He didn't say 'my wife and I.' I would've noticed."

She pointed at the family picture of the Gills on her cell —a confident patriarch and a loving mother holding a cute, *alive* baby. "Most papers ran this picture with their articles about the trip."

"Little Clementine looks rather alive and well," Alex said.

"Exactly."

"So, Joseph Gill might have lied to the papers to...cover up her death? Have you seen articles published later reporting on their trip? Or their return?" Tom asked Claire-Lune.

"No. But I didn't dig much past the sale of the house. I wish I had."

"I'd love to know if they even left the country," Serena chimed in.

"I'm asking Renaud to look into this," Alex said, texting on his phone.

"Good. Ask him to find out where they're buried too." Tom looked at Elenora. "Maybe Yukiko could get some answers from their graves."

"I'll assist her if she wants me to," Elenora said. A grave-side séance was nowhere near her bucket list, but as long as she didn't have to dig up coffins to read remains, she was okay with it.

"Noted." Tom returned his attention to the image on Serena's tablet. "So, what do we have here? Jane and Clementine Gill. A man's hand—"

"Probably Joseph Gill's. Our poltergeist," Serena declared with confidence.

"What makes you so sure he's the poltergeist?" Alex asked her.

"The poltergeist's an asshole. And Joseph Gill looks like one." She jerked her thumb at Claire-Lune's phone to prove her point.

Alex chuckled. "That argument wouldn't hold water in a court of law."

"Well, we won't be dealing with a court of law. The guy looks like an arrogant asshole. Period." She shot him a defiant look. "Tell me he doesn't."

Alex shook his head and kept chuckling. "Okay, maybe he does."

Elenora studied Joseph Gill on the cell. She had to agree with her friend. Arrogance leaked from the man's air and posture. A guy determined to show the world who was boss.

Tom headed to the wall and examined the cracks while pondering out loud. "So, this wall is showing us a deceased child, and the poltergeist is obsessed with this spot—it's willing to kill over it. I'm pretty sure there's nothing special about the plaster, so it must be about the baby, the mother, or the father. Something behind the wall is related to one of them?"

CHAPTER TWENTY-FOUR

Elenora stared at the damaged wall with queasy curiosity. What gruesome mystery awaited them on the other side?

"Time for a little demo?" Alex asked before turning to the witches. "Can you guys blast a hole in there or something?"

"If this were an ordinary wall, we might be able to string together a bunch of spells and make a suitable hole." Claire-Lune lifted her chin at the wall. "But this one's way too unstable. Throwing that kind of magic at it in an enclosed space could have dire consequences."

"Let me try a revealing spell." Wren approached the wall but stopped at a safe distance and turned. Her eyes went to the harness still tethering Elenora to Serena and the banister.

Serena caught on. "You want us alert?"

Wren nodded, and the witches prepared to react.

"Gimme a minute." Alex grabbed the sledgehammer still under his foot and jogged down the stairs with it.

"Lunie, when he's back, throw a sealing spell at the top of the stairs," Serena suggested.

"Good idea."

A door slammed. Footfalls on the stairs announced Alex's return.

Wren took a few more cautious steps closer to the wall. She studied the spiderweb cracks before murmuring a string of words. Her fingers twitched, and the wall lost some of its opacity, causing enough transparency to reveal a form behind it. Unfortunately, the form remained hard to discern.

Wren added words to her spell and moved her hands in front of the wall. Her soft voice became louder, betraying her struggle to reveal more of the mystery item. She groaned in frustration. "I think the dark spell is interfering yet again. I'll keep working on it. Sorry for wasting your time, everyone."

"At least now we know there's something back there," Juniper said, having none of her colleague's apology.

"Wren, we'd be nowhere without you. Except maybe in a hospital or a morgue," Tom quipped grimly. He pointed between himself and Alex. "Can you imagine the two of us investigating this case without you? Without any of you?"

Elenora hated reminders that she could lose Tom in the line of duty. Now that he dealt with paranormal threats and she, too, was involved, the risks were even greater. She hated that so much.

Wren smiled at Tom. "That's generous of you to say."

"It's true, though..." Alex agreed before turning pensive. "Hey, Juniper, did I imagine things, or did the tornado take longer to strike this time?"

"It did take longer."

"Because you were holding it off and Wren's spell was cramping its style?"

"It would appear so, yes."

"If you'd known the exact moment Elenora would be pushed, could you have tempered the blow?"

Juniper narrowed her eyes at Alex with suspicion. "Maybe?"

"Is the air still okay?" he asked.

Juniper, Elenora, and Yukiko all nodded.

"Great! Gimme a minute." Alex headed for the stairs, leaving everyone guessing.

Claire-Lune deactivated her sealing spell in time before he reached the landing. He went down and reappeared a moment later with the sledgehammer.

"Juniper, would you please have my back?" He swung the tool over his shoulder like one would a baseball bat.

The witch threw a hesitant look at her fellow witches.

"Hold it right there, cowboy!" Serena yelled at Alex. "You think you can just swing that thing at the wall?"

"Worth a try."

"Are you insane?"

"Juniper's on board, and I could punch a hole in that wall with my bare fist if it wasn't for the dark crap. There are answers"—he pointed at the wall where the hidden object was—"right there. We're wasting time."

Serena pursed her lips, crossed her arms over her chest, and glared at him.

Alex prepared to take a swing at the wall.

"Wait! At least let us figure out a way to protect you before you kill yourself," Serena said.

"I don't think the harness would fit me or the banister could withstand my weight," Alex retorted.

"I don't mean the harness. I mean a spell."

"You'd cast a spell on me?" His face fell.

"We'd *protect* you like we did with Elenora. So that you, you know, don't die."

"I don't know about that." Alex turned an uncomfortable gaze on Elenora. "Did it feel funny?"

"No funnier than if your reckless alpha bullshit gets you killed." Serena looked like she wouldn't take no for an answer.

"The spell is fine, Alex," Elenora confirmed.

"I've got just the thing for you," Wren said to him. "You won't feel anything, and the spell won't linger once you're done and I've broken it."

Alex shot Elenora another look.

"I'm still standing." She gave him a reassuring smile. To think he was so strong and courageous but could be such a baby.

Alex leaned close to Wren and dropped his voice. "Will I still be able to have kids?"

"Yes. It's totally safe."

He rubbed the back of his neck. "Fine, then."

Wren moved her hand in front of his chest, and he cringed with apprehension.

"Done," she said.

"That's it?"

"Yes."

"Thank you," he mumbled and stopped making a face. He shook his arms and legs, as if testing to see if anything had changed, and seemed reassured. "I can go ahead now?"

"Well, I'm not keen on you doing this, but yes, you can proceed," Wren answered.

After a brief hesitation—he clearly valued the witch's opinion—Alex picked up the sledgehammer with nervous energy and prepared to swing. Elenora had seen him play baseball in friendly tournaments with colleagues. He was an agile and powerful amateur athlete, and she expected half the wall to fly to pieces when he hit it.

"Tell me when, Juniper."

"Okay—on *go*. Three... Two... One... Go!"

Alex took a swing and seemed to meet an invisible resistance that slowed him down to a near halt. Despite his impressive strength, the sledgehammer's connection with the wall barely chipped the paint. At least, he didn't fly across the room—no doubt thanks to Juniper's intervention.

He frowned with surprise and annoyance at the lack of damage. Bringing the sledgehammer up to his shoulder again, he prepared for another swing.

Juniper took the hint. "Three. Two. One. Go!"

He swung, and this second attempt also hit a metaphorical patch of molasses in mid-swing, but at least it made a dent, furthering the damage Jérémie Marsan had made. Not much progress, but at least some.

Alex grunted in frustration and took another swing, meeting resistance again. The soft blow produced a new network of delicate cracks. At this rate, it would take days to even pierce a hole.

The detective let the sledgehammer dangle from his hand and called to the poltergeist, "Fine, you win." He made a big show of putting down the tool, only to pivot quickly and roundhouse kick the weakened spot in the wall. His foot and calf went through. A triumphant smirk spread across his face.

"I wouldn't keep my foot in there if I were you," Serena taunted with a smirk of her own. "Who knows what might grab your toes..."

Alex's cocky grin died. Panicking, he scrambled to dislodge his foot from the hole. He skittered away from the wall, his eyes shooting daggers at Serena. She chuckled.

Claire-Lune shook her head at them and joined Tom, who was shining a light in the hole with his cell and peering inside.

Elenora observed them from a distance, hoping nothing nasty would jump out at them. "What do you see?"

"Looks like a white box," Tom answered.

"I concur." Claire-Lune grabbed a loose piece of wood lath and plaster, wiggled it, and ripped it off, further opening the hole. But it was not enough to access the mystery box.

Wren daintily picked up the sledgehammer and mumbled a spell. The handle briefly glowed yellow. She turned to Alex, who eyed her with guarded curiosity from across the room.

She brandished the tool at him with an inviting smile. "Would you care to give it another try?"

He cocked a brow. "You did some..."

"Woo-woo to it? Yes."

He laughed and hesitated a bit, but curiosity quickly won out. "What the hell, right?" He took the tool before glancing at Juniper.

"I still have your back," she assured him.

"Awesome. Let's go for a home run this time."

Tom and Claire-Lune moved away from the hole.

Before Alex launched the mother of all swings, the sledgehammer handle glowed. Unhindered, the swing was swift and powerful and made an impressive impact on the wall this time. Major cracks now spanned over several feet, and a considerable amount of lath and plaster fragments had caved into the hole.

"And the crowd goes wild," Claire-Lune said humorously.

Yukiko and Juniper golf clapped.

Alex took in the damage he'd caused, flabbergasted. "Jeez. Where were you guys when I was in little league?"

Claire-Lune and Wren laughed.

"You two should stroke his ego some more. He obviously needs it." Serena rolled her eyes and went to help tear away dangling bits of wall to enlarge the hole.

With some effort, they managed to create a sizeable entrance to the cavity. Juniper called Wren over before anyone reached inside.

"I don't detect anything threatening, but would you please check for dark magic?"

Wren crouched in front of the hole and trailed a hand over its edges. After a moment of assessment, she put on gloves and reached into the cavity. She struggled to retrieve something—no doubt the object itself. Juniper snapped on a pair of gloves too and gave her a hand.

Together, they hauled an elongated container out of the hole.

A tiny white coffin.

It was in pristine condition and adorned with pretty carvings of flowers and angels. The mood in the attic turned solemn.

"I'm going to open it," Wren said reverently, glancing at her fellow witches.

They all stood to attention, eyes glued to the coffin, fingers ready to react.

Elenora's heart lodged in her throat in shocked anticipation of seeing the remains of a baby. She wasn't sure she wanted to look. She was, however, pretty sure she didn't want to touch whatever was left of the little one. Sadness and dread overwhelmed her.

The coffin lid creaked under Wren's delicate touch but didn't put up a fight.

There were no remains inside. Several breaths of relief whooshed at once. The funeral box was lined with burgundy velvet and contained a lone black-and-white photograph—the one from Elenora's mind of Jane Gill holding Clementine.

Wren picked up the photo and held it close to Tom and Alex for them to examine. Without warning, the top edge of the print glowed crimson and burst into flames.

"Let it go, Wren!" Juniper shouted, and with her magic, she yanked the picture out of her colleague's hand and made it float in the air.

Claire-Lune cast a spell on the flames, but it only slowed the fire down. Wren and Serena jumped in with two other spells, but none kept the picture from burning. Its ashes rained down on the floor until the last bit was destroyed.

"The coffin!" Juniper's cry called everyone's attention to the funeral box, which now glowed grayish green.

"We need it out of here, stat!" Claire-Lune barked.

Wren waved her hands at the coffin before taking a few steps back. "Okay, go!"

Juniper spread her fingers at the coffin and made it levitate. She carefully but swiftly guided it toward the staircase. Wren and Yukiko followed closely behind her.

"At least we have the picture from Ele's mind," Alex said.

Serena cleared her throat loudly and brought a finger to her lips to shush him.

Catching her drift, he mouthed a contrite *Sorry.*

Claire-Lune threw one last spell over the pile of ashes on the floor. "Let's go."

They rushed down the stairs and soon caught up to the others. Juniper was steering the coffin in the air ahead of herself at an impressive speed.

"Dammit! It's back." Yukiko groaned.

Elenora felt the air thickening again. The poltergeist was after them.

"We're on it, Junie!" Claire-Lune shouted as she, Serena, and Wren waved their hands wildly at the coffin and around the group.

They all stampeded toward the main floor.

As Elenora neared the bottom of the stairs, a hair-raising coolness glided along the back of her neck. She recalled feeling a cold chill around that spot on her first visit. She didn't know what this meant—if anything—but it didn't feel like Mary's or Angéline's summons.

She hoped it didn't mean something worse.

Yukiko grabbed the front door handle and waited for a signal.

"Cloaking in three, two, one," Wren said, and the coffin disappeared.

"Go!" Juniper said, and Yukiko flung the door open for Juniper, who was presumably still moving the invisible coffin.

Everyone followed them out of the house.

The lightness of the air outside struck Elenora. The weather had cleared, and it was no longer as oppressive as before—or as it had been inside the house.

"Are you okay?" Tom asked her, recovering by her side.

"Yes," she panted.

Next to them, Alex breathed hard through his nose. In his case, it was probably due to being creeped out more than physical exertion.

A warm breeze skimmed Elenora's arm, and she perked up. Had Angéline or the poltergeist followed them outside? She scanned the front lawn. Nothing seemed suspicious or out of place. She glanced at Yukiko and Juniper to see if they'd noticed something, but they were deep in conversation with Wren around the now-visible coffin nestled in the tall grass. They seemed unbothered.

Maybe it's just a breeze.

"What are you guys gonna do with it?" Alex asked the witches about the coffin.

"Wren detected dark magic on it," Claire-Lune replied. "If it's okay, we'd like to bring it to the OPO so we can analyze the magic. It might give us clues about the dark spell or the poltergeist."

"That works," Tom said.

"You're not afraid it's gonna burst into flames or attack you on the way to the OPO?" Alex asked with genuine concern.

"Our colleague Hassan is on his way. He's gonna transport it with the OPO's ambulance," Serena said.

"The one I rode in to bring Rolland to the hospital?"

"That's the one. The back doubles as a secure compartment for quarantine and hazardous materials."

"Oh. Wow." Alex's eyes stayed on Serena.

"What?" she asked sharply.

"It's just that I thought *my* job was stressful. I don't know how you guys do this. It's draining." The admiration in his voice was unexpected.

Serena's eyes narrowed. Maybe she wondered if she'd heard him correctly.

"This dark-magic thing is a real pain in the ass," he went on. "Doesn't the OPO have a dark witch or someone who takes care of that shit?"

"How many serial killers are on the payroll at the precinct?" she countered bluntly.

"Actually, we do consult with psychos from time to time."

"Good for you."

The witch's hostility didn't deter him. "Seriously—not being sarcastic. Wouldn't it be a plus for you guys to have such a resource?"

"Pray tell, kind sir, where would we find such a delightful, morally challenged individual? Online classifieds?" Serena sassed.

His lips twitched in amusement.

"Few of us practice dark magic—thank goodness—and those who do rarely roam the streets nonchalantly in search of opportunities," Claire-Lune explained calmly.

Wren came to join them, frowning. "Were there pictures of Jane Gill among those you found in the basement?"

"I don't think so," Tom said.

"I gather they're at the precinct?"

"Yes, they've been logged as evidence and scanned." Tom reached for his phone. "I can email them to you."

"Thank you for offering me a copy, but I'm worried about the originals. If they contain dark magic, it might be best not to keep them at the precinct."

Tom's face darkened. "I'll swing by the station and take them out."

"I'll go with you to check. If there's a spell on them, I'll try to subdue it. But maybe there's nothing to worry about."

If the pictures held a spell, maybe that was why Elenora had sensed little from them, aside from a feeling of distress. Come to think of it, she had only tried to read one picture. She should give them another look.

And now, she itched to hold the pictures from the basement in her hands.

CHAPTER TWENTY-FIVE

After arriving at the precinct, Tom offered for Wren, Serena, and Claire-Lune to scrutinize the pictures inside. He got a cryptic reaction from the twins.

"We might run into a certain chief." Serena elbowed her sister with a little smirk.

Claire-Lune ignored her and said to Tom, "I think it's best if our presence goes unnoticed."

"I guess you can't go wrong with that," Tom replied, seeming to read between the lines.

Did Claire-Lune have a history with Chief Costa? *Intriguing*. Elenora would have to ask Serena about it on a rainy day.

"I'll go fetch the pictures," Tom said. "Let's meet in the parking lot behind the precinct."

Alex went with him while the others gathered in a secluded corner of the back parking lot, shielded from prying eyes. The pair returned a few minutes later. Alex held up the clear evidence bag with the pictures, and Wren moved a hand over it.

She bit her lips. "There's indeed something dark on them."

He threw the bag to the ground as if it were radioactive.

"It's just a minor spell," she specified, picking up the bag. "Or maybe stray bits from the dark spell settled on them." She moved her hand over the bag again, mumbling words in Latin. Then, with gloves on, she took the pictures out and mumbled more words. After a few minutes of work, she had stripped the photographs of their magic.

"Will they self-combust like the other one?" Alex eyeballed the bag warily.

"It's unlikely. Wren just covered them with a fire-repellent spell to prevent that from happening again," Serena said to him before turning to Elenora. "Do you remember which photograph you already read? Maybe start with that one as a baseline."

Elenora nodded, liking the idea. Wren fanned the deck of pictures like a card dealer at a casino and held them up for Elenora to peruse. Her gaze skimmed various faces from the past in search of a young brunette sitting in the brocade armchair and surrounded by a handful of male relatives. She found the photograph and picked it up. As her fingertips made contact, she felt the same distress as before, except the intensity had increased tenfold. The feeling slammed into her, startling her.

She recovered, dialed down the overwhelming emotion to a bearable level, and brought her full attention back to the picture. She studied the suffering on the young girl's face. Her stare was intense.

Clutching to the distress emanating from the picture,

Elenora closed her eyes and tried to connect with the girl. As with her previous attempt, the connection failed.

She handed the picture back to Wren and moved on to another one. It showed a young man in his early twenties sitting in the same chair and surrounded by grief-stricken family members. The subject wore the same intense look as the young woman in the previous photo.

Upon touching the picture, the same sensation of distress hit Elenora in full force. This time, she expected it and promptly toned it down. She took in the young man's expression, willing herself to connect with him. But once more, nothing came of it.

She moved on to the next picture, one depicting a little boy around four or five years old with his mother. He, too, sat in the middle of the big armchair, which threatened to swallow him. Like the two other subjects, he looked intense. Elenora focused on connecting with him but, again, to no avail. Her attention shifted to his mother, who hadn't bothered hiding her devastation, and she tried to link with her. But the past remained silent.

The same scenario repeated itself with the remaining pictures, a failure across the board to get anything more than misery from either the subjects or their relatives.

"Anything?" Serena had moved closer to Elenora and was looking at the last picture over her friend's shoulder.

"Nothing more than the distress I felt before. Except this time, it isn't muffled. It's loud and clear." Elenora wished she had something more exciting to say. There were stories behind the pain and the sharp stares, and they called to her like a siren's song. It was frustrating.

"There you are!" A familiar male voice came from across the parking lot.

Alex stealthily took the pictures from Wren's hands, dropped them back into the evidence bag, and casually hid them behind his back.

"What's up?" Tom went to meet Renaud, who was heading toward them with a folder.

"Demontigny thought he saw you back here."

Tom picked up the pace, no doubt to meet his young colleague away from their group and keep him away.

"I have some info for you guys." Renaud kept walking past Tom, his curious gaze taking in the three witches.

"I'm all ears," Tom tried, trotting after the kid.

Renaud only stopped when he reached the group. "Hey," he said to everyone, his eyes lingering on Serena.

"Anything we can do for you, Detective?" she asked with a fetching smile.

"Oh, please, none of that. Call me Renaud," he stammered and blushed, looking charmed.

Understandable—Serena was a dashing woman who deceptively looked his age.

"A pleasure to meet you, Renaud." She offered him her hand to shake. "Serena."

"Serena, the pleasure's all mine."

Elenora could swear Alex bristled at the witch flirting with Renaud. He clasped a big mitt on his colleague's shoulder to get his attention. "All right, what's up? You're keeping the dead waiting."

"They're in no hurry." Renaud gave Alex a distracted glance before going back to Serena.

Tom slipped the folder out of the young man's hand. *That got his attention.*

"Oh, about that, um..." Renaud eyed the witches again, hesitant to talk.

"You can talk in front of them," Tom said.

"Oh?"

"Yeah, they're contractors," Alex explained.

Renaud cocked his head. "What type of contractors, if you don't mind me asking?"

"They do mind," Alex objected.

"No, we don't," Serena replied daringly.

"Well, I do." Alex's voice became gruffer.

His aggravation seemed to amuse her. She smiled at Renaud again. "We specialize in witchcraft. We're witches." Her amusement grew with Alex's shocked expression.

What the hell? Elenora shared Alex's shock at the witch's casual revelation. It had taken a severe case of spiritual possession for them to be introduced to her very secret world. But right here, right now, she was joyfully spilling the beans like she was discussing a shoe sale.

Renaud stared at Serena, slack-jawed, before a tentative smile appeared on his lips as if to say, *She's pulling my leg, right?*

"Seriously, Serena, what the fuck?" Alex growled.

"Stop goofing around, Reena," Claire-Lune scolded her sister.

Serena rolled her eyes. "I'm just having a little fun to blow off steam. Can't a sorceress have some fun? Sheesh."

"Please don't mind my sister, Mr. Renaud. She's a prankster. Now, please tell us what you found."

"Okay. But I hope you're not easily shocked." Renaud

turned his attention to Tom and Alex. "So far, I've found nothing in the media about the Gills' big trip around the world. Maybe the announcement was a red herring. At least, it looks like Joseph Gill never left Montréal..."

He let that piece of information sink in, reveling in the suspense.

"Go on!" Alex barked.

"Right. I'm still waiting to hear back from cemeteries, and the only info I found so far on Jane Gill is that she was an orphan. But—drumroll, folks—Mr. Joseph Gill hanged himself in the house on Maple Street."

"Where in the house?" Elenora asked. The coolness she had felt near the first steps... Could it have been him?

"At the bottom of the main staircase," Tom replied, his nose buried in the file.

Elenora sucked in a sharp breath and shuddered. Tom looked up at her inquisitively. She gave him a small "not now" headshake—she couldn't tell him about the cold chill in front of Renaud.

"That's a stellar find, Mr. Renaud. In my searches, I found nothing about his death." Claire-Lune looked impressed.

"And I almost didn't either." Renaud pointed at the file in Tom's hands. "The report of death was misfiled in the morgue's archives. If I were paranoid, I'd say it was buried on purpose. It's almost a miracle I found it. Also, Joseph Gill's name was misspelled—"

"And the date and signature are conveniently smudged," Tom finished for him.

"You think the misspelling and the smudges were deliberate?" Alex asked.

"The sloppiness adds up and does feel deliberate," Renaud agreed.

"But why do this?" Serena asked, no longer playful.

Renaud drank her in as he replied, "Maybe the author of the report wanted to remain anonymous—didn't want it known they'd logged the body but still wanted Gill in the system. In some very inefficient capacity."

Elenora tried to understand the circumstances motivating an officer to produce and then hide such a report. While she'd been working with the police for a long time and had learned a lot about detective work from Tom, there were endless strange scenarios she had not yet encountered. And this one was particularly baffling.

"Maybe they did this to avoid scandal. The press would have had a field day," Tom added. "Or maybe Gill himself bribed someone before his death to keep it under the radar."

He looked at Renaud. "Great work. I can't wait to see what you dig up next."

"That makes two of us. This case is getting creepier by the minute." Renaud beamed a giant smile at everyone and then settled it on Serena. He showed no signs of leaving.

"It *is* getting creepier." Alex glared at him. "We'll see you inside."

Serena offered her hand to Renaud again. "It's been a pleasure."

He shook her hand happily. "Maybe I'll see you around?"

"Who knows what fate has in store." She kept his hand in hers and added, her voice like velvet, "Now, please humor me, dear, and take a good look at these two lovely ladies." She wagged a finger at Claire-Lune and Wren.

Renaud complied.

"Now, look at me."

His gaze obediently moved back to hers.

"When you walk over the threshold of the precinct, you will forget ever meeting the three of us." She gave him a playful smile.

He laughed, convinced she was joking again. "The witch thing. Right."

She winked at him and let go of his hand. "See you around, Renaud."

"Can't wait." He nodded goodbye to her and everyone else and headed back to the building, chuckling to himself.

"Is he seriously gonna forget about the three of you?" Tom asked the witches.

They all nodded, and Serena snickered. "He couldn't identify me in a lineup even if I were the only one in it."

"Is your woo-woo gonna leave a scar, like brain damage?" Alex's expression was dark.

"Oh, no. Nothing like that. It's a rather inoffensive spell," Claire-Lune said reassuringly. "Though we use it only when it's *really* necessary because we endeavor not to reveal ourselves in the first place." She gave her sister a pointed look.

"Yeah, well, exceptions exist for a reason. Detective Cutie was already curious about our presence, and he would've kept digging. That's what he does, and he's damn good at it," Serena argued. "I can't think of an excuse that would justify us being privy to information on this case. Even as *contractors*." She offered Alex a taunting smile. "I simply cut to the chase and saved us time."

Serena made a valid point, but her prank had nearly given Elenora, Tom, and Alex a heart attack. Elenora had heard about the memory spell before but had never seen it in action. Considering the stress they were under, a heads-up would have been nice.

"So, with Joseph Gill dying in the house..." Tom started pacing, crunching gravel underfoot. "Odds are good that we do have a second ghost, right?"

"My money's on it," Serena said with smug glee. "Asshole in the house. Called it!"

CHAPTER TWENTY-SIX

"It's the eyes," Rolland said, pointing at the face of a man staring oddly at the camera. "See?"

Tom had printed a copy of the pictures found in the basement of the old house after Elenora had told him something about them was nagging her. They had scattered them over their dining room table to see if they could figure out what it was.

It was early afternoon. Their friend Rolland and his girlfriend, Anna, had swung by unexpectedly to return one of Tom's power tools and see the baby. They were smitten with Aubrey, and any reason to visit was a good one for them. Elenora loved to have them over and often helped them find excuses to stop by.

"What about the eyes, Rolly?" With Aubrey on her hip, Anna leaned over the sea of printouts to see what Rolland meant.

"The gazes are too realistic to be postmortem touch-ups." He moved a finger over the portraits. "And yet, the people sitting in the armchair all seem dead to me."

"The gazes don't match the bodies?" Tom summarized.

"That's what I'm thinking. That might explain why the pictures are bothering you, Ele."

Elenora nodded. The oddness of the stares certainly added a layer of eeriness to the distress coming off the pictures.

"Okay. Concretely, what does this mean?" Tom asked.

Rolland shrugged. "It's like... It's like they're at once dead and alive, but that doesn't make sense."

"Serena would say that anything can make sense," Anna pointed out before taking a sip of tea.

They all chuckled. Serena would totally say that, and in this case, she could be right. Elenora sensed truth behind Rolland's perplexing observation.

She surveyed several of the pictures. "How can they at once be dead *and* alive?"

Rolland shrugged again. "That's a billion-dollar question."

Like Serena and Claire-Lune, Rolland had lived through most of the nineteenth century and was familiar with the practice of postmortem photography. Back then, he had also worked in morgues before becoming a doctor, which gave him a singular expertise with corpses in various states.

Anna narrowed her eyes at a picture. "What makes you think these people are dead?"

"The hints are subtle." Rolland scanned the pictures. His finger landed on the portrait of an elderly lady. "This woman's posture, for example, is slightly unnatural for a living person. It would have been awkward for her to take it and maintain it, especially at her age. Unless she had a physical deformity, I see no reason for it. So I'm thinking rigor mortis."

He perused other pictures for clues and pointed at other elements. "The sunken eyes here... This man has rouge on his cheeks... The sallowness of the skin despite makeup."

Elenora, Tom, and Anna followed Rolland's roaming finger.

"And then the armchair. Its back seems quite reclined. It makes me think the photographer had it custom-made— maybe to help prevent the head of a deceased from slumping forward."

"So the chair means a deceased subject," Tom said. "Yet everyone sitting in it is staring sharply at the camera. While most of the relatives have softer eyes. Interesting."

"And you're convinced Joseph Gill couldn't have doctored their eyes to this degree of realism?" Elenora asked Rolland.

"Well, even with insane talent..."

"His insane talent was his claim to fame, though. Making the dead look alive was his marketing angle," Tom remarked.

"Okay. For argument's sake, let's say he did have the talent to produce such realism," Rolland said. "Then why choose to paint a tormented expression in his dead clients' eyes? Why not make them look serene?"

"You think he gave them a tormented expression on purpose?" Anna brushed a lock of hair away from Aubrey's forehead. She then sat, shifting the baby onto her lap.

"I think it makes no sense for him to do so, which is why I'm stumped."

"So, we have dead people with eyes too real to have been faked." Tom stroked his chin.

"That's my theory. Take it with a grain of salt." Rolland kneeled in front of Anna and asked the baby, "What do you think, sweety?"

Hopefully, Aubrey is blissfully unaware of our conversation and doesn't have an opinion, Elenora thought and hoped that things would remain that way for a long time. Someday soon, though, Tom would have to stop using the dining room for work. And they would have to watch what they said beyond swear words.

"Come see Uncle Rolly." Rolland offered his arms to Aubrey, who became excited. He picked her up, and a huge grin appeared on both their faces.

Rolland had delivered Aubrey—under insane circumstances—and Elenora liked to think that he shared a special bond with her daughter. They certainly liked each other. And from the way both he and Anna were crazy about their honorary niece, Elenora wouldn't be surprised if they had a little one of their own sooner rather than later.

Tom grabbed the ceramic teapot on the table. "I'll go make another pot," he said on his way to the kitchen. He probably wanted a few quiet minutes to himself to mull over Rolland's thoughts more than he craved a tea refill.

"Anyway, I don't want to mislead you guys." Rolland bounced Aubrey on his knee. "Maybe your photographer really did have one hell of a magic touch."

Tom stopped in his tracks in the doorway. He turned, and his eyes caught Elenora's. "A dark magic touch," he mumbled.

A dark magic touch...

At once dead and alive.

A horrible thought crossed Elenora's mind. "Necromancy?"

Elenora rocked Aubrey on their garden swing on the back patio. After hours of scrutinizing suffering souls, she was desperate for fresh air and a quiet mind. She got a meager lukewarm breeze and racing thoughts.

Joseph Gill might have been a necromancer.

The unsettling notion wouldn't stop rattling around her head.

When Elenora left the dining room after Rolland and Anna had gone, Tom was telling the necromancer theory to the witches on a video call. Wren apologized for not seeing that one coming. Serena reminded them that while necromancy was sinister as fuck, it changed nothing in their quest to stop the violent poltergeist. She was right.

Now they might better understand what had gone on under the Maple Street roof and what Joseph Gill might have subjected his departed clients to. But that knowledge didn't bring their team any closer to stopping the malevolent spirit—whether or not the dead photographer himself had been raising hell in the house. Though Elenora could totally picture him as the aggressive poltergeist. So much more than Angéline de Montbleu.

She forced herself to appreciate the breeze and the little sweetness in her arms. Aubrey was sound asleep and limper than a rag doll. Elenora loved watching her sleep. Was there anything more peaceful looking than a sleeping baby?

Could Joseph Gill have killed himself in the house to remain close to his baby daughter? Grief made people do crazy and desperate things sometimes.

Had he thought Clementine's spirit lingered in their

home and he could reunite with her in death? If so, then she must have died there too.

But could an adult spirit connect with a baby's? Could a spirit get in touch with any other spirit?

If Joseph Gill had been a necromancer, maybe this was within his power.

Elenora tipped her head back against the plush cushion and squinted. The sun shone brightly on her face, a jolting contrast with her lugubrious thoughts. She took in the lush greenery of their backyard. The grass was getting long. She made a mental note to mow the lawn one evening when the heat relented.

The patio door slid open. Tom appeared with two glasses of iced tea and joined her on the swing. The seat depressed a little under his weight.

"Claire-Lune located Joseph Gill's burial plot. He's resting in peace all by himself. There's no grave for Jane next to his. Nor Clementine. But given we found her coffin in the attic, it's not a surprise. Yukiko would like to try summoning him again in the house, but if he's still uncooperative, she said we should try the grave."

"Sounds like a lovely plan," Elenora deadpanned.

Tom chuckled. "Sounds like your definition of *lovely* has evolved drastically."

"Why does she think we'll have better luck at the house than at his grave? We've already struck out a few times."

"The coffin has already helped Wren better understand the dark spell on the house. She thinks she's close to a breakthrough in lessening it further. And Yukiko said that since Gill killed himself in the house, his spirit should be strongly present there—unless he's moved on or it's not him. Anyway, the odds of reaching him outside the house, even if we are physically close to his remains, are less good."

"Hmm."

Good grief! Could the spiritual world be any more complicated? She ought to start writing everything down.

Tom took her hand in his. "Ultimately, it sounds like our best bet is for Wren to have another go at the dark spell and for Yukiko to give it another try."

They swung in silence for a moment.

"Why do you suppose Joseph Gill would have used necromancy on his clients?" Elenora asked.

"Prestige? Power? Money?"

"But he already had plenty of prestige, power, and money."

"Even more prestige, power, and money? For some people, plenty is never enough."

The case occupied most of Elenora's mental real estate for the rest of the day and became particularly consuming as she prepared a salmon filet for Tom to put on the grill. The familiar dinner preparation gave her too much time to reflect, and her mind kept churning out dark questions.

Clementine's coffin was empty. Where were her remains? Had Joseph Gill kept them in the house?

Jane Gill wasn't resting at the cemetery with her husband, and her whereabouts were still unknown. Had her husband killed her and...kept her remains too?

Would they find her at the house?

Could the body in the rosebushes belong to Jane?

Wait, no. Jane Gill was a delicate woman, and the mystery arms and hands had been male. No cigar.

Elenora rinsed a pair of bright-yellow lemons and sliced them for the fish. A deliciously tangy mist spritzed from the citrus and filled the air.

So, Joseph Gill might not have pushed his wife from the attic, sending her into a bush of roses, but Jérémie Marsan had plunged to his death that way. The construction worker had come too close to Clementine's coffin and her post-mortem picture. Was this the reason for the deadly shove?

If so, how could he have been a threat to these two items? Because he could have stolen and pawned them?

A young life was sacrificed over a picture and a coffin belonging to a family that had perished long ago, two objects that meant nothing to anyone anymore. Except maybe to the spirit of a destructive and troubled dead patriarch.

Elenora sighed and wrapped the gorgeous piece of salmon in tinfoil. Balancing the tray carrying the fish in one hand, she opened the patio door, offered the packet ready for grilling to Tom, and shared her latest thoughts about the Gills and Jérémie Marsan's death.

She then returned to the kitchen to finish the potato salad and rejoiced at the sight of the leftover fresh dill. Just the right amount for the potatoes.

Something right for a change.

CHAPTER TWENTY-SEVEN

In her dreams that night, Elenora was surprised to find herself in the backyard of the old house on Maple. Had there been another casualty? But now that the coffin and picture had been found, what reason would Joseph Gill's ghost have to strike against an innocent trespasser?

She readied herself to witness another murder. Instead, in a delightful and unexpected turn, Angéline appeared. Elenora reminded herself that, while Joseph Gill was a much better suspect and it seemed ridiculous to even consider Miss de Montbleu as their poltergeist, they hadn't ruled her out yet. She kept that in mind and tempered her enthusiasm.

"I apologize for summoning you, my dear, but I didn't know what else to do," the elderly departed medium said, agitated. "I am so glad it worked this time."

Wait, what?

Had the spirit really summoned her in a dream? Or was this a premonitory dream in which the spirit claimed to have summoned her? Either way, Elenora was intrigued. And besides, Yukiko and Dr. Brent had trained her to not question the dreams, unless they made her uncomfortable or scared, and to just go with the flow.

"What happened?" Elenora asked.

"I got kicked out of the house." Angéline stared piercingly at her home.

"How? What makes you say that?"

"I've never been able to leave the house before and come outside—and trust me, not from a lack of trying."

Elenora put a hand on the ghost's shoulder to calm her, and the touch took her aback. She could feel the dead medium nearly as much as if she were in the flesh.

Angéline looked just as stunned. "I can feel your hand on my shoulder."

The spirit mirrored Elenora and brought a hand to her shoulder. Her eyes widened even more as she touched the sleeve of Elenora's nightgown and brushed her bare arm.

"Do you know how long it's been since I've felt anything?" Angéline let out a giddy laugh of disbelief. "Oh my, this is crazy."

Indeed. This and everything else. Elenora would allow her mind to be properly blown later, when she had time to process this astonishing encounter.

"Can you feel anything else?" Angéline asked with intense glee, her eyes scanning the backyard.

Elenora looked down—she didn't feel the grass under her bare feet. She lifted her gaze and saw the rosebushes where Jérémie Marsan and the mystery man had landed.

The rosebushes... She headed to the fatal spot and brought her fingers to a rose, careful not to get pricked. Her hand went through the flower. She pivoted and went back to touching Angéline once more, and again, the old lady's wrinkled skin was tangible and soft under her fingers.

Huh.

"I can only feel your presence," Elenora said.

Her neck prickled like she was being watched. She looked at the house, expecting to catch someone spying on them. She checked each window but saw no one. Her gaze roamed some more and settled on the plywood securing the hole in the attic.

Dropping her voice to a whisper, she asked Angéline, "Have you ever seen anyone other than the young construction worker fall from the attic? At any time in the past?"

Angéline frowned. "No. Why?"

"I had a vision of a man lying under Jérémie Marsan in the rosebushes, but I got very little information."

Angéline went as pale as her spectral state allowed.

"What is it?" Elenora asked.

"You've seen..." The spirit's face lit up with hope. "Maybe my Anselmo? What did you see?"

Anselmo?

"That's the thing. I couldn't see enough to identify him. Only that he was male."

"Where was he?"

Elenora went back to the rosebushes, crouched, and pointed at the base of a shrub. "Around here."

Angéline fell to her knees next to her, as if to worship the area. Anselmo must have meant a great deal to her.

"We dug but found nothing," Elenora said gently.

"He's buried in a family plot in the east end."

"May I ask who he was?"

"He was my everything." Angéline's breath hitched. "My beloved. We had planned to elope, but then he died building this house. A freak accident, we were told... You said he fell from the attic and landed here?"

Elenora put a hand on the senior's shoulder once again to comfort her. The medium's sad tale echoed what had happened to Jérémie and his fiancée. *Another star-crossed couple.* The unfairness touched her.

"I didn't see him fall," she replied. "But he was so close to where Jérémie was—I assumed that's what happened to him too."

"Ah, I see. Did you see anything else about him?" Angéline roamed her hands under the bushes, as if searching for clues.

"No. I'm sorry. If we'd found remains, I would've tried to read them, but I didn't get that opportunity."

Angéline straightened up and stared at the ground where her fiancé once might have been.

"I know it seems like nothing, but this sliver of new information means a lot to me. I had long lost hope of learning more about his death. Even after buying this place. I thought I'd find answers here, but no."

"You lived here because of him?"

Angéline nodded. "I naïvely thought I could reach him."

"With a séance?"

"Yes. Before buying the house, I tried so many times to connect with him at his grave. But I only managed to summon just about every other spirit in the cemetery." A bittersweet smile curled the specter's lips. "Let me tell you, some of his relatives are a handful. And that's putting it politely."

Elenora laughed, and Angéline joined her for a while before becoming serious.

"Since he never answered me, I thought I'd have a better chance here since his death hadn't been a kind one." She sighed. "I guess some things just aren't meant to be."

"I'm sorry for your loss."

"Thank you, dear. I could never tell anyone, you know. Not a soul. You're the first."

"Your family would not have approved?"

"That, too, is putting it politely." She gave a thin smile.

Elenora's heart pinched. How lonely and awful it must have been to keep the love of her life a secret and grieve alone.

"Anyway, water under the bridge," the departed senior muttered before shifting her focus to the house. A steely resolve hardened her features. "I can't believe I got thrown out of my own house. How dare they?"

"Maybe it's for the best. For your safety. We found some seriously disturbing things in the attic..."

"The coffin and the picture that caught on fire?"

Elenora's eyes widened. "How do you know this?"

"I was there. I tagged along with you and your friends and tried to answer your summons, but the connection failed each time."

"Huh." Had the dark spell or Wren's tweak on it hindered the summons as Claire-Lune had guessed? Or did the poltergeist not want them to converse again and had interfered?

Or was Angéline simply playing her?

"Tell me what happened, how you ended up here. What happened before you got here?"

Angéline looked unsure of how to answer the question.

"Well, I was going around the house—*my* house—" the dainty specter shouted at the building before lowering her voice. "And I..." She rubbed a bony hand along the back of her neck and grimaced. "I may have gone back to the attic to see if you had missed something."

Elenora could see where this was going. Joseph Gill must have caught Angéline snooping and thrown her out of the house. But why would that upset him now that they'd discovered what he didn't want them to find?

Unless there was more to find...

"And then?"

"And then, I must have lost consciousness because there's a blank in my memory. I don't remember getting here. And yet, here I am. I tried to reenter the house but failed. I tried every door."

"But you wouldn't be able to open a door..."

"True. I meant I tried to move through the doors as I do around the house. I tried going through the walls, too, but something's keeping me out."

"It must be the dark spell."

"I thought about that. But then, how did I go through that barrier in the first place and end up out here if I can't make it back through that same barrier?"

"Maybe it's a one-way barrier. Or the person controlling the spell did this to you."

"That sounds logical. But what am I to do now?"

Once again, Elenora got the uncomfortable impression she was being watched. Her eyes swept between the windows and saw nothing. But if Gill was spying on them, would he let himself be seen?

And was this even possible? She was dreaming, for heaven's sake!

"Do you feel safe here?" she asked Angéline.

The elderly spirit pondered the question for a moment and studied her surroundings. "I don't feel unsafe."

"Good. Contact me if that changes. In the meantime, please just stay put. I will ask Yukiko for advice, and we'll be in touch as soon as possible." She lowered her voice. "We think we're getting closer to dealing with the...*vermin issue*." She tipped her head discreetly toward the house.

Angéline snorted and whispered, "Oh, goody."

Her relief seemed genuine. In fact, her behavior during the whole encounter had seemed genuine. Elenora refused to believe she was being fooled.

"Hang in there." Elenora squeezed the gentle spirit's hands. She then let go, pictured herself waking up, and found herself in bed.

It was morning, and she heard the rustling of sheets as Tom turned behind her. He snaked an arm around her waist and murmured in her hair, "Good morning."

"Good morning," she replied. "Angéline says hi."

***

Elenora wondered if she'd imagined her talk with Angéline. Maybe it had been nothing but a very realistic dream.

When she told Yukiko and the witches in a video call

about her unexpected meeting with the spirit, she emphasized her uncertainty. The women were stunned to hear she'd been in touch with the departed medium in her sleep. Yukiko said that dream visitations were usually not so complex or intentional. They grew enthused and proposed a visit to the old house to check on Angéline and test another tweak on the dark spell.

On the drive to Maple Street, Elenora couldn't wait to see if the spirit had indeed visited her. It would be amazing if the encounter had been real. She almost asked Tom to be liberal with the speed limit so she could get to Angéline faster.

They were the first ones to arrive, and sure enough, Angéline de Montbleu was giddily waiting for them on the front lawn, an expression of pure delight on her face.

She greeted Elenora with open arms. "You came! It wasn't a figment of my imagination!"

"Well, I did dream our encounter, but that's the way it works on my end," Elenora quipped.

Angéline giggled. "Aren't we marvelous?"

"We are."

Angéline pulled her in for a hug. Elenora expected to embrace air, but the contact surprised her yet again. Unlike in the dream, it was barely perceptible, but she still felt a trace of solidity. The word *semiopaque* came to mind—if such an equivalence for touch existed. She also felt the ghost's elation.

Leaving a respectful amount of space for Angéline, Tom positioned himself in front of Elenora so she wouldn't appear to be hugging air and conversing with herself.

"Do I look deranged?" she asked him.

He chuckled. "Or like you're doing improv."

She snorted before pulling back to look at the spirit. "I can still feel your presence a bit. Nowhere near as much as last night—in fact, it's barely perceptible. But if I focus on the sensation, I can feel you. This is..."

"Marvelous?" Angéline smiled wider.

"What's going on?" Tom asked. "You can feel her?"

"Faintly, but yes. About as much as I feel the warm chills. Like an airy mass," she explained to Tom before saying to Angéline, "It is indeed marvelous."

"It's mind-blowing," Tom said.

Marvelous. Mind-blowing. Potentially scary. For sure, other adjectives would join the list once Elenora understood what this meant for her.

Angéline turned to greet Tom. "Hello, sir. I apologize for not saying hello earlier. This is more excitement than I've had in a century."

"She says hello." Elenora relayed the full greeting and apology.

"Hello to you, too, Miss de Montbleu."

The spirit nodded and turned back. "Please tell him to call me Angéline."

"Call her Angéline," Elenora said to Tom before focusing her attention on the departed medium. "How are you? Has anything happened since we talked?"

She shook her head. "It's been quiet as far as I can tell. From the outside anyway."

A motorcycle pulled up next to them.

"Is Angéline here?" Yukiko asked with excitement before she took off her helmet.

"She is!" Tom answered.

"Wonderful," Yukiko beamed and clapped her hands with delight.

A series of closing car doors farther down the street announced everyone else's arrival. Within seconds, they were all gathered on the sidewalk.

"How about we go to the backyard so we can do this properly? We'd love to meet the lovely Miss de Montbleu and be part of the chat," Claire-Lune said.

"Please call her Angéline," Elenora said as the specter opened her mouth to speak.

Minutes later, with Yukiko doing a proper summons and Serena throwing a revealing spell, Angéline materialized in the backyard. Despite the harsh sunlight, the spectral being was still visible to everyone. In broad daylight. Thankfully, mature trees obscured the space, so no neighbor had a clear view of what was going on.

"Angéline, how did you summon Elenora in a dream?" Yukiko asked her expectantly.

Behind her, Alex stared at the spirit, his lips parted.

"I'm not entirely sure how it happened. I wished I could talk to one of you. And then, Elenora was right here with me, in this backyard. I'm still recovering from that lovely surprise."

"Elenora is remarkably sensitive to the subconscious realm," Yukiko said. "We're still trying to figure out the extent of her abilities. But she bowls us over regularly."

Elenora's face flushed. "I don't deserve much praise, though. These things just keep happening to me."

"Oh, pshaw. Give yourself some credit." Serena gave her a side hug. "You're dedicated and working hard on yourself and evolving, whether or not you want to admit it."

"Elenora told us you've been thrown out of the house," Tom said to Angéline.

"Indeed."

"And nothing else has happened since?"

"Correct."

"Good." He turned to Wren. "Would you still like to try something new with the dark spell?"

Wren grimaced. "Yes, but it's half-baked. I still haven't found a foolproof way to cancel the spell." She blew out a breath of frustration. "This one's a real...tough nut to crack."

"But you still got something to try," Tom said. "Might as well try it, right?"

"Yes, but I think this will just run a different kind of interference on it. It's like trying to bring down the Great Wall of China with a peashooter. Maybe it will make a dent."

"You're doing great, Wren." Juniper patted her colleague's shoulder encouragingly.

"Everyone ready to bring this party inside? This time's the right one," Serena called confidently.

"You got a good feeling?" Alex asked her as they headed to the house.

She shrugged. "I got fuck all, dude. I'm just tired of getting my chain yanked."

⁕

Wren's new magical maneuvers took a while to take effect. The witches didn't know yet what impact—if any—it would have on the poltergeist, but at least it weakened the dark spell barrier enough for Angéline to reenter the house. The spirit's relief was obvious and beautiful to see.

"Thank you so much, my lovelies! I was growing worried I'd never see the inside of my home again."

As Elenora set foot in the foyer, a crushing wave of angst and despair unfurled over her—so violent and visceral her knees buckled. Tom and Alex caught her by the arms before she hit the floor.

"What's happening?" Tom didn't bother to conceal his panic.

"It's okay, Tom," Yukiko said reassuringly before turning to Elenora. "I feel them, too, Ele. It's overwhelming, but just like your eyes adjust in the dark, your emotions should steady as well. If they don't, try dialing them down."

"You feel them too. Who's *them?*" Alex asked Yukiko as his worried eyes scanned the room.

"We might have a new guest," she replied, her voice level. "And we shouldn't assume they are unfriendly."

"You think it's little Clementine? Or Mr. Rivard?" Claire-Lune tried.

Elenora recognized the distress saturating the air. Thankfully, its intensity had dimmed to a manageable level. "Joseph Gill's clients from the pictures... This is how they felt to me."

"The victims of his necromancy? You think one of them is here?" Serena asked.

Elenora gave her a tentative nod.

"Shiiiiiit." The witch whistled through her teeth.

Elenora shared the sentiment. The prospect of one of those poor tortured souls being around the house made her gut churn.

But it also made her curious.

"The poltergeist might be one of the clients?" Tom asked no one in particular.

"Your guess is as good as mine," Claire-Lune replied.

"Do you see them, Angéline?" Yukiko asked.

The specter's eyes swept the foyer. She glided around to peek into the adjacent rooms and shook her head.

A strong desire to seek them out bloomed inside Elenora. "Maybe they're downstairs."

CHAPTER TWENTY-EIGHT

The emotions intensified as Elenora neared the dark basement, and she had to dial them down. She, Juniper, and Yukiko led the way, each carrying a candle to light their path and expedite a séance.

Elenora entered the former photography studio, and an overlay appeared on top of her reality, revealing twenty or more specters floating around the vast room. Men, women, and kids in various physical conditions and states of dress and undress—likely how they were when they'd taken their last breath. Elenora gasped softly at the sight of them and their sheer number.

Yukiko and Juniper halted by her side. Angéline floated nearby.

"Do you see them?" Elenora whispered, her eyes glued to the crowd of ghosts.

They looked shy and disoriented.

Yukiko shook her head.

"You see someone?" Angéline whispered back.

"I see about twenty of the departed clients. They're scattered across the room."

"Oh." Angéline drifted a few feet into the room and swept a hawkish gaze around the dark space. "Now that you mention it, I see dark-gray blurs. Only blurs, but I do see blurs. Several indeed."

"I gather they look skittish?" Yukiko jumped on the whispering bandwagon.

Elenora turned a puzzled look on her. "How did you know if you can't see them?"

Her mentor chuckled. "Well, I'm used to being hyper-aware of every little thing. But also, you're whispering and acting like the room is filled with wounded animals needing help, and you're afraid to scare them away. That's a dead giveaway. No pun intended."

"Puns are always intended," Serena whispered loudly from behind them. "Whether consciously or subconsciously—"

Someone shushed her, probably Claire-Lune or Alex.

"Do they know we're here?" Yukiko asked, her voice still low.

"I don't think so. They all look like deer caught in headlights." Elenora observed the awkward body language of the wild-eyed spirits. "It's as if they just noticed their peers and are struggling to recover from the shock."

Wren hummed. "Maybe the latest tweak to the dark spell has drawn them out and revealed them to one another."

Claire-Lune nodded. "Makes sense."

"If they can see one another, why can't I see them too?"

Angéline's question stumped Yukiko and the witches for a moment.

"Maybe the dark spell affected them differently than you?" Wren shook her head. "I honestly don't know."

"How about we summon and reveal them and see if we can get some answers?" Serena asked, quietly this time.

Yukiko nodded.

"Okay. Stealth mode engaged." Candle in hand, Serena slunk toward the pentacle. An older male spirit saw her coming and recoiled out of her way.

"Sir, we come in peace," Elenora called in a friendly voice, freezing Serena in her tracks. "We mean you no harm."

Serena looked at Elenora over her shoulder, waiting for her signal.

"You may carry on. Just no sudden movement, I guess."

With the deliberate carefulness of a bomb squad member on duty, the fiery witch set her candle on the nearest pentagram tip before returning to the crowded doorway. By now, every spectral eye in the room was on her.

"They're all staring at me, aren't they?" she hissed and shuddered.

"Yup." Elenora barely held back a smirk.

"I hate it when they do that."

Juniper laughed. The departed all turned their attention to her. She abruptly stopped laughing and shuddered too.

Yukiko took Elenora's candle and advanced toward the pentacle, a soft smile on her face. The spirits retreated to the back of the room, some cowering but all watching the mellow medium with interest.

"Hello, everyone. My name is Yukiko. I'm a medium. I cannot see you just yet, but my colleagues and I will set up candles on the floor and start a séance so we can see you and talk with you. You have nothing to fear. And I cannot wait to meet you."

While some ghosts still eyed her with fear and suspicion as she put her two candles down on the floor, her words seemed to put most of them at ease.

Claire-Lune and Juniper positioned their candles on the remaining pentagram tips and then sat with Yukiko, Wren, and Serena in a circle.

"Gentle spirits in this room, I respectfully summon you," Yukiko started softly. "Please show yourselves."

One by one, the specters came forward, and their glow became brighter. As if no longer needed, Elenora's overlay vision vanished. Judging by Yukiko's delighted smile, the spirits had responded to her summons, and she could see them now.

Yukiko gave Serena a small nod to go ahead, and the witch murmured the revealing spell. A soft collective gasp from her colleagues told Elenora that they, too, could now see the new visitors.

"Whoa! That's quite the party." Juniper pivoted her head to look at the spirits. She stood to study them more comfortably.

Her fellow witches and Yukiko followed suit.

"D'you see him?" Elenora heard Tom ask Alex barely above a whisper.

The two detectives scanned the crowd with piercing stares, probably looking for Joseph Gill, who could be hiding in plain sight among these innocent spirits. Elenora's heartbeat increased as she scrutinized every male ghost in the room.

None of them fit the man from the photos.

"Hello, again," Yukiko said to the departed. "It's such a pleasure to meet you all. Would you please tell me who you are?"

Her question was met with hesitant silence and puzzled looks. A handful of spirits looked away.

Yukiko waited awhile before adding, "Do any of you know why you're here?"

More silence.

"Not the response I was hoping for," she told Tom and Alex.

"Maybe they don't know the answers or are afraid to talk," Tom replied.

"Or a spell is preventing them from talking," Wren added.

Or maybe they are still recovering from the trauma of their necromantic ordeal.

Alex whipped out his phone and brandished a picture of Joseph Gill at the ghosts. "Yo! Anyone knows this dude?" His voice was low but the tone expedient.

His gauche intervention caused them to flinch and gasp.

"You're freaking them out." Serena elbowed him in the ribs.

"I can see that." He lowered his phone. "Sorry, folks. Didn't mean to freak anybody out." He turned to Tom. "What the hell do we do now?"

That was a good question. How could they get answers from unresponsive, traumatized spirits? The ghosts were facing a bunch of strangers from the future, who must look like aliens to them. That certainly didn't help.

"We're intimidating. May I try talking to them alone?" Elenora asked her friends.

"Sure. We'll wait outside." Tom led the living and Angéline to the antechamber.

Elenora addressed the spirits. "Hello, everyone. I'm Elenora. We know you've been through a harrowing ordeal. We are trying to understand the details and help you."

Her kind gaze surveyed them one by one. They weren't warming up as a group. Maybe that was the problem. While they shared a spiritual scar, they didn't seem to know each other. So, even without Elenora's contemporaries around, these lost souls were still in a room full of strangers.

Try establishing a rapport with one of them.

She scanned the crowd for a good candidate and spotted a little boy studying her from behind the ample skirt of a dark-haired woman. She recognized him from one of the photos.

Kids are usually more malleable...

An idea struck her. She offered him a friendly smile to gauge his reaction. He ducked behind the woman, but soon a small pair of eyes peeked out. Elenora pulled one of Aubrey's rubber zebras from her purse. The young boy's face lit up with fascination and awe.

She took a few tentative steps toward him. He no longer seemed intent on hiding from her, so she approached and crouched near him. She gave him a closer look at the rubber toy.

"This is Marvin the zebra."

"Malvin," he whispered and pointed at the figurine before shyly burying his chin in his shoulder.

"That's right. Marvin. Isn't that a great name?"

He nodded, squirming closer to her and the toy.

"What's your name?"

"Ed—" He caught himself, suddenly aware of the others in the room, and kept silent. The crowd of specters had floated nearer to observe their interaction.

"Would you like to whisper your name in my ear like a secret?" Elenora asked the boy playfully.

He seemed keen on the "game." She leaned forward to invite him to talk. He cupped his small hands around her ear, and she felt a tickle.

A little wet whisper said, "Edward."

She leaned back a bit. "Oh, what a lovely name."

He gave her a proud smile.

"May I say your beautiful name out loud?"

He nodded.

"Wonderful. You're an awesome boy, Edward. Marvin thinks so too."

Elenora brought the rubber zebra back into view to redirect his attention so maybe he wouldn't notice her touching his arm lightly. She was curious to know if she would feel something like she did with Angéline.

Her fingers detected a light density, and she found herself transported into a memory. Joseph Gill was there, facing her—Edward—taking a picture of the boy. While there was nothing scary about the photographer's demeanor or his old-fashioned camera setup, uncontrollable fear overwhelmed her. She heard a choked sob next to her and felt Edward's desperation to ask his mother to hug him.

But he couldn't speak or move.

Elenora sensed the eerie paralysis that held him in place. And she now knew for certain that when Edward's picture had been taken, he'd indeed been dead, but his spirit had been around. His eyes, the windows to his soul, had seemed alive in the picture because he *had* been alive. His gaze had looked so real because it *had* been real.

A shiver ran down her spine. Her hunch about Joseph Gill's necromancy had been right. He had recalled Edward's spirit into his dead body to immortalize him.

For a photo op.

The poor child had been terrified and too young to understand what was going on. But then again, had any of the other spirits understood the deranged situation? Had they known they were dead?

Elenora dragged herself back to the present, eager to shake off the horror of the wicked magic.

Edward was staring at her with round eyes. Maybe her gray irises had turned almost white, as they often did when she was lost in a vision.

She forced herself to smile reassuringly. "Tell me, Edward. Did the photographer take your picture?"

He gave her a confused frown.

"Perhaps he doesn't know what a photographer or a picture is," Tom said quietly from the doorway.

Elenora glanced at him over her shoulder. He and their colleagues were gathered and spying into the room.

She turned back to Edward. "Was there a man looking at you next to a big cam—a big funny-looking object?" She used her hands to mime Joseph Gill's camera, her poor job making her cringe. But how else could she explain this to him?

Fortunately, he caught her meaning and nodded.

"Your mommy was with you, and she was sad. You wanted her to hug you. But you couldn't speak?"

Panic rose in his eyes.

"It's okay now. I've got you." She touched his arm to comfort him, and he let her.

His eyes traveled to her hand, and he looked more curious than frightened. He must have felt the touch too.

"It must have been scary, and you were very brave," she added, opening her arms, on the off chance that he would accept a hug.

Surprisingly, he launched himself at her, and she felt his semisolid form hug her back as a strong sense of relief—his and her own—filled her.

Without ending the hug, she turned her head toward the doorway. "Mr. Gill's wonderful talent for bringing his subjects *back to life* was not just artistry indeed." Her tight voice dripped with contempt.

"You're confirming necromancy?" Claire-Lune asked.

"Unfortunately."

"If that ain't cheating..." Alex scoffed.

"I know, right? Great artist, my ass," Serena concurred.

"If he recalled them specifically for pictures, then why are they still here? Was he not powerful enough to release them once he got what he wanted?" Tom asked.

"Maybe these spirits could not move on for whatever reason," Yukiko said. "Or maybe they wanted to remain here, though they don't strike me as keen on being here."

The specters were staring at the living, engrossed in their quiet conversation.

"What happened to me?" the ghost of a young gentleman asked, his gaze traveling from Yukiko to Elenora.

"After you passed, a photographer brought your spirit back into your body to take pictures of you," Elenora explained delicately.

"We are dead?" another man asked.

"I'm afraid so."

She expected a fierce reaction from him, but he only said, "Oh." Either he had already suspected he was dead, or the news would take some time to sink in.

"Do you remember being photographed in this room?" she asked the two men who had spoken.

The two men and the other departed nodded.

"Did you feel trapped in your body, unable to move or speak?"

Again, the spirits agreed. Edward reacted to her words too. She smiled at him and ruffled his hair. It barely moved.

"Can you please tell us more about what you remember? Every little detail can help us," Tom called politely from the doorway.

Spectral gazes dropped to the floor faster than gravity, Tom's question making them clam up.

Was it his intervention or something else holding them back?

Elenora went to Tom and dropped her voice. "Maybe they're uncomfortable sharing such a personal experience in front of a crowd."

"The men might also hesitate to open up in front of female company," Angéline added.

Elenora and Tom exchanged a knowing glance.

"I'll interview the women. You talk to the men?" Elenora said to Tom.

CHAPTER TWENTY-NINE

Elenora invited the female specters to talk with her, one by one, in a corner of the studio while Tom did the same across the room. He advised her to be on the lookout for any behavior or discourse that seemed out of place. There was a slight chance that one of the spirits was the poltergeist if Joseph Gill wasn't their man.

The first lady who came forward seemed eager to talk in private. Tall and thin, she glided over to Elenora with a grace that gave her elegance despite her stained, tattered nightgown and the gruesome black marks marring her skin. In the pictures, the marks had no doubt been touched up because Elenora sure would have noticed and remembered them. She tried not to show disgust or avert her eyes.

"Hello."

"Hello." The woman rubbed her hands together.

"Please call me Elenora. What's your name?"

The spirit's lips spread into an amused smile. "Elinor."

Elenora returned the smile and chuckled. "A beautiful name."

"Isn't it?" she beamed, and her humanity surpassed the unsettling grotesque nature of her appearance.

"Tell me, Elinor, what do you remember from the moment of your passing?"

Elinor thoughtfully considered the question. "I remember darkness and seeing a light in the distance. It beckoned me, and I moved toward it. But then, it was as if someone brought me back with smelling salts. I was suddenly facing a man—the photographer you must be after."

"Is this him?" Elenora showed her the picture of Joseph Gill on her cell phone.

Elinor recoiled from the phone and eyed it with interest from a safe distance. "Is this apparatus...dangerous?"

"It's not magic. It's perfectly safe technology. Please look at the picture."

Elinor looked at the screen and expressed delighted fascination at seeing the digital image, though she scrutinized the phone as much as the picture. "Marvelous."

The other ladies, who patiently waited in line a few paces away, made no efforts to conceal their eavesdropping and eyed Elinor's reaction with curiosity. The line had been short at first but had grown bigger since Elenora had started talking with Elinor. The spirit's easygoingness and relaxed posture conveyed trust and must have helped convince the more guarded ones to join.

Elinor's piercing gaze took in every detail of the picture like her afterlife depended on it. "I believe it's him."

"Thank you for confirming." Elenora lowered her cell phone. "Do you remember anyone else in the room when he took your photograph?"

"I'm certain there were other people. I heard sounds on

either side of me. Occasional whimpers. Coughs. I tried to see who was there, but I couldn't move. I couldn't even turn my head. I remember being quite frustrated about it." She frowned as she recollected. "I wondered if I'd been given a strong dose of Godfrey's Cordial. Or if I was dreaming."

"It must indeed have been frustrating. And terrifying."

"It was. I grew worried that I was paralyzed. I tried to talk, but my lips wouldn't move. I panicked and tried to calm myself, thinking that someone would eventually ask me what was wrong and help me." The spirit's voice caught. Her eyes were glassy with unshed tears. "But no one did. It was as if they didn't even know I was there."

"They didn't." Elenora laid a comforting hand on Elinor's arm, forgetting it might trigger a vision.

Oh, no! She caught herself unprepared and put on mental brakes. As if reacting to her desire to avoid it, the vision switched to an overlay, leaving Elenora aware of Elinor before her. She got a quick flash of Gill looking her—Elinor—in the eye. Knowingly. He knew her soul was in her dead body and that she had no choice but to stare right back at him. Elenora also picked up on the female spirit's growing sense of dread and distress in the memory.

It must have shown on her face because Elinor frowned at her with concern. "Are you fine, my dear?"

Elenora moved her hand away from Elinor's arm. "Yes. But I feel for what you've been through." *Literally.*

The specter leaned in and murmured, "Was I truly brought back from the dead?" She seemed to find her words ridiculous.

"It would appear so."

"Oh." Elinor seemed disappointed. "Then I wish I could

have seen my dear sister Penelope one last time when I came back. What a cruel missed opportunity."

The woman visibly longed for closure, which was only natural. Not only had she survived a soul-scarring ordeal and was newly aware of it, but now she also felt regret, which might follow her in the afterlife.

Would she be dejected for all eternity?

How awful and unbearable that would be.

A crazy idea struck Elenora. She hesitated a moment before fiddling with her cell phone to see if she had Elinor's postmortem photo.

She did.

In it, the departed woman sat in the brocade armchair, flanked by two women who bore a family resemblance. Both looked shattered with grief, and each held one of Elinor's hands, as if unwilling to let her go.

Elenora's gut churned. Would it be cruel to show Elinor the picture? If she were in her shoes, would she want to see it? She imagined she might be shocked at first but ultimately grateful for having seen it.

"Elinor, I'd like to show you something. This might upset you, but please know that's not my intention," she prefaced.

Intrigued, the specter craned her neck to see what was on the phone. Elenora flipped it to show her.

Elinor's face lit up, then she cocked her head. "Hmm. I don't recall that dress..." As realization dawned on her, she gasped and brought a hand to her mouth. A whimper and a tear escaped from her.

"I'm so sorry," Elenora blurted out, taking her phone away. "That was insensitive of me. I shouldn't have—"

"No, no. Please let me see again," Elinor pleaded, her hands gesturing wildly at the cell phone.

Elenora turned the screen back toward her, unsure she was doing the right thing.

"My sister Brigitte..." Elinor shook her head in disbelief. More tears fell, wetting the edges of her deeply moved, grimacing smile. "I can't believe she came after all." She lifted her eyes to Elenora. "We were estranged, you see. I never thought we'd ever be together in the same room again." She blew out a breath and chuckled before giving a huge smile.

How odd it must be for her to see herself dead. While still looking alive. And to know that her sister had shown up. How could she be coping this well? *The emotions alone would have killed me.*

"Thank you so much," the specter said, and Elenora felt a feather-light squeeze around her hands.

No vision came from the impromptu contact this time, but a wave of elation and appreciation washed over Elenora. The outcome of Elinor seeing her postmortem picture had turned out much more positive than expected, and that made Elenora's heart soar. That said, if she were to show any more postmortem pictures to other deceased, she needed to prepare them better.

Elinor's smile dimmed. "Do you think I might ever see Brigitte again?"

Since the picture had been taken well over a century ago, surely Brigitte was no longer alive. Elenora had no idea whether the sister had gone to a place where people could be reunited. Thanks to her brush with the Gray Court, she knew that hell existed but also had very little knowledge of the preferable alternative. She ought to ask the girls about it.

"I honestly don't know. But my colleagues and I will seek the best resolution for all of you."

She turned to the doorway and saw Angéline on the look-out. Before starting the interviews, Elenora had asked the departed medium if she would mind chatting with the female spirits once she was done talking with them. The idea had delighted Angéline. Elenora waved her over.

"Elinor, thank you so much for talking to me. This is Angéline, a fellow departed. She would love to chat with you."

Angéline led Elinor to the anteroom. Both women looked keenly at one another and were already engaged in lively conversation before they disappeared from view.

Elenora welcomed the next woman in line. She was named Mildred and looked near middle age. Her cause of death was concealed and would likely remain a mystery. Her swanky dress and flawless skin suggested that, unlike Elinor, she hadn't died in her bed of an agonizing illness. Mildred's story, however, matched the other spirit's. The darkness and the light, the odd encounter with the photographer, the feeling of paralysis... She also mentioned she'd been plunged into darkness again after the photo shoot, with no light in sight. Then she'd drifted through nothingness, all alone with her anxious thoughts, for what seemed like an eternity. Until now.

"Did you see anything while drifting around the house?" Elenora asked.

Mildred answered with a perplexed look. "What house?"

"You were floating here, in this house."

The ghost looked around the room before returning her gaze to Elenora. "I don't remember being in a house. But everything was so dark. I could have been anywhere, I suppose."

Hmm.

Elenora showed her the picture of Joseph Gill on her phone. Mildred, too, confirmed he was the photographer she had seen. Elenora put her phone away, and the ghost's eager eyes followed it.

"Isn't there something else you'd like to show me?" Mildred's voice was full of expectation.

Dang it. Elenora held back a sigh. She didn't like to torture people, but the cat was out of the bag now, so to be fair, she had to let the other spirits see their pictures if they wished to.

She swiped through the gallery of postmortem photos on her phone and found Mildred's. The departed woman sat in the brocade armchair, surrounded by family members, and she looked stunning. After giving the specter a more explicit warning about what she was about to see, Elenora showed her the picture.

Even though she was better prepared than Elinor, Mildred still let out a small gasp, and her hand flew to her mouth as she took in the photo. Her eyes glimmered, and a smile escaped around her fingers. "Oh," she said in a moved whisper. "Didn't my William look dashing?" She pointed to the man sitting stiffly on her right and wearing a solemnly destroyed expression. "I wish death weren't so painful for loved ones."

Elenora nodded in agreement. She readied herself to put a comforting hand on Mildred's arm and wondered if, by focusing on her interlocutor and wishing to remain aware, she could replicate the overlay vision she'd had with Elinor—

somehow influence the form of the vision by anchoring herself to reality. It would be wonderful to have some level of control.

Stay with her, she ordered herself.

With her fingers landing on the deceased woman's arm, a flash of Mildred's ordeal with Joseph Gill appeared over reality. *Yesss.* Though the effect was jarring—the photographer was staring at Elenora from over Mildred's shoulder as the ghost thanked her warmly for letting her see the picture.

Elenora removed her hand, pulling the plug on the overlaid vision. She escorted Mildred to the doorway. In the anteroom, Angéline and Elinor joyously greeted the third spirit as if they were long-lost friends having a much-anticipated reunion.

Elenora peered at Tom, who was now conversing with the men as a group. She returned to her corner and waved the next lady in line to come tell her story. Adeline was her name.

Then came Gertrude, Fiona, and Caroline.

Georgia, Charlotte, and Eliza.

Catherine, Beatrice, and Marianne.

They all said roughly the same thing as Elinor and Mildred had. All had been kept in the dark, both literally and figuratively. None of them had a recollection of wandering around the old house.

Once Elenora and Tom finished speaking with the spectral victims, she noticed that the intense feeling of distress previously permeating the room had waned dramatically, replaced with hope. Like the women in the other room, the men mingled with each other, no longer looking grim and skittish.

"May I please have everyone's attention?" Tom asked the group cordially.

The voices dropped to a murmur and then stopped.

"Thank you again for agreeing to talk with us," he said. "We will work on figuring out your predicament and resolving it in the best and quickest way possible. We will be in touch."

He received several thank-yous and grateful nods. After a polite pause, the ghosts resumed conversing.

"Let's go rescue Alex," Tom joked to Elenora.

In the next room, they found him waiting near the staircase with Serena. The space, filled with the female spirits, buzzed with conversation. The women looked like they were having a great time. Tom waved Angéline over. She excused herself and glided to them.

"Have you learned anything from them that could be relevant to the case?" he asked her as Alex and Serena joined them.

Angéline laughed. "Not unless the fashions of yesteryear are the key to solving it. I'm afraid to say we've essentially been catching up on gossip and idle topics. And what an immense pleasure it's been."

"I'm glad to hear that," Elenora said happily. Angéline's joy was infectious.

"But rest assured, I asked every single one of them if they remembered anything else. I tried to jog their memories. Unfortunately, no one could think of anything they hadn't already shared with you, Elenora."

"Thank you for your help, Angéline. We'll see you soon," Alex said before motioning to Tom and Elenora to follow him.

"Is she not coming with us?" Elenora's face fell as she worried about Angéline's safety in the house, especially now that they'd seen and talked to the spirits.

What if Gill retaliated against them? She didn't know what he could do to them, but she sure wasn't keen to find out. She wanted to ask Yukiko and the witches to bring the elderly spirit with them, at least for the time being.

Serena cleared her throat loudly. "Ele, Angéline's having fun, and I sure could use some coffee." She gave Elenora an exaggerated wink, linked her arm with hers, and pulled her toward the stairs.

Okay. Elenora was being asked to play along.

"See you around, ladies," Serena said to the group.

They replied with little waves and murmured goodbyes.

"Take care," Elenora managed to tell them before Serena dragged her up the stairs.

CHAPTER THIRTY

"What if Gill's spirit hurts them because we spoke to them?" Elenora asked Yukiko and the witches, her anxiety spiking again. "He's not taking kindly to us sticking our noses in his business."

"When you told us that Angéline got kicked out of the house, Wren prepared a protection spell for her. And she extended it to the other specters when we found out about them," Claire-Lune said. "So they're all protected."

"Also, moving Angéline might have raised suspicion," Serena added.

The gang had gathered at a nearby coffee shop, away from prying spectral ears. They were huddled around a table over coffee and pastries and kept their voices low out of habit, though few patrons were around. They didn't have to be overly concerned about what they said.

Tom and Elenora shared their comparable interview findings with the group. The darkness the specters had experienced, their alarming encounter with Joseph Gill, their anguish at being paralyzed, and the endless, tormenting darkness again. Elenora mentioned showing the spirits their post-mortem pictures, and Tom admitted to doing the same once he caught on to what she was doing.

While they had interviewed the departed, Serena and Alex had stood guard in the anteroom, on the lookout for party crashers, and Yukiko, Wren, Juniper, and Claire-Lune had tried summoning Joseph Gill's spirit upstairs in the ballroom. The summons had failed again—he was apparently still hiding from them.

"Won't Gill notice the spell protecting the spirits and undo it?" Alex asked.

"I don't think so. I encrypted it and used some of his own spell-crafting logic to hide it in plain sight." Wren rarely spoke with such pride and confidence.

Elenora took it as a good sign.

"Mind you, it's not impossible for him to find out about it," Wren added, "but it's unlikely."

Elenora chuckled. *There it is. Wren's typical caveat.* What was it with the two of them and their insecurities? Wren was so bright and talented, and yet she seemed to doubt herself at every opportunity—even more so than Elenora. But why? Why couldn't they just be confident and acknowledge when they did something cool? Seriously.

"So..." Serena said, pensive. "None of the spirits knew they were stuck in the house after their forced return to their bodies in the photo studio. They weren't there voluntarily. So, either they were left there on purpose or because Gill's magic failed... But his magic's been spectacular so far—I don't see him failing Necromancy 101."

"So, we're left with *on purpose*." Claire-Lune absently

played with her coffee cup, swiveling it back and forth with her fingers.

"And they were kept in the house because...? Surely not to haunt it," Serena continued. "I mean, even if they were drifting around the place, they couldn't scare anyone. They didn't even know they were there, and no one could see them. So what was the point of that?"

"Hmm," Claire-Lune said.

"They didn't answer my summons until Wren's latest tweak on the dark spell," Yukiko joined in. "I wonder if they were being kept on a different spiritual plane."

"There's more than one spiritual plane?" Elenora's eyes widened. Her ignorance felt like a bottomless well. Just as she understood one thing, two new, baffling things would pop up for her to scratch her head over.

"It's a vast world of possibilities out there, my dear," Claire-Lune replied with a kind smile.

"Especially with dark magic involved," Serena muttered.

Alex let out a long, despondent sigh but said nothing. The sigh itself spoke loudly.

Serena bumped shoulders with him. "Hey, it's not like we have to understand everything at once to solve this."

"Maybe, but it feels like we're going in circles."

"Like this?" She made a circling motion with her index finger at his coffee cup. The level of coffee rose with every complete circle. She smirked at Alex's stupefaction.

"Did you just ruin my coffee?" He made a face at his cup.

"It's just a glamour." Serena snapped her fingers, and the newly added coffee vanished. "My point—my *very tenuous* point, 'cause I just felt like showing off—was that circles aren't always a bad thing. We're chipping away at the case, sure, but we're still making progress."

"Speaking of which, so far, we have..." Tom flipped to a fresh page in his notepad. "Jérémie Marsan's death started this investigation. Joseph Gill, a dead, necromancing warlock, is our prime suspect. Innocent souls are trapped inside the house, and their presence might have something to do with Marsan's death." Tom scribbled as he talked. "We found a tiny coffin behind the attic wall—presumably Clementine Gill's—and her postmortem picture. Both items seem to be a sore spot and the source of the poltergeist's retaliation and possibly the reason for Marsan's death. We presume the poltergeist didn't want the coffin and the pictures to be found."

"We have Angéline, a spectral ally," Alex added to the list. "There are no records of either Jane's or Clementine's deaths, and their graves haven't been located."

Tom added Alex's facts to the page. "Jean-Luc Rivard's bizarre death occurred on the premises but might just be a fluke and unrelated. The mystery victim Ele saw under the rosebushes might be a man named Anselmo, Angéline's sweetheart. What am I missing?"

"Just the way for us to grab Gill by the collar and banish his ass," Serena replied dryly.

Elenora scanned her surroundings as Yukiko and Wren put away the candles. They were at Joseph Gill's grave in an old part of the Mount Royal Cemetery, where several mausoleums and monuments of various sizes stood here and there.

The afternoon was sunny, but the general mood was gloomy and defeated. Yukiko had tried several times to summon the photographer's spirit unsuccessfully, and Elenora had attempted to get a read on the headstone, also unsuccessfully.

Wren had also cast her awesome revealing spell over the grave to see if they could confirm a body was indeed buried there. Similarly to what she'd done with the wall in the attic, she had made it possible for them to see below the grass in front of the epitaph, revealing an imprecise image—but an image nonetheless—of a casket and its contents. A form suggested a skeletal presence. But short of digging up the bones, they had no way of confirming the remains belonged to Joseph Gill.

Serena pointed at the grave. "Maybe it's a John Doe in there."

"Burying a John Doe would be consistent with how the police report was handled," Alex said.

"What an odd choice of location for a famous man. Especially since it was public knowledge that he had a family," Claire-Lune remarked.

Joseph Gill's grave lay in a single plot wedged between two mausoleums. Fancy engraved plaques on both stone buildings claimed they'd been built decades before the photographer's death. The awkward, narrow location of the man's grave explained why his wife and child had not been buried by his side.

Tom took pictures of the plaques. "They seem unrelated to the Gills, but I'll still ask Renaud to look into them."

"Maybe the person who hid the report of death had something to do with why he was buried here," Alex said.

"Someone who maybe also knew his wife and child wouldn't need burial plots?" Tom added.

Both Jane's and Clementine's remains could be at the house.

Elenora massaged her temples and noticed she wasn't the only one showing signs of a headache or frustration. Serena held her forehead. Alex scrubbed a hand over his face. Wren and Yukiko looked like they'd given up.

"How about we call it a day to gain some perspective?" Claire-Lune suggested. "Standing around here, banging our heads against headstones, is counterproductive."

CHAPTER THIRTY-ONE

"It's time to learn Mandarin?" Tom quipped when he dropped Elenora home. He needed to head back to the precinct for another case.

She chuckled. "While playing chess *and* the piano, yes." Doing something that required a lot of concentration was a great way to take her mind off concerns, and Elenora craved a respite from the case.

On their drive from the cemetery, her tired mind had latched onto an unpleasant question: by showing the spirits their postmortem pictures, had she further scarred them?

Had it been the right thing to do?

She had felt genuine elation and closure in all the women, sure, and she still felt high from the astounding experience and from making them happy. But had it been worth the potential long-term devastation? No one in the history of humanity had ever seen themselves in death. It had to leave one hell of an impression.

How do they feel about this now?

Elenora's tortured mind had then moved on to worrying

about the specters' fates. She trusted that Wren's spell would keep Gill at bay for the time being. But what would become of the other ghosts in the long run? Of Angéline?

"Tell that brilliant mind of yours that whatever's troubling it, we will find a way to make things right." Tom squeezed her hand knowingly.

While both Elenora and Tom were passionate and had an equally hard time leaving everything in the office at the end of the day, he managed to keep an emotional distance that she had a much harder time achieving. It was her job to be empathetic. It was who she was. And with her growing psychic abilities, she had an even harder time getting out of her head when she needed to.

Elenora badly needed to rest and relax, but resting and relaxing would give her more time to think, and that would lead to rehashing every thought and reliving every feeling. Her mind and emotions were stuck on an endless spin cycle. She needed to get off this unhealthy merry-go-round, keep her mind busy, and exhaust herself in a constructive and unemotional manner.

She thought about bringing Aubrey on a run to the drugstore. Shopping with the baby never failed to keep her in the moment. Her eight-month-old daughter was a wild card. If she was in a sunny mood, a trip to the store meant exploring a variety of new sights, shapes, and colors and interacting with strangers. If she became cranky, the shopping expedition turned into an obstacle course and a mad dash to the cashier.

Hmm.

Shopping with a baby might not be the best distraction

after all, especially when Elenora felt *this close* to losing her own shit.

Pierre offered to stay and hang out with them, and Elenora wisely took him up on his offer—joking that maybe he should move in—and decided to go easy on herself. She would keep her mind busy without putting herself through unnecessary stress. And thankfully, Pierre understood her delicate state. He avoided mentioning anything related to the day's events or the case and entertained her in the best ways.

The three of them went for a swim at a neighbor's pool, where they had a standing invitation. Then, back home, the baby went down for a long nap while Elenora ate ice cream and did a puzzle with Pierre in the living room to the sound of a baseball game on TV. Before she knew it, a relaxing afternoon had gone by, and they ordered Indian for dinner when Tom came home.

When Elenora hit the sack that night, she focused her thoughts on those pleasant, carefree hours as her mind drifted to sleep, hoping to prolong her peaceful state of mind.

She found herself in a dark room. A full moon shone through a large window, allowing her eyes to adjust fast. She recognized the ballroom of the old house on Maple. Angéline must have summoned her again. Elenora's heart skipped a beat. Did something happen to the affable spirit?

She searched for a spectral presence. Her eyes caught movement to her right, and she expected to see the friendly medium. Instead, a tall and slender man in dapper clothes stood at the other end of the room, one elbow resting against the mantel of the imposing fireplace. He snapped his fingers, and a fire roared to life in the hearth, illuminating his face with harsh shadows.

Joseph Gill.

Panic rose inside Elenora, but she made it recede just as fast. *Relax, it's just a dream.* Still, here she was, facing the ghost of a cruel, stylish psychopath while she wore a light summer nightgown.

Classy.

And fierce.

"Miss Elenora, is it?" the man asked with smug disinterest.

"Yes. Mr. Gill, I presume."

"Indeed. A pleasure to make your acquaintance." He gave her a feral smile.

"Likewise. I would love to talk." She successfully kept her voice steady, even though she felt like prey.

"Then have a seat." A glimmer of malice filled his eyes.

Elenora found herself in a comfortable chair. She glanced down to understand the source of his amusement and recognized the chair she was sitting in—the postmortem brocade armchair. Her stomach lurched at the thought of all the corpses that had sat in it.

She leaped to her feet, and Gill's derisive chuckle echoed in the room. She wanted to run away but reasoned with herself. *He wants to psych you out. And if he succeeds, he'll gain the upper hand.* The thought was enough to fill her with indignation and awake her stubborn streak, forcing her to regain her composure.

This is just a dream. The chair isn't real. Get over yourself, and focus.

And even if the chair were real, so what if dead people had sat in it before her? People like Elinor. Mildred. Gertrude... Good women—and men—who had been helpless in an impossible situation and had had to endure this monster before her. Elenora remembered their distress, their terror at being paralyzed in their own skin, and she became angrier. She sat back in the chair, schooling her features to keep any hint of revulsion off her face.

Gill sneered. His eyes hardened, and he straightened.

Elenora let herself sink farther into the chair, making herself comfortable. Two could play his mind game.

"Tell your little friends their efforts are futile," he ordered. "They shall cease at once, or I will annihilate them."

Right to the point. Gotta give him that. And he knew they were trying to banish him. Of course he knew. As a powerful warlock who had been flirting with the dark side and spying on them, of course he would be on to them. But why did he want her to deliver a threat to them? As a weird courtesy? That seemed unlikely. So far he'd acted ruthlessly, both with his victims and as a poltergeist in the house. He should have struck the witches without warning.

Elenora wanted to ask him why he didn't tell the witches himself or why he even needed to warn them, but being antagonistic would lead her nowhere good. Instead, she studied him. His expression and posture were menacing—he wanted to intimidate her. He wanted her to be afraid of him. But she didn't feel afraid. While the dream felt real—and she suspected this encounter wasn't imagined—she felt strangely calm and assured. And grateful, too, for this odd opportunity to question him.

Gill's eyes bored into hers as he waited for her to respond.

"I will give them your message," Elenora said in a professional tone. She needed to change the subject. She needed to establish a rapport with him—that was what she needed to do. But how?

To connect with clients, she usually enjoyed searching for common ground or highlighting people's strengths or accomplishments when they thought of themselves as failures.

Gill's strengths and accomplishments were horrendous, and he clearly didn't see himself as a failure.

And as for common ground...

Okay. There goes nothing.

"It's quite something to meet you, sir." She meant it, though not in a flattering way. How often did one get to meet a murderous poltergeist warlock?

Her words surprised him. He gave her a curt nod.

"I've seen your work. Very realistic and haunting," she continued, walking the fine line between truth and lie. She almost added, *Who knew that art and necromancy could mingle so well?* but kept the dig to herself.

He eyed her suspiciously.

"Those who commissioned your work must have appreciated your artistry," she added. "I'm sure it comforted them to see their departed loved ones' likeness immortalized so masterfully."

Gill observed her silently, still guarded, but his mood seemed to mellow. Elenora was dying to ask him if his wife had known about his "artistry" or why he'd felt the need to kill Jérémie Marsan, but it was too early to poke the bear. If she started out too direct, she might not get answers.

"I've encountered some of your former clients in the house," she tried cautiously.

"So I have noticed." His face darkened.

He knows we talked with the spirits.

"You enjoy their company?" she fished.

He shrugged. "We float in different circles." A slow smirk appeared. He was toying with her.

"Do you intend to let them go?"

"And lose leverage?" His brow quirked.

Leverage? He was...holding the spirits hostage? But how would that work?

Elenora must have frowned because he chuckled condescendingly, as if he wanted to pat her on the head. "I've kept the spirits here in anticipation of this very moment. I saw you and your coven coming decades ago."

Her coven? He thought she was a witch? And he had foreseen them confronting him?

"You saw us? Are you psychic?"

A mocking grin seeped underneath his well-kept mustache. "Not you specifically. But I always knew someone would eventually want to banish me from my home."

And therefore, he had trapped the spirits as a bargaining chip.

"If you get banished, what will happen to the spirits?"

"They will be tethered to this place forever, never able to move on."

Crap.

"Even if someone undid the spell you placed on them?"

Gill snorted. "I'd like to see anyone try."

"Why is it so important for you to remain here?"

"Why would you possibly care?"

"I'm trying to understand," Elenora said.

"Are you, now? Understand what?"

"Why you need to stay here at such a high cost."

He looked at her silently, sizing her up.

"Please help me understand," she said. "Is it because of Clementine?"

He ignored her question, his face betraying no thought or emotion. "Even if you were to understand, which I very much doubt you would, your coven will still try to banish me. I can't let that happen."

"Maybe there's an alternative?"

"How naïve you must be to think such foolishness." His tone became impatient. "Tell your coven their efforts are useless, and make sure they understand. I have all of eternity to defeat their silly spells. Theirs is a lost cause. That will be all."

"Wait!" Elenora wasn't ready to be dismissed. "What if they bring your case to the Gray Court?" She knew the question was bold, but this was also a dream, and he hadn't harmed a single hair on her head. He was unlikely to do so.

At least, that was what she wanted to believe.

"What if I'm in the court's good graces?" He picked at an imaginary piece of lint on his frock coat, feigning indifference.

Why would he be in the Gray Court's good graces? No one should ever be in the good graces of a judicial system—the term "judicial" being used loosely in this case. Gill's statement reeked of corruption, which didn't surprise her.

She made a wild guess. "Then maybe the witches would wonder why that is and investigate to find the source and terms of these good graces... And then argue collusion between you and the court."

She braced herself for verbal vitriol. Instead, Gill's face fell, and he struggled to hide his reaction. Her supposition had set him off-balance. She caught a shred of vulnerability in his eyes.

"Sir, please help me understand..." she pleaded softly.

The ghost briefly considered her plea before letting out an exasperated sigh. He started pacing in front of the fireplace, hands clasped behind his back.

He stopped and turned a flaming gaze on her. "What's their price?"

"Whose price?"

"Your zealous sisters. To let me be."

Bribery. Of course.

Elenora burned to tell him that her *sisters* would never let him be at this point and they all had way too much integrity to be bought. But saying so would shut down their already shaky dialogue. "Why don't we all talk?" she proposed.

He let out a snort of contempt.

"Please," she insisted. "What do you have to lose, compared to what you have to gain?"

"Talking is impossible. The moment I show my face, they will try to banish me."

"But your magic is so powerful. You know they're struggling to get to you."

He puffed up his chest, liking the sound of that.

"What if I got them to agree to listen? Surely we can all have a civilized conversation," she added. "What if we found an amenable solution?"

He shook his head in disbelief before staring into the darkness of the room, entertaining the notion. Until something—the dry crackling of the fire, maybe?—reminded him of where he was and who he was talking to. His face turned to stone. "Nice try."

Ugh. This was going nowhere, and Elenora could get yanked out of the dream at any time. She needed to speed things up. "Why did you kill Marsan?" she asked bluntly.

"The insufferable little fool vying for Satan's attention?"

"No. That was Jean-Luc Rivard."

Gill's brows drew together in genuine puzzlement. He didn't know who she was talking about.

Hmm.

He scrambled for an answer, and Elenora saw a hint of fear flickering in his eyes before his face became impassive. "Marsan, yes," he said.

He was lying...

"Why?" Elenora asked.

"She had to go, of course..." he drawled, looking like he was trying to buy himself time. "She was at death's door, anyway."

Whoa! Was he thinking of Angéline? Had he killed her too?

Focus!

How could he not remember killing Jérémie Marsan? His death was so recent. Unless...

Gill didn't kill him?

"If you didn't push him out of the attic, then who did?" Elenora watched for his reaction. Her gaze met his, and she caught another hint of apprehension.

But then, his mood turned nasty in a split second, and he lunged at her, stopping a few inches from her face. He grabbed her arm and hissed, "What game are you playing, wicked woman?"

Elenora barely had time to register Gill's unexpected outburst and his hold on her arm when his touch revealed what was on his mind: a female specter, looking down as she stood at the edge of the opening in the attic's exterior wall, from which Jérémie Marsan had fallen to his death.

Jane.

Before the flash was over, it conveyed grief and yearning.

And panic.

CHAPTER THIRTY-TWO

The image of Jane vanished from Elenora's mind, and she found herself staring into Joseph Gill's fiery eyes, his fear now mixed with anger.

He doesn't want me to know about Jane...killing Jérémie?

The spirit tightened his hold on Elenora's arm, shifting her focus to the pressure. It was strong enough to notice, but being in a dream, the squeeze came out as muffled and didn't hurt her as much as her aggressor surely intended it to. Yukiko and Dr. Brent suspected Elenora couldn't get hurt in a dream, but this wasn't an ordinary dream, and the man before her was no ordinary dream intruder. He was a warlock well-versed in dark magic.

Maybe *he* could hurt her.

Fear spiked inside Elenora, but she curbed the feeling. Giving in to fear would not help her. She needed to focus on what she could control.

She pictured the radio dials in her mind and diminished the squeezing pressure on her arm until she felt nothing. The result reassured her, but she knew better than to be overconfident. It was better to remain vigilant. Maybe Gill could get to her in other ways.

He didn't seem to notice she had suppressed his aggression, and it was best he didn't find out. *Make him believe he has power over you.*

"Answer me! What game are you playing?" he spat.

She lowered her eyes to not further provoke him. "This isn't a game, sir." *Tread carefully.* "If you didn't kill Marsan—"

"I certainly did." He let go of her arm and straightened, looking peeved and uncomfortable. "Now, go tell your witches to move on." He pointed a finger at her. "And you..."

A grim smile lifted the corner of his lips, and Elenora felt her limbs grow numb.

She tried to move her fingers but met strong resistance. Was he trying to paralyze her? A chill went through her.

"You stay away from me." A glimmer of menace shone in his eyes. She could tell he enjoyed terrifying her. Having power over her.

She focused on dialing down the numbness in her limbs and fingers. It took a struggle, but the sensation returned. *Good!* She could still fight back. That was all she needed to know.

"And I will not tell you again," Gill added for good measure. His eyes searched her face for a sign that his threat had been thoroughly understood.

Elenora recognized desperation in his dangerous gaze. He was threatening her because he felt threatened by her. He desperately wanted her away from his business. She was too close to the truth for his comfort. Jane might have killed Marsan, and he didn't want her to know.

"You're protecting Jane," she tried, observing him.

Gill's nostrils flared. The flames in the fireplace shot up, burning brighter, mirroring his temper. Judging by the panicked fury on his face and her limbs losing sensation again, Elenora had guessed right. Jane had killed Marsan, which meant she would go to hell. Gill knew it, and the prospect terrified him.

"If she took a life, she will be held accountable," Elenora rasped. The ghost was trying to affect her vocal cords now. She struggled to add, "Someone will—"

"I will make sure your coven can do nothing," he said forcefully.

She dialed back the pressure around her neck and cleared her throat. The noise took him aback. He hadn't expected her to overturn his power.

"But the next coven that comes along might be stronger and able to do something," she retorted, her voice still a bit hoarse. "Now, stop this nonsense, and listen to me."

The sharpness of her tone ruffled his feathers, but at least he complied. He eyeballed her with perplexed interest as she dialed down the rest of his magical control over her. Her limbs tingled as the sensation returned.

"If Jane killed someone, she is marked for hell, regardless of who successfully brings down your defenses," Elenora said.

The color drained from Gill's face, and he shook his head violently. "She doesn't deserve to go to hell. She's not a killer." He ran a nervous hand over his face. "She's such a sweet soul. She would never kill someone on purpose. You must believe me." He looked at Elenora with pleading eyes. "She is very protective of Clementine. She lost her once and couldn't bear to lose her again."

Elenora could believe Jane was protecting her daughter. The poor woman had lost a child and lived with an unscrupulous dark-magic-wielding madman. Joseph Gill had abused his clients. He had likely abused her too. He had trapped spirits in his house. Had he trapped his wife as well? Both in life and in death?

He and Elenora had been talking only for a few minutes, but she could tell he was a cruel bastard with serious control issues.

"If she felt she was protecting Clementine, it could make a difference," she said. "Intent matters." *In a regular court of law, that is.* But would the Gray Court even consider intent?

Gill's face lit up with hope. He wanted to believe her.

"Is she a poltergeist too?" she asked. Was this how Jane had been able to push Marsan to his death?

The departed warlock took a while to answer, but Elenora didn't get the sense he was trying to deceive her this time. Rather, he simply seemed unsure of what to say.

"I don't know for certain. She avoids me," he finally said.

He looked troubled by his own admission, and she could understand why. If his wife was avoiding him—and why wouldn't she?—and they were forever stuck in a house together, then being eternally rejected ought to hurt.

"What happened?" she asked gently.

Gill started pacing again in front of the fireplace, debating whether to talk. Elenora prayed that he would open up to her before her time in the dream was up. If the magic broke before he talked, she might never get him vulnerable enough again to cooperate.

He settled stiffly close to the fire and stared at the flames. His shoulders dropped in resignation.

"When Clementine passed, Jane's grief was infinite. She was inconsolable. Then she became ill, and I couldn't bear the thought of losing her too." He choked on his words and became silent.

"So, you made sure she'd remain in the house?" she nudged.

"I..." He cleared his throat. "I relieved her of her pain and grief. I reunited her with our daughter. I gave her everything—I always gave her everything."

In other words, he *did* kill her. And he made his wicked deed sound noble.

Elenora kept her breathing steady and made sure to show no judgment—quite a feat considering how appalled she felt.

"But I think she never forgave me for keeping them here," he said, baffled. As brilliant and powerful as the man was, he was also profoundly clueless. Jane must have hoped to escape him in death, but even *that* peace he'd denied her.

"You used magic to keep them here," Elenora said to make sure she understood correctly.

"Yes."

"The dark spell around the house?"

He hesitated before confirming her guess. "That's part of it."

"Then you hanged yourself in the house to be with them?"

"Someone had to protect them. And I needed to be here when she came around, to show her I did this for us—so we could always be together. She will always be mine."

Poor deluded fool.

Elenora didn't dare to tell him that an eternity would

never be long enough for his estranged wife to come around and forgive him after what he'd done.

"Where is she?"

Gill's anger returned. "Don't try to trick me, witch! You think I will tell you and make her vulnerable? So that you and your coven—" He sputtered with outrage.

Stay cool. Elenora took a deep breath, kept her voice soft and steady, and interrupted him. "Mr. Gill, if Jane killed an innocent person, she is already vulnerable. If I could read her remains, I might find out what happened from her perspective. I could understand why she did what she did and include this information in an appeal. If she felt threatened and the resulting death was an accident, then maybe we can help her avoid a sentence in hell."

As the words escaped her lips, Elenora wondered if she could make such bold claims. Had Jane Gill been alive, she would have had the right to a fair trial. But what were the rules and laws regarding spirits committing crimes, especially those who might otherwise have gone to a peaceful afterlife had they not been kept here against their will?

Would the Gray Court have a say in this? And if so, where would that ruthless assembly stand?

The one time Elenora had had the displeasure of dealing with the Gray Court, she'd quickly found out that fairness and compassion—understanding even—had no room in it. Joseph Gill had acted deliberately, both while alive and in death, and he must have known that he would be going to hell sooner or later. He sure acted accordingly, like he had nothing to lose. But in his wife's case, the situation was much less black or white.

The dead photographer scoffed. "How can you even think you can help her?"

"I would like to *try* to help her."

"Then tell your coven to stay away," he growled.

"And then what? Wait for the next coven to come around? What happens when one of them is powerful enough to banish you?"

"I've already told you. The spirits will remain tethered here."

"And Jane will eventually go to hell. Without Clementine. Is this what you want for her? A miserable nonexistence until someone manages to release her?"

His lips pinched tightly. Maybe it hadn't occurred to him that Jane would also be collateral damage if he ever were banished. He kept a stony façade, but hints of vulnerability and helplessness came through again.

"I know it's hard to understand, but I honestly want to help her. And I might be the only one who can," Elenora said. "Will anyone else be able—or even willing—to advocate for her?"

His pained look suggested he realized she might be right.

A familiar noise echoed in the distance. The sound of Aubrey crying. *Shoot.* Elenora felt a pull. Her return to reality was inevitable, but dang it, she felt so close to reaching an agreement with the ornery spirit.

The crying intensified.

"You are being summoned. You are quite sought after," Gill said dryly. And with resignation. "Go, Miss Elenora. I'll grudgingly admit I appreciate your stubborn willingness to help, but I dug my grave too deeply for a solution to exist."

"Jane didn't help you dig."

He hung his head in shame. "It doesn't matter. It's too late."

Elenora felt another pull away from the ghost and raised her voice, at once to be heard and to emphasize her words. "Tell you what. I'll visit Jane tomorrow and do my best to help her. You will *not* interfere."

She barely finished that last sentence before she got yanked out of the dream.

Joseph Gill didn't get a chance to protest.

"Teeth?"

Elenora walked into Aubrey's bedroom, dazed from sleep and her intense encounter with Joseph Gill's spirit. Her red-faced daughter clutched Tom and wailed in his ear. The shrill sound made him wince, and his left eye blinked on its own. He paced the room, trying to soothe Aubrey, but the tactic seemed inefficient.

"Teeth, yeah," Tom said gruffly.

Elenora held out her hands to take Aubrey and relieve him, and he dumped the baby in her arms. The wailing calmed a tad before launching into a different frequency. *If only there was a dial for this.*

"I can't believe you were sleeping through this," Tom nearly shouted to be heard over the gum-related meltdown. "You must've been really deep down some rabbit hole."

"You have no idea. The weirdest thing just happened."

Tom turned an apprehensive gaze on her. His left eye blinked some more.

Great. Could she have chosen a worse time to bring up

her discussion with a murderous warlock? She shouldn't have said anything just yet.

"Before you worry, nothing happened to me. I'm all right, see? And I'm not traumatized, I assure you."

"You say that, and I'm supposed not to worry?" Blink, blink.

"Listen—"

Of course, Aubrey took that as a cue to pump her volume up a notch. Elenora grimaced and swung the baby away from her ear. Surprisingly, they never mentioned hearing loss in baby books.

She started bouncing Aubrey around, if not to soothe, at least to distract. That gave the wailing a bumpy vibration. The baby noticed and switched to vocalizing, the result amusing her. An odd-sounding mix of sobs and giggles ensued.

"You tried rubbing her gums?" Elenora asked Tom.

"Yeah. And her teething ring, but she threw it across the room. Almost hit the cat."

"Okay. Then maybe a breadstick will do the trick."

They headed downstairs to the kitchen, and sure enough, Aubrey happily grabbed the stiff little breadstick and gnawed on it greedily. Elenora found the sudden silence almost jarring, her ears still ringing. She settled her daughter in her high chair.

"You're both killing me," Tom said.

"I talked with Joseph Gill in a dream."

"You *what?*!"

Aubrey made a startled peep, and they both turned to her and held their breath. Thankfully, she resumed biting the breadstick.

"Nothing bad happened, Tom. I'm right here, as you can see," Elenora said in a very, very soft voice.

He matched her soothing tone through gritted teeth. "But something could have happened. Remember Barlow in the mirror?"

The murderous spirit of Oliver Barlow had connected with Elenora through a mirror and almost strangled her. Not something one could easily forget.

"Barlow showed up through self-hypnosis. That's different. I have never been harmed in my dreams."

"You mean, aside from psychological scarring?"

"Fair enough. Though I am getting better."

A heavy silence ensued, disturbed only by Aubrey's sloppy munching sounds.

Tom let out a long sigh and grabbed his wife's hands. "You saw how Yukiko and the witches reacted when you told them you met with Angéline in your sleep. It blew their minds. They didn't think the two of you could interact like that. So, how can we know for sure that you can't get hurt in your dreams when it's uncharted territory?"

"You're right. We can't. But I didn't seek to see him, and I was vigilant."

He drew her into a hug. "I know you are. And I certainly don't want you to fear your own thoughts. I'm just afraid of what you can't control."

So was she. But she was even more tired of being afraid. "Aren't you curious about what he said?"

"I want to know every detail. Let me grab a notepad."

Elenora peered outside the patio door and saw a faint light on the horizon. There would be no going back to bed. She sighed and turned on the coffee maker.

"I asked him to consider talking with us," Elenora said to Alex, Yukiko, and the witches on a video call on Tom's laptop later that morning. Pierre was also there, drinking coffee in their dining room headquarters.

"Perfect!" Serena replied. "We'll chitchat with him, banish his ass, and then go back to our regular programming. Can't wait."

"Not so fast. He saw us coming over a century ago. He's keeping the other spirits in the house hostage as leverage."

"So he doesn't get banished..." Claire-Lune groaned. "Crafty bastard. What happens if he does get banished?"

"He's tethered them to the house so they can't move on. If he goes down, they're screwed forever," Tom answered.

"How Machiavellian," Wren said, pursing her lips.

Serena crinkled her nose. "You say *Machiavellian*. I say *typical vindictive asshole*."

"Why is he doing this? Why is he hell-bent on staying in the house?" Alex asked.

"He got irate with me and grabbed my arm," Elenora said. "And the contact showed me the ghost of his wife on his mind—"

"You touched a specter in a dream and got a vision from him?" Yukiko interrupted her, bowled over.

"Well, technically, *he* touched me—"

"Dude! Just own it already!" Serena shook her head.

"Okay, so, what's up with his wife?" Alex tried to steer the conversation back on track.

"Well..." A smile bloomed on Elenora's face. "I might have the opportunity to ask her that myself."

CHAPTER THIRTY-THREE

"Hmm." Wren moved her hand over the front door of the old house to assess the state of the dark spell. "That's unexpected."

"What is?" Serena looked full of nervous energy.

"The dark spell is gone."

"*Gone* as in *no longer there?*"

"Mm-hmm."

"Gill took it down?" Claire-Lune asked, incredulous.

"Why would he take it down?" Juniper asked, just as suspicious.

"As a sign of good faith?" Elenora tried. Could he really have reconsidered his position after their conversation?

"Or as a sign that he's fucking with us," Serena replied sarcastically.

The witches had been skeptical of Joseph Gill's willingness to let Elenora interact with his departed wife and play nice. To be on the safe side, they'd asked their OPO colleague Hassan and another crew of witches to stand by in a surveillance van parked across the street. Should things go sideways, the crew would know and could rush inside to their help.

"I concur with my foul-mouthed sibling. It might be a ruse," Claire-Lune said. "He could have changed the spell and made sure we couldn't detect it."

"Yeah, my money's on *ambush* or *psychological warfare*," Serena said.

"Maybe I'm too naïve for my own good," Elenora argued, "but I hesitate to think the worst just yet. He was devastated over his wife going to hell. He needs our help and knows it. I suspect he understands the benefits of cooperating."

"I agree that if he's as smart as he thinks he is, he might get it." Claire-Lune glided her hand over the front door. "But let's not take any chances. He's proved to be morally impaired, and he might still play dirty. Let's assume this is an ambush so he doesn't take us by surprise."

The other witches nodded in unison.

Juniper put a hand on the door handle. "Everyone ready?"

After another round of nods, she gave the door a push and leaned back. The door creaked open slowly. Nothing stirred in the house—the coast seemed clear. The witch poked her head inside, sent a round of magical waves to assess the main level from the doorstep, and waited expectantly.

"Seems good," she finally declared and stepped inside.

Everyone followed her in.

A luminescence up the stairs caught Elenora's eye. Angéline was sitting there, hunched over her knees as if trying to make herself inconspicuous. She gave a little wave, and Elenora discreetly waved back. The spirit stood up and carefully came down.

"Angéline?" Serena asked Elenora quietly.

She nodded.

The witch whipped a small candle out of her pocket, lit it with a finger snap, and shoved it in Yukiko's face.

"Angéline-de-Montbleu-I-respectfully-summon-you-please-show-yourself," the medium murmured expeditiously, and Serena threw a revealing spell at the stairs.

Angéline's ghost appeared to everyone and pointed warily at the ballroom. "I think he's in there," she said in a low voice.

Gill? Juniper mouthed.

She got a vigorous nod from Angéline.

"Don't worry, girlfriend. We got this." Serena gave the specter's shoulder a symbolic air pat. "Though, may I suggest you keep a safe distance from that crackpot?"

Angéline snorted. "Sounds good."

A whoosh was heard, followed by crackling noises.

Juniper raised a hand to halt everyone and pressed a finger to her lips for silence. *What was that?* she mouthed, straining an ear.

Elenora recognized the familiar soundtrack from her latest dream. "He's got a fire going in the fireplace."

They poked their heads into the ballroom. Sure enough, a fire roared in the hearth at the other end of the room.

Elenora noticed a shimmering next to the fireplace. *Gill?* She dialed the distortion mentally. Her tweaking provoked an overlaid vision and exposed the photographer.

Whoa.

Nifty.

Leaning against the mantel, the specter was waiting for

them, arms crossed and sharp eyes shooting daggers at the witches.

"He's by the fireplace if you'd like to summon and reveal him," Elenora said to Yukiko and Serena.

"No need for amateur tricks." Gill snickered and swiped a hand in front of his lanky frame, revealing himself.

"Impressive," Claire-Lune said frankly to the spirit.

He sneered at the compliment.

"You mean *impressive display of arrogance*," Serena mumbled with a sneer of her own.

Gill huffed.

"Guys..." Hoping to put a stop to the escalating tension, Elenora gestured at her colleagues to stay put and let her handle this. She noticed Tom stiffen and smiled at him—*I've got this, love.* She straightened her posture, made herself look agreeable, and marched to the departed warlock. "Thank you for showing up, Mr. Gill. I gather you are considering my proposal?"

He nodded at her coolly.

"As I mentioned last night, I would like to do my best to help Jane. If you are on board, you need to let me work without interfering. As you know, I'm only psychic. I have no magical powers that could harm her. My colleagues also understand what is at stake here and don't want to interfere. You have our word that we are here in good faith."

Gill's piercing gaze studied her for a moment before moving past her and assessing everyone else. His eyes narrowed. Behind the detached hostility in his eyes, Elenora could see genuine concern. She sensed he was willing to give her a chance but was unsure about her colleagues.

"Do we know for certain that Jane is marked?" he asked.

"Yes," an assured male voice boomed from the foyer.

"Who is this intruder?" Gill asked snootily.

This intruder is your only chance for a positive outcome, Elenora itched to retort. Instead, she said, "This is my esteemed colleague Jeb Morsy. He works with the devil's advocates at the Gray Court."

Before the visit, Elenora and the witches had consulted with Jeb over Jane Gill's unusual predicament. He thought the Gray Court was unlikely to be convinced to overturn a marking. However, despite his laid-back, surfer-dude looks, Jeb had never met an impossible fight he didn't like, and he'd proposed to file an appeal with the Sovran Council—a judicial entity above the Gray Court. Apparently, the council was more objective, its scales not tipping so much in favor of evil.

"We discussed Jane's case with him," Elenora continued, "and he thinks it's a very long shot since the situation is rather complex and there's no precedent. But he agreed to take time out of his very busy schedule to evaluate the special circumstances of the murder your wife committed." Her voice was patient, but she held Gill's stare, willing him to be on his best behavior with Jeb. "We're talking murder *singular*, correct? Or is there something else we should know?"

"Singular," the specter grunted.

"And just to be clear, Jane pushed a construction worker to his death through an opening in the attic, correct?"

The spirit's face distorted with pain. "It appears she did."

Elenora remembered Gill had mistaken Jérémie Marsan for Jean-Luc Rivard when she'd first mentioned him. He likely hadn't witnessed the death itself, but he knew it was

Jane's doing, or he would deny the accusation. He knew she was marked, or he wouldn't be talking to them.

"Thank you. Now, if Jeb thinks the Sovran Council might be receptive to Jane's predicament, he will file an appeal with them to reexamine her sentence. Again, this won't be easy, considering what happened. And unless we have your full cooperation, there's no point in pursuing this. So, can we count on your help and goodwill?"

Gill blew out an annoyed breath. "Very well."

"We have your full cooperation?"

"Yes."

"Then, very well indeed." Elenora broke into a relieved smile. "Now that we are all on the same page, shall we proceed?"

"Wait," Gill said with the stiff politeness of someone squashing their ego for a greater good. "I would like to be there when you read my wife's remains."

"Does anyone object to Mr. Gill's request?" she asked her colleagues.

They conferred with each other for a moment.

"It seems reasonable," Wren announced on their behalf.

Elenora looked at the warlock.

He hesitated a moment before nodding gravely. "I will lead you to her."

He floated to and up the stairs, and they followed him.

"Her body's in here?" Tom asked, surprised, when they reached the attic.

"Yes. Behind the wall." Gill pointed at the infamous inside wall with the jagged hole.

"Hmm. We found a small coffin with a picture back there but not your wife."

"And you call yourself a detective?" the spirit goaded him with a smirk.

Tom didn't take the bait and remained cordial. "I'm also a good cook and a fair pool player, but I have no illusions of being able to compete with a cunning magician."

Gill accepted the compliment. "She's behind the back wall of the cavity you found. The coffin was meant partly as a distraction."

Tom and the others exchanged looks.

"Clever." Tom considered something. "And speaking of clever distractions, I'd love to hear more about how you bribed a member of the police force to bury the report of your death."

The request took Gill slightly aback, but then he grinned. "Why pay a bribe when you can threaten for free?"

Tom answered with an inquisitive smile, urging the spirit to elaborate.

And he did—no doubt showing off. "Detective Harrington was the brother of a client, and I showed him what necromancy can do. I told him to take care of me discreetly after my death or I would revive the city's worst dead criminals and sic them on him and his family. The good man didn't argue."

Serena snorted with contempt. "What a peach."

In contrast, Tom nodded at the specter, impressed. "I can't say I've heard this one before..." His eyes skated to the infamous wall. "Anyway. May we make a hole in the back wall so Elenora can meet your wife?"

Gill made a mocking grand gesture at the wall, inviting them to go ahead before crossing his arms over his chest.

As Tom, Alex, and Juniper approached the opening in

the wall to enlarge it, the air thickened in the room. Elenora's hackles raised. Had they been played? Was Gill about to unleash hell on them again?

Yukiko and Juniper turned an accusatory stare at the spectral warlock. The other witches caught on and prepared to retaliate. A breeze kicked up in the room.

"Stop it right now!" Serena snapped at Gill.

"Sir, you are jeopardizing your wife's chances!" Elenora added.

Gill raised his hands in surrender. "It's not me, I swear. It must be Jane." He drifted closer to the hole.

Tom, Alex, and Juniper stepped away.

"My love, please calm down and come talk to us. It's of the utmost importance," the ghost pleaded.

The breeze defied him and blew stronger.

Gill took it as a personal affront. "Please don't make me calm you down," he hissed through his teeth, his voice carrying the authority of a man used to being obeyed. But the wind only amplified and made him bellow, "Don't make me fetch you!"

That escalated quickly.

"Mrs. Gill, we only want to talk to you. It's very important for you and Clementine. If you don't want to end up in hell," Elenora pleaded softly.

But her words fell on deaf ears. The witches didn't waste another moment and worked on countering the poltergeist activity.

Joseph Gill beat them to the punch by suspending the forceful winds with the flick of his wrists. He stretched an arm in front of him dramatically and made a come-hither gesture at the hole in the wall. A spectral glow reluctantly came out of it, struggling against the departed warlock's magic.

The figure of Jane Gill materialized. She held Clementine while cowering in fear. Her feral eyes were locked on her husband through her lashes, regarding him with horror and dread.

She's afraid of him.

Elenora had witnessed this look countless times at work, especially in cases of domestic abuse—emotional, physical, or both. Gill had no doubt pushed his wife beyond the breaking point. He must have stripped her of her ability to trust, too.

"My love," Gill said, his voice strangled with emotion at the sight of his estranged wife.

Jane flinched violently at his words. Her protective stance toward the bundle in her arms increased. She would not be messed with.

Elenora now better understood why Jane might have perceived Jérémie Marsan swinging a sledgehammer near her and her baby as a threat to them—the reason she had struck back so fast.

"Jane, I'm Elenora. We mean you no harm. We want to help you." She slowly approached the skittish specter. "No one will touch Clementine. I promise."

Jane moved her gaze to Elenora and took her in. Distrustful and traumatized. And here they were, using force against her to bring her out into the open and expose her.

Elenora took a few more tentative steps closer to mother and child, determined to connect with Jane. She looked at the baby's ghost. Little Clementine's spectral appearance showed no sign of illness, and her real gaze—not the one magically doctored by her crazy father in the picture—conveyed sweetness and intelligence.

"Your daughter is beautiful," Elenora said, aware that Jane was still scrutinizing her sharply. "You must be very proud of her. She looks like a wonderful baby."

The specter's face softened slightly at the kind words.

"She is," Gill said proudly.

Both women whipped their heads his way. Jane's eyes became murderous while Elenora's pleaded for him to shut the hell up and stay out of it.

He raised his hands in surrender again. "Carry on," he mumbled, looking away.

Things would be so much easier if he weren't there. But he had requested to be present, and Elenora couldn't renege on her word.

She leaned closer to Jane and dropped her voice to a whisper so only the spirit could hear. "Your husband's actions were misguided, and you have all the right in the world to be upset, to be angry with him. And fearful and sad."

Jane gave her a confused look.

"He let his pain cloud his judgment. He couldn't bear to let you and Clementine go. It's the reason he kept you here. You matter a lot to him." Elenora couldn't bring herself to say he *loved* them—love rarely had anything to do with control and possessiveness. "Even if he was truly awkward and unforgivable in the ways he showed his feelings for you and your daughter."

Jane stared pointedly at Gill. At least he had the good sense to look contrite.

"I have a young daughter too," Elenora said, regaining Jane's attention. "And I would do anything to protect her. I understand why you felt that way... I would like to show you a photograph."

Elenora opened her purse to get a printed picture of Jérémie Marsan. She had figured that if given a shot to talk with Jane, using her cell phone could be distracting.

Jane watched her dig through her purse with interest. The bag's fashion must have seemed odd to her.

"Do you recognize this young man?" Elenora showed Jane a recent picture of Jérémie taken at a construction site.

The specter brought Clementine closer to her chest.

"You thought he was going to harm your daughter?" Elenora asked gently.

Jane gave her a barely perceptible nod, but the sadness and regret in her eyes could neither be missed nor mistaken.

"You pushed him away to protect Clementine?"

Her nod was clearer this time.

"Do you know what happened to him?"

Jane averted her eyes, her features tightening. "Did he survive the fall?" Her voice was meek, rusty, and unexpected.

Hearing her speak took everyone in the room by surprise.

"I'm afraid he didn't make it."

Elenora gave Jane time to let the horrible truth sink in. She wondered if she could get a read of the tragedy by touching the ghost instead of her remains. That would save the two of them a lot of grief if it worked. But touching her now might send Jane into a frenzy. Or destroy the meager trust they were slowly building. Elenora kept her hands to herself.

"I didn't mean to harm him," the spirit said.

"I know." Elenora gave her a thin smile of sympathy.

"You've had traumatic experiences, Jane. Your reaction is understandable."

"But I will go straight to hell..." she whispered, her sorrowful eyes on Clementine.

"If we don't intervene, yes. But we want to try getting you a more lenient sentence."

Whatever a *more lenient* sentence meant. Jeb had hinted at another place aside from heaven and hell—maybe he'd meant purgatory, though he hadn't used the word and had remained fuzzy on the details. Was there a gray area, neither awful nor pleasant, where spirits could spend their afterlife? Or even have a shot at redeeming themselves?

A glimmer of hope appeared in Jane's eyes. "Thank you."

Elenora took the ghost's gratitude as a chance to comfort her with a touch. She offered Jane a kind smile and gently placed a hand on her arm, willing herself to remain rooted in reality. Jane's turmoil hit her like a slap along with a jumble of moving lights and shadows. Elenora fought not to react to the powerful mix of emotions assaulting her while attempting to sharpen the vision.

"How?" Jane asked.

"My colleague Jeb will explain what we intend to do." Elenora kept her hand in place, working on clarifying the images as Jeb approached.

He must have guessed what she was doing because he slowed, reached for a folded document in the inner pocket of his jacket, and pretended to review it. "Indeed... Mrs. Gill, just gimme a second if you don't mind..." he drawled, capturing Jane's attention.

Elenora quickly turned her mental dial up and down on the images and tried tweaking their frequency, but no trick got rid of the fuzz covering them. *Dang it.* She wasn't getting anything usable from the spirit's mind, and further stretching the moment would only make things awkward. It looked like she would have to read Jane's remains after all. Elenora let go of her arm.

"Here's what we need to do," Jeb said, his mellow voice and commanding presence seeming to put Jane at ease. "With your permission, we would like to access your remains so Elenora can make a record of the event as you lived it and gather other related proof to build a strong appeal. I promise we will treat your remains with the utmost respect and not harm your daughter. Do you find this acceptable?"

She nodded timidly.

"Good. Once we know the outcome of your appeal, we will bring your remains and those of your daughter to a more suitable resting place of your choosing."

Elenora noticed Gill stiffen in her periphery.

"That said," Jeb went on, "for your protection until the trial, we will bring your spectral form and Clementine's with us—"

"I didn't agree to that!" Gill exploded.

Jeb raised a calming hand in his direction. "Sir, this is not a trick or a game of chicken. We are not trying to take away your leverage. We just need to ensure Mrs. Gill's safety until we know where we stand. The other spirits will remain in this house as a sign of good faith, with the understanding that you won't be a threat to their safety, of course."

Jeb's eyes drilled into Gill's as he waited for the man's agreement.

"Of course," Gill said curtly.

"By advocating for your wife and attempting to reverse a

potentially unfair verdict of *eternal damnation*," Jeb enunciated the words harshly to drive their importance home, "we are putting our necks on the line. Do you understand this?"

Gill gave Jeb a stiff nod.

"As part of this agreement," Jeb added, "once your wife's status has been resolved—regardless of the outcome—you will release the other spirits in this house, lift any spells you have cast on this place, and make it possible for us to vacate you from the premises. Are we clear?"

Gill's jaw ticked, and he fumed in silence. Eventually, he reluctantly bowed to Jeb. Had he thought he could keep the status quo in his favor once his wife's fate was reviewed?

"Juniper? Tom? Alex?" Jeb pointed at the wall. "Please go ahead."

CHAPTER THIRTY-FOUR

Juniper, Tom, and Alex worked on enlarging the hole in the wall, with the help of delicate magic this time to carefully fragment the structure around the opening. Alex shot Jane and Joseph Gill a wary glance over his shoulder as he pulled on a loose chunk of wood and plaster. Elenora suspected he was right to second-guess the photographer. She kept an eye on him, too, wondering if—or rather when—the spirit would blow another fuse and do something rash.

His type can be so unpredictable, she thought right before noticing wisps of spectral mist emanating from him and pooling at his feet. They hovered close to the floor and spread in several directions, sneaking up behind Jeb and the witches, who seemed oblivious to them. Couldn't they see or feel the mist?

"Yukiko?" Elenora said quietly, getting the medium's attention.

She tipped her head discreetly at Gill. Yukiko threw a

side-glance in the man's general direction. Elenora gave him a side-glance too. He looked guarded but innocuous, as if he was watching the progress on the hole with detachment.

Yukiko frowned, leaned close to Elenora, and whispered, "What is it?" It appeared she saw nothing wrong.

"The mist," Elenora whispered back.

Yukiko's frown grew deeper.

By now, Gill's vaporous minions had traveled up their unsuspecting victims' bodies and wrapped around their necks. Serena coughed, Claire-Lune cleared her throat, and Wren absently pulled at the collar of her dress. What the hell was the ruthless spirit up to?

A feather-like touch of air caressed Elenora's neck, and her throat began to constrict. The rat bastard was trying to strangle them. "You're only gonna punish Jane, you fool!" she shouted at Gill, getting his attention and everyone else's. "Stop this right now, or the deal is off!"

His face registered a hint of surprise before he quickly recovered his bored expression. The misty tendrils vanished. "Whatever do you mean?"

The asshole. Elenora's quick accusation might have stopped him from hurting them, but now she had no proof. Thankfully, her fury carried her past that detail. She got in his face. "You think you can sneak up on us and strangle us with no one noticing?"

His eyes went wide. "What? You...?"

"Yes, I saw. And felt. Very clearly."

A zap of light shot past Elenora and struck Gill in the face. He jerked back and then tried to retaliate but found himself frozen in place. His seething gaze swept the room, looking for the culprit.

"Now, now, Reena," Jeb said placatingly to his ex. He and Serena had known each other for centuries and had been a couple on and off a few times. It was complicated. "Use your words, dear. Like this..."

Jeb invaded warlock's space and leveled his gaze at him. "It is quite unfortunate that you deemed it acceptable to renege on your word, *sir*. Problem is, now that you're forcing my hand, I might be tempted to cut corners with your wife's appeal—assuming I feel charitable enough to pursue it now."

Jane whimpered. Gill glared at Jeb.

"Tell me, Mr. Gill, should I even bother?"

The ghost huffed and puffed but was smart enough to contain his temper. "Yes, please do," he finally said with forced politeness.

"You're skating on thin ice, and I won't give you a second chance if you screw up again. So here's the new deal—take it or leave it. I will ask the Gray Court to send a custodian to collect you—today."

"You can't do that!" the specter scowled.

"Watch me."

"No, wait!" Gill backpedaled and made himself look contrite. "Please, no—I need to be here to protect Jane and the baby. I'm so sorry. I promise I won't do anything to compromise your generous agreement again. Please—"

Jeb lifted a hand to silence the ghost's apologetic rambling. "While we wait for the custodian to show up, you will untether the spirits you're holding captive and eradicate any spells on these premises. You will also disclose the location of your remains so they can be handed in quickly. Every single condition will have to be met to our satisfaction before I proceed with the appeal. Do we still have a deal?"

"How can I be sure you will keep your word?"

Jeb shrugged. "You can't." He turned his back on Gill. "Wren, Claire-Lune, and Serena, please get him to eradicate the spells, release the spirits in the basement, and tell you where he's buried."

"With pleasure," Claire-Lune said, barely containing her enthusiasm.

"On second thought, start with his remains so Hassan's crew can fetch them while you tackle the rest. And if he gets nasty, don't hesitate to hit below the belt. Decorum has long left the building."

Serena smirked and made a show of cracking her knuckles.

"I'm gonna go contact the Gray Court." Jeb headed down the stairs.

Elenora took Serena aside. "Why is Jeb handing Gill over to the Gray Court?"

"Because once the appeal is done, our favorite jackass is heading straight down south—and I don't mean Florida."

"Okay. But wouldn't he get there just the same if you guys banished him?"

Claire-Lune joined the conversation. "He would likely get there, yes. Except he's a dirty-playing warlock, and he might find a loophole along the way if we banish him."

"This way," Wren added, "he gets a direct trip to hell, ensured by one of Satan's lackeys."

"And no one fucks with those guys." Serena gave Gill a taunting smile. "Though I'd love to see him try."

The specter glowered at her.

"Also, the Gray Court will keep him confined effortlessly

for the time needed. Whereas he could try to wear us out or outwit us if he were in our care while the Sovran Council considers the appeal," Claire-Lune added matter-of-factly.

Elenora admired that the witch wasn't threatened by Gill being more powerful than them and even recognized that fact gracefully.

"Thanks for the clarification," she said.

"You're always welcome, dear." Claire-Lune turned to Gill. "Now, let's get cracking. Where are your remains, sir?"

His face darkened, his expression calculating.

"And don't bother saying *the cemetery*," Serena warned him.

Gill opened his mouth to talk but reconsidered. Elenora understood that once he gave away the location of his remains, there would be no turning back for him. No hope of escaping his fate.

"Under the front porch," Jane said, making them all turn. She had crept up behind them and wore a steely resolve.

"My love?" Gill gave his wife a baffled look.

"Look for an urn," she added in a chilly voice.

Serena lifted her wrist and spoke into her watch. "Hassan, you got that?"

A male voice escaped from the device. "Yup. Reaching for the shovel right now."

"Thank you, Jane," Claire-Lune said.

"Of course he's near the front door," Wren mused. "Easier to control the dark spell. Smart."

Gill was still too shocked by his wife's betrayal to notice Wren's appreciation of his twisted cleverness. His eyes remained intent on Jane, who floated away from them.

"Jane! How did you know?" he called after her with a pained expression.

She stopped and pondered her answer before facing him. "I know more than you think." She stared him dead in the eye, her head held high. Only a slight quiver of her bottom lip betrayed how rattled she truly was. She resumed her glide to the other side of the room.

Elenora caught up to her. "It takes a lot of bravery to do what you just did. To face an abuser."

Jane briefly glanced at her cruel husband, and fear returned to her eyes.

"Don't worry—they've got him. He won't be a threat to you anymore," Elenora reassured her.

"Maybe not now, but if I land in hell, he will." Jane's voice trembled. "Neither the witches nor anyone else will have control over him down there. He'll come after me."

She made an unfortunate and indisputable point. If both spouses ended up in hell, Gill would indeed be out of the witches' reach, and he might make his wife's afterlife even more atrocious. Unless Jeb succeeded in having her unmarked.

Jeb had to succeed.

Or if not, maybe he could cut some deal to keep Gill away from Jane? Would that be an option?

"We got a second hole!" Alex announced triumphantly from inside the wall cavity.

"Please be careful. Their remains are fragile!" Gill yelled with seemingly genuine worry.

How could one care so much for someone and yet be so monstrous to them at the same time? Elenora wondered as she headed toward the craggy entrance in the wall.

"Chill! We're not amateurs!" an annoyed Juniper yelled from behind the wall.

As Elenora grabbed the sides of the first opening to enter it, she heard Alex say, "Let me shed some light." And after a beat, he let out a strangled gasp.

CHAPTER THIRTY-FIVE

Elenora struggled to an upright position inside the cavity behind the wall. Already crammed there, Tom, Alex, and Juniper were staring, slack-jawed, into the new hole in the back wall. They moved aside to let Elenora see their discovery.

Leaning in, Elenora caught sight of the infamous brocade armchair. An adult skeleton sat in it, its arms encircling a mangy blanket in which tiny bones were nestled.

Jane and Clementine.

Elenora's breath caught. While her visions were often emotionally charged, seeing the decayed mother and child in person was something else. Even though she'd interacted with Jane's ghost just a moment earlier, the sight of her remains—at once eerie and oddly dignified—made the woman's horrific situation even more real and shook Elenora to the core.

Get a grip and focus. Jane deserves it.

Her eyes dropped to the skeleton's feet, where over twenty framed pictures lay interspersed with unlit candles, much like a shrine. The first ones Elenora looked at depicted Jane and Clementine while still alive. Then was the post-mortem picture of Clementine that they'd seen, with Gill's necromancy present in the baby's eyes.

The other images—not previously seen—showed Jane sitting in the postmortem chair, her gaze shooting daggers at the lens. She maintained the same position her skeleton had settled in, clutching a pristine blanket in her arms—the mangy blanket before it degraded. Its hidden contents were no doubt Clementine's remains. The pictures all showed Jane holding the blanket but wearing different fashionable dresses. *Maybe she was still alive in these despite the chair?*

But then Elenora started noticing the little telltale signs Rolland had mentioned—too much rouge on the cheeks, eyes sinking, sallow skin... It became apparent that she was no longer alive in those pictures and that Joseph's necromantic skills had been limited to controlling souls. As more sickening pictures proved, he'd been powerless to stop his wife's body from decaying. And he had kept photographing her well after it'd been decent to do so.

Elenora fought a wave of nausea and looked away from the ultimate proof of Joseph Gill's inhumane treatment of his wife.

"The bastard made sure she was conscious until the very end," Alex gritted through his teeth.

Elenora's eyes couldn't help returning to one of the most disturbing pictures and noticed the tortured gaze typical of the photographer's victims. Like them, Jane had been conscious during the morbid photo sessions. But unlike them, she might also have been aware of her own perishing.

How deranged would you have to be to do such a depraved thing? And why? Being unable to let go?

Tom's arm wrapped around Elenora's waist. He gave her a gentle side hug and murmured, "It's a lot to take in. Would you like a moment before you read her?"

She gave him a weak smile and shook her head. The sooner she read Jane, the sooner she could process her shock in peace. She reached for the remains through the opening, but the access was too restricted and awkward. She fought to get close enough.

"Ele, how about we enlarge the hole first?" Alex asked.

"Better yet, it'd be easier from the main room. Let's enlarge both holes and get them out," Juniper suggested. "We'll have to get them out anyway."

Elenora exited the cavity, and her gaze locked with Gill's. She shot him a murderous look, and he averted his eyes.

"I couldn't bear to let them go. Can you blame me?" he muttered.

Elenora used considerable restraint to not scream *Hell yes!* at him. She knew there was no point in shouting at a deaf man. Instead, she shook her head in disbelief at him and shifted her attention to Jane, who cowered in a corner, upset. Elenora went to comfort the specter.

"I'm so sorry," Jane whispered.

"For what?"

"I wish you didn't have to see *that*." She spat the last word with disgust.

She's ashamed to have strangers see her remains. Of course she would be.

"Jane, what I saw is a mother cradling her beloved child. You are a loving mother."

A sob escaped the spirit, and tears fell down her face. Elenora drew the translucent figure in for a hug, mindful of the baby. She felt an airy presence against her, as if she were hugging cotton candy. The tremors from Jane crying were noticeable.

"Thank you for being so kind to me," Jane mumbled into Elenora's shoulder, and a trace of warm air tickled Elenora's neck.

"You deserve so much more than my kindness," she replied. "And you deserved none of the bad. It's all on him. Please always remember that."

Another round of sobs shook Jane. Soon, Elenora felt the spectral form relax. However, the spirit's peace was short-lived—Juniper, Tom, and Alex emerged from the hole, painstakingly carrying the chair with her skeleton.

Jeb appeared at the top of the stairs, followed by a tall blond guy in a midnight-blue suit. The stranger carried a grimy funeral urn and looked more like a car salesman than a threatening bodyguard on Satan's payroll.

"Ugh," Serena scoffed.

Everyone's attention turned to Jeb and the newcomer.

"This is Thelonious from the Gray Court," Jeb said in a monotone that barely disguised his annoyance.

"Hey, everyone!" The visitor waved at them cordially, flashing a blinding smile.

He seemed quite approachable and the polar opposite of Stefan, the other member of the Gray Court Elenora had had the displeasure of meeting. But judging from Serena's reaction and the stiffness in Jeb's posture, she guessed that once again, looks could be deceiving. She was relieved to not have to deal with Stefan, but at least that insufferable man wore his contempt and malevolence on his sleeve. Whereas this Thelonious guy oozed devilish charm—he might be even more insidious. She ought to keep herself off his radar.

"This is the guy?" Thelonious jerked his head at Gill.

"Yes," Jeb answered.

Thelonious gave Gill a once-over before an unreadable grin spread across his face. "Excellent." His gaze then swept the room before settling on Jane's spirit, and a glimmer of mischief appeared in it. "And this lovely lady?"

"Stay away from my wife," Gill growled.

Thelonious chuckled, clearly not threatened by the dead warlock's warning.

"As I explained, Mrs. Gill is off-limits for now," Jeb said flatly.

"For now. You really think the Sovran Council will give a rat's ass about her sob story?" He wore a discordantly affable smile.

"There's a first time for everything."

"Spoken like a man who's never pissed them off for wasting their time." Satan's emissary glanced at his watch. "Speaking of which, I love the company, but I need to get going."

"Hold your apocalyptic horses!" Jeb interjected. He turned to Wren and indicated Gill. "Did he take down every spell and undo the tethers?"

"Yes."

"The spirits are free to go?"

"Yes."

"Thanks." Jeb turned back to Thelonious. "He's all yours."

The custodian slapped a hand behind Gill's neck and gripped him, making him flinch.

"Wait!" Gill freaked out at the realization that this was finally the end. "I need to say goodbye to my wife."

"Dude, take a hint. She can't wait for your ass to be gone," Serena said.

The ghost fell to his knees, but Thelonious's grip stopped him midway to the floor and kept him dangling in an awkward position. He didn't fight back, too busy throwing his wife a devastated look.

"Jane, my love, please do everything they tell you to do. For your sake and Clementine's. I'm sorry if I've hurt you. I didn't want you to leave me. I will love you forever!"

"All right, enough of that," Thelonious declared, pleasant smile still in place, and he yanked Gill back up effortlessly. "Jeb, always a pleasure. Ladies and gents." He gave everyone an exaggerated bow, then both he and Gill vanished.

"Good riddance times two," Serena said, unfazed by the two men's sudden disappearance. She took a deep breath and moaned, "Could the air ever be sweeter than after evil has left the room?"

Elenora snorted at her friend's colorful remark before noticing that Serena wasn't entirely joking. The air in the room had perceptibly changed. It was...purer? Even though Jane and Clementine's musty remains were just a few feet away.

That sure said something about the foulness of immorality.

Elenora read Jane's remains, capturing the departed woman's experience of Jérémie Marsan's unfortunate demise. She also retrieved a substantial number of incriminating memories proving Joseph Gill's pernicious spousal abuse. Serena successfully downloaded everything in digital format. The collection of clips provided a perfect context for Jane's visceral reaction to the young construction worker and gave Jeb everything he needed to craft a solid appeal to convince the Sovran Council that she didn't belong in hell. He was cautiously optimistic.

With Jane in tow, the group headed to the basement to help the other spirits move on.

"Any chance Thelonious might ignore the agreement?" Tom asked Jeb and the witches on their way down. "Could he, say, release Gill somewhere else on earth to wreak more havoc? Surely the forces of evil would see value in the spirit of a corrupt warlock with dark-magic abilities."

"He knows better than to screw me over," Jeb replied, "especially when I'm about to address the council. He's a brilliant strategist and doesn't want to get dragged in for interfering—not for something that means nothing to him anyway. Besides, we go way back, and I know where his bodies are buried."

Tom laughed. "Nothing beats having good old dirt to keep people on the straight and narrow. Even the minions of hell can't escape that principle."

Jeb chuckled. "Amen to that!"

They reached the last steps, and a glow from the former studio caught Elenora's eye. The spirits were waiting for them. And the atmosphere was...light.

She smiled. "Hello, everyone! It's good to see you again."

The specters greeted her with smiles and hellos. They seemed upbeat.

"They're all here?" Yukiko asked.

"I think so."

"Awesome."

The medium fished all her candles out of her backpack, set them on the floor, and the witches promptly lit them. Yukiko pronounced a general summons, Serena threw her revealing spell around the room, and every specter appeared.

Elinor glided to Elenora. "Did something change? I feel so much better. Like a tremendous weight has been lifted off my shoulders. It's wonderful."

"Indeed," Elenora said. "You are no longer tethered to this place. Mr. Gill's spirit is gone and no longer a threat. And Yukiko will now be able to help all of you move on so you can finally rest in peace."

A hum of surprise buzzed around the room.

Tom had asked his OPO colleagues whether they should keep the spirits around as witnesses in case Jane needed their testimonies. Claire-Lune thought that since their grim experiences with Joseph Gill had already been recorded in Elenora's mind and downloaded, it seemed unnecessary, and they deserved to move on as soon as possible. Jeb pointed out that, at the very worst, the Sovran Council could always summon them back. Thus, it was decided that Yukiko would send the spirits to a proper afterlife.

The medium stepped forward and addressed the crowd of ghosts. "The process is very simple and painless. I just need to know your full name to release you from this plane, and then you'll be on your way. Any questions?"

"Am I heading to heaven?" Gertrude asked.

Yukiko considered her answer. "We assume you'll be moving on to a peaceful afterlife. However..." She raised a questioning brow at Jeb and the witches.

Serena shrugged. "If someone's marked, they might as well find out now. Not that it will make a difference."

Yukiko turned back to the ghosts. "If you think you might be heading to hell, tell us, and we'll check to see if you're on the list."

Gasps of horror and a wave of panic spread among the departed.

"Hold on!" Yukiko tried to appease them. "It's much rarer than you think!"

"Listen, everyone." Serena came to her colleague's rescue. "Unless you've murdered someone in cold blood, you need to have been a major turd to land on the devil's shit list."

Rounded spectral eyes gaped at her, either in reaction to her statement or her colorful words. Or both. At least she had stopped their frenzy.

"Believe us. Unless you committed a very serious crime, you shouldn't have to deal with the big guy downstairs," Claire-Lune added. "Again, if you have any doubt, just say so, and my colleague Jeb will check the registry before you're released."

One of the male ghosts raised his hand.

"You have a question, sir?" Claire-Lune asked him.

He stared at his feet as he talked. "What if we haven't killed anyone but haven't been choirboys either? Where does that leave us?"

She smiled at him. "You should be fine."

"What awaits us?" Eliza asked.

"Well, honestly, we mostly deal with the clear-cut cases

bound for hell," Claire-Lune replied. "We don't know all that much about what's beyond the veil otherwise."

"That said, I've summoned countless spirits after they've moved on, and I can tell you that the vast majority are serene," Yukiko volunteered warmly. "Most had reunited with loved ones. I've never asked them for extensive details about their resting place, but I can't see it being any worse than the state of limbo in which Mr. Gill had trapped you."

Her answer seemed to reassure them.

"Any more questions?" Serena asked.

"Could you please tell me if my sister Charlotte made the..." Mildred cleared her throat. "*Naughty* list? I love her to bits, but she was always a handful. I'd love to know if I'll be able to look for her."

"Sure." Jeb waved her over.

After a slight hesitation, the ghost glided to him. They exchanged a few quiet words, then he closed his eyes to consult the registry. The specters watched with quiet anticipation. Based on Jeb's grin and Mildred's excited reaction, things had turned out just fine for Charlotte.

Mildred thanked him profusely before bravely declaring, "Well, then. I believe I am all good to go." She floated to Elenora. "Thank you for listening."

"My pleasure." Elenora smiled. "I hope you find peace, Mildred."

"Thank you. And I wish you a wonderful life." The specter's lively gaze swept over everyone else as she said, "I wish you all a wonderful life or afterlife." Then she went to Yukiko. "My name is Mildred Victoria Notman. What do I need to do to proceed?"

"You're ready?" Yukiko asked.

"Yes."

Yukiko picked up a candle from the floor and held it between them. "Then please look at the flame."

Mildred's eyes traveled to the fire, and she gazed at it. She exhaled a jittery breath, bracing herself for departure.

"Mildred Victoria Notman, I release you," Yukiko declared in a serene voice.

As Mildred's spectral form faded, an expression of bliss washed over her face.

"Who's next?" Yukiko asked the remaining ghosts with a smile.

The release ceremony took nearly an hour, but it was worth every minute. Each spirit consulted with Jeb before embarking on their final voyage, and thankfully, none of them got a terrifying answer from him. Before leaving, they, too, showered the living and their fellow departed with well-wishes and words of gratitude. They then moved on to their afterlife wearing peaceful expressions.

Elenora's cheeks ached from smiling, and her colleagues looked equally delighted. Even Jane, who observed from a corner, seemed moved.

After the last of the deceased left, Yukiko bound Jane's and Clementine's spirits to a candle to transport them to the OPO, along with their remains. They would be safe there while waiting to hear from the Sovran Council. Dr. Brent had also offered to give Jane psychological counseling so she could begin to heal. Whether or not the council ultimately had mercy on her soul, Jane could at least get a sense of closure, maybe even forgive herself.

To Elenora, this felt like a small victory.

CHAPTER THIRTY-SIX

As they returned to the main floor, they called to Angéline. The spirit came out of hiding in the ballroom near the foyer, looking apprehensive.

"We come bearing good news. No need to look so freaked out," Serena said.

"Is he gone?" Angéline whispered.

"Yes. The fool broke the agreement and was escorted out of here. He will soon be in hell, where there's a bag of briquettes with his name on it."

"That is good news," the spirit said with guarded enthusiasm.

"What's wrong?" Elenora asked her.

The ghost looked away before clearing her throat. "I imagine you'll want me gone as well…"

"Releasing you is not a punishment," Yukiko said softly.

"Oh, that is not the issue…" She searched for words.

"Is it Anselmo?" Elenora tried.

Angéline's voice quivered. "I don't think he was able to move on. If I'm released now, I might never find him."

"I see." Yukiko exchanged looks with the witches.

"Would you object to us trying to track down Angéline's beloved before we release her?" Claire-Lune asked Tom and Alex. "Given that she's never caused trouble in this house..."

"I promise I won't interfere with the construction crew," Angéline blurted out. "Even if some of the aesthetic choices are questionable."

Tom briefly pondered the request before raising an inquisitive brow at Alex, who shrugged.

"I think we can trust our esteemed Miss de Montbleu to be considerate and discreet while—"

A loud gasp came from the other end of the ballroom, catching Angéline's and Elenora's attention. They turned their heads and saw three young male ghosts staring at them. One wore modest work clothes from over a century ago and a shell-shocked expression.

"My love, is that you?" His deep voice broke.

Angéline glided closer to him, absently passing through Wren. "Anselmo?" she yelped.

Anselmo? Elenora recognized the man's shirt sleeves as that of the rosebush mystery man, confirming Angéline's suspicion. Had his spirit been here all along?

"What's going on? Is her hottie here?" Serena asked Elenora.

"Looks like it. And he's got company." She pointed at the newcomers for her friend's benefit.

Serena and Yukiko performed their express summon-and-reveal schtick, and the three ghosts appeared to the living.

"Jérémie Marsan," Tom said at the same time as Alex

identified the other man, "Jean-Luc Rivard." They were both right.

Jérémie Marsan wore the same dusty black T-shirt and jeans Elenora had seen him wearing on his last day, whereas Jean-Luc Rivard donned the blood-soaked hooded robe in which he'd been found. The disciple of Satan looked skittish and stood slightly behind the two other spirits, as if fearing an attack.

"Angéline, it's really you," Anselmo whispered, slowly getting over his shock. His gaze roamed over the spectral woman, who looked several decades his senior. But the outrageous age difference didn't seem to bother him one bit.

"And you!" Angéline rushed to him. She reached for his hands and clutched them tightly.

"My love, I thought I'd never see you again." He looked at her lovingly. "You're even lovelier than I remember."

Angéline snorted. "Either you missed me tremendously to say that or your eyesight needs checking, my love."

Anselmo frowned, not catching her meaning.

"I'm an old bat!" She chuckled.

"You certainly aren't," he replied reverently. "You simply lived a longer life than I did. A good one, I hope?"

Her eyes flooded with emotion. "A good life but a lonely one. I spent most of it trying so hard to summon you. Trying to get you back... But you're here now."

She threw herself into his arms, and he held on to her passionately.

"About time, girl!" Serena whooped and whistled with two fingers.

The three young men froze and looked at her, utterly stunned.

"She can see us?" Anselmo whispered to Angéline.

"Yes! Yes, she can!" she replied enthusiastically. "They all can. Isn't that amazing?"

Anselmo took in the small crowd. "Who are they?"

"It's a long story. But in a nutshell, they're the best friends I've ever had."

———⁂———

After explaining to Jérémie, Jean-Luc, and Anselmo what had been going on and listening to what they'd gone through, Yukiko and the witches concluded Joseph Gill had stashed them away on other spiritual planes, and their reappearance had resulted from the warlock lifting his spells. Yukiko did a summons to make sure there were no spirits left in the house, but no one answered.

She then told the specters that she would help them move on to a proper afterlife. Jean-Luc Rivard reacted strongly to her announcement, terrified of going to hell. Jeb confirmed he was not marked, but that did little to assuage the former satanist's paranoid worries. He begged to be released quickly, convinced there must be a catch or an error or that someone was bound to change their mind and send him to hell, where he still thought he belonged. He admitted to having experienced paranormal events in the house and was shocked to learn it was not the devil but a dead warlock who had messed with him for his own cruel entertainment.

It had been nearly a week since they'd vanquished Joseph Gill and freed the spirits in the Maple Street house. With Chief Costa's blessing, they'd declared Jérémie Marsan's death an accident. Claire-Lune helped Tom and Alex produce the final report and close the case. As it was standard procedure for cases involving the OPO, the report went into the police system, but the witch cast a repelling spell of disinterest on it to dissuade people from ever looking at it—from seeking it, even.

They also updated Jean-Luc Rivard's file, listing Joseph Gill as his killer and his murder as solved. Claire-Lune also spread a generous layer of her repelling spell over it.

In an unprecedented—and surprising—move, the Sovran Council not only accepted Jeb's appeal but also promptly ordered for Jane's abused spirit to be unmarked and awarded a peaceful afterlife with her daughter. The news overjoyed Elenora.

She was also relieved when Serena agreed to meet with Harold Sanschagrin, Jérémie Marsan's traumatized colleague, to cast a forgetting spell on him if he wanted it. The man was single and had kept the traumatic episode to himself as requested. But the memory of it was eating at him and affecting his quality of life immensely. He was grateful for Serena's help and accepted to have the trauma erased. The following day, he returned to work and to being his usual self, happily oblivious.

And now, Elenora and Serena were on their last mission, waiting for Jérémie Marsan's fiancée to come home after work. Before crossing over, the young man had asked for a white flower to be sent to his fiancée so she would know he was okay. With his criminal past and him being a magnet for trouble, Jérémie had often joked to Kirsten that when he died, he would certainly end up on the wrong side of the heavenly track. And she'd always argued that she had never met a kinder soul, way too pure for hell. In jest, they had decided that whoever left this life first would give the other a sign of their eternal destination. Something red for hell, something white for heaven.

To Jérémie's massive relief, Jeb had confirmed that Kirsten had been right.

So here were Elenora and Serena, waiting in the witch's car to fulfill Jérémie Marsan's last wish, a giant bouquet of white lilies on the back seat. They could have phoned in the order, but they suspected Kirsten would be in shock and thought that subjecting an innocent delivery guy to a heart-wrenching meltdown was a dick move.

Elenora also craved to witness the emotional closure the lilies would hopefully bring the young woman.

She glanced at the time on the car's dashboard. Kirsten was due to come home at any minute.

"I hope she doesn't flip too hard," Serena said.

"I think it's going to be nearly impossible for her not to flip," Elenora replied. "Let's hope the shock is manageable and she recovers fast. Giving her a heart attack would be awful."

"Like Angéline and Anselmo almost did to one another? Aren't they cute?"

Elenora chuckled. Seeing Angéline and Anselmo reunited had gotten a strong emotional response from everyone present. She would never forget the touching moment. It had made her so happy to see the spirit back with her love after decades of mourning. Yukiko had released them together, hand in hand, so they would never lose sight of each other ever again. Elenora loved that so much.

She sure would miss the charming departed medium.

"Here she comes." Serena elbowed Elenora's arm, her eyes glued to the rearview mirror.

Elenora glanced at her side mirror and spotted Kirsten crossing the street toward her home.

They waited for her to get inside, and after a moment, Serena declared, "All right. Showtime."

They got out of the car, and the witch retrieved the bouquet from the back seat.

Elenora found waiting for Kirsten to answer the door nerve-racking, even though Serena was supposed to take the lead and seemed laid back about it. The witch was also ready to keep the flowers and erase the encounter from the fiancée's memory if the shock proved too great.

The door swung open, and Kirsten appeared in the doorway. She greeted them with a polite smile that didn't hide her sorrow.

Elenora expected Serena to launch into a comforting explanation before giving her the flowers, but her friend didn't utter a single word. Instead, she offered Kirsten the white lilies with a warm, knowing smile.

The young woman took in Serena and the flowers with a confused frown, but then realization sparked in her eyes. She drew in a sharp breath and faltered. Serena swooped in to catch her. Kirsten clutched her tightly, shaking with all the grief in the world.

Elenora's throat thickened, and her eyes watered. Had this been a mistake?

Please, let this not be a mistake. It would be too cruel.

Elenora looked away and wiped a tear from her cheek, reluctant to look at Kirsten. She felt like she was intruding on a private moment of raw vulnerability. Thankfully, they were on a quiet street with no other witnesses.

"He loves you so very much," Serena said to the grieving woman.

"I love him so very much too," she replied with a strangled sob.

"And he wants you to be happy."

Kirsten pulled back abruptly. "Is he going to be okay?"

Serena looked her in the eye. "Yes. He will miss you dearly, of course. But he hopes you will live a full life so that when you two meet again, you'll have so much to tell him."

Smiling through her tears, Kirsten accepted the bouquet. "Then I will do my best to make him proud and have so much to tell him."

CHAPTER THIRTY-SEVEN

Elenora called Serena and Rolland for an emergency meeting over coffee and pastries at Café Jackalope. A dream the previous night had rattled her oddly. It had felt more like a garden-variety nightmare than a premonition, but it had lingered in her mind. Something had seemed off, and she didn't know what to make of the dream. She hadn't had the chance to tell Tom about it, but there was no sense in alarming him if it turned out to be nothing.

The eerie dream had started at the old house on Maple. Elenora instantly recognized the very familiar place. Since they finally had no unfinished business over there, she concluded her subconscious must have needed more closure.

Unworried, she let herself drift through the familiar rooms.

Suddenly, she was holding Aubrey, asleep in her arms—a typical dream non sequitur. *Maybe a nod to Jane and Clementine,* Elenora thought, still rolling with it.

But then, frigid water stung her bare feet. The sound of rushing water grew to a deafening level as a forceful stream gushed over the floor and evolved into a quickly rising flash flood.

It's just a dream.

Elenora calmly waded toward the front door to leave the house. The water reached her waist, and she lifted Aubrey above it, willing her mind to wake up. But she remained in the dream. Her heartbeat sped up. She struggled to keep her composure despite her panic rising as fast as the flood.

A second later, she found herself submerged, sitting cross-legged on a riverbed, with Aubrey still asleep but now in her lap. Elenora knew this place. She had dreamed about it countless times and expected the creepy little boy to appear.

She looked around for him and saw something she'd never noticed before—a clutter of dark structures falling apart in the distance. Like an underwater ghost town. She squinted to see it better, but a nearby presence caught her attention.

The little twerp was uncomfortably close to her, leaning over Aubrey. Studying her.

And then he said the most horrible thing.

"She's mine."

Elenora woke up with a jolt.

She breathed hard, struggling to recover her wits. It was morning, and she was alone in bed. She heard Tom downstairs, getting out the door for work. *It's just as well,* she told herself, still too rattled for a calm and coherent conversation.

She pulled herself out of bed and spotted Willem staring at her with feline intensity, his tail flicking. Ominously.

Not helping.

"Don't give me the creeps just because you want food," she grumbled at him.

The more awake she became, the more the dream's

impact confused her. A knot of dread sat in her stomach. The little jerk had said that Aubrey was his, echoing Muriel's disturbing declaration about Elenora's daughter. Why? What did it mean?

Was it a sign?

Or was it just a dream, her subconscious making up a connection and her reading too much into it?

Still. Something didn't feel right.

"If he's just a kid, what could he possibly do?" Rolland took a careful sip of latte.

Aubrey slept, cradled against his other arm.

"*I* look like just a kid..." Serena retorted, waving a hand in front of herself. "Wanna see what I can do?" She gave him a perturbing smile.

Rolland laughed and raised his free hand in capitulation. "No, ma'am. I'm good."

"Don't ma'am me."

"Jeez. Tough crowd."

"You think he might be more than a kid?" Elenora blanched.

Having just seen how powerful magic could be—especially the dark and nefarious kind—she didn't like her friend's implication.

"I'm sorry, Ele," Serena backtracked. "I was just sassing Rolland. Didn't mean to freak you out even more."

"But you might have a point."

"Anything's possible, of course, but like you said, it could just be your exhausted subconscious playing tricks on you or trying to find answers where there are none. That'd be normal and logical. Now that the Maple house case is closed, maybe your brain moved on to the next worry to fill the void."

"How about you guys try to download the kid's latest guest appearance?" Rolland's words came out inelegantly around a mouthful of peaches-and-cream muffin.

"Hmm. Why not? Maybe it'll work this time." Elenora offered her hand to Serena.

The witch dusted off her fingers and took a sip of coffee before doing her magic. Once the download finished, they huddled over her tablet. The clip showed Elenora's dream, from the flash flood in the old house to the bottom of the river, but the little boy was a no-show. Again.

"Ugh. What the hell's his problem?" Serena muttered.

Elenora's throat felt dry. The boy's recurring vanishing act suddenly didn't seem innocuous.

Rolland noticed her uneasiness. "Maybe he's the psychic equivalent of a computer virus or a spam caller. Just there to be a nuisance."

Serena snorted at his comment but then became thoughtful. "Huh. Actually, that's interesting, Rol. Maybe he *is* like a glitch..."

She turned to Elenora. "You first saw him when you were, like, a toddler, no?"

"Yeah, when I was three."

"Right. So, back then, your abilities were dormant, and your mind was far from mature. Maybe your subconscious was trying to cope, using images that your young mind might understand...but without meaning anything?" Serena frowned at her words. "Okay, I dunno. That sounds half-baked. But something like this could explain why we can't capture him."

"You mean he might be more like a figment of Elenora's imagination than an actual threat?" Rolland asked.

"Right."

Right. That could make sense. Well before she discovered her psychic abilities, Elenora already knew from her work how powerful a mind could be—and that the brain tended to protect itself from trauma. Maybe the little boy was just her brain still struggling with old trauma from the accident and repressed memories. Maybe her recent stress had rekindled the whole thing.

Maybe.

"Maybe you're right, and I shouldn't worry. But that's the hard part, not worrying when I'm exhausted," Elenora said.

"I hear you, sister. You've been through the wringer lately. Hopefully, some rest will do the trick. But that said..." Serena's gaze surveyed the room as if checking for witnesses. She then leaned toward Aubrey.

"You want to hold her?" Rolland asked, his tone suggesting he wondered what the witch was up to.

"Not yet. Keep holding her." Serena put her hands softly on the sleeping baby's arms.

Trails of glittery blue-and-purple particles appeared and roamed all over Aubrey before fading quickly. Elenora and Rolland watched with fascination.

Elenora knew that whatever spell Serena was putting on Aubrey wouldn't be harmful. Still, she couldn't wait to find out about it but kept quiet in case her friend wasn't done.

Rolland, however, didn't have the same patience. "What's this for?"

"It's a protective spell that tethers her to me—Ele, I hope you don't mind?" It seemed to just occur to Serena that she should have asked permission first.

"No, of course I don't mind. But what does it do?"

"It's like an alarm. Should anything malignant come close to Aubrey, I will know, and the spell will fight back. It won't hold off a threat for long, but it will get us a head start and a chance to react. That way, you can sleep in peace. And I can always cancel it if it makes you uncomfortable."

"No! This is great! It's genius." Elenora felt enormous relief. The spell sounded wonderful, and maybe it would even help her psyche calm down and stop worrying about the little boy and get over him once and for all. She smiled widely. "It sure pays to have witchy friends."

Serena returned her smile. "My pleasure to be of service. Plus, I dare anyone to harm a single hair on my goddaughter's head."

They parted ways in front of the coffee shop. Despite the broad daylight, Rolland and Serena both offered to walk Elenora and Aubrey to their car in case they bumped into Mary Gallagher's ghost. But Elenora politely declined their help, feeling at once silly and emboldened by her recent dealings with Joseph Gill.

But now that she was getting closer to the haunted vacant lot, her thoughts snapped to Mary, and she almost regretted refusing their help. Earlier, running on adrenaline and with the street full of people, she had speed-walked to the café and avoided the spirit. But after discussing and analyzing her dream at length and with the implications of Serena's spell on Aubrey sinking in, Elenora was drained.

What if she couldn't elude Mary this time? What if the ghost cornered her? Or worse, followed her home?

Get a grip. It's the middle of the afternoon, and you handled Gill. Surely she can't be worse than him.

Maybe not worse, but certainly much harder to look at. If only it wasn't for all the blood. And the severed head.

Elenora shivered and picked up the pace. The street block was suspiciously empty. *Gah!*

Serena thought that the famous ghost had barely shown herself to Elenora in Yukiko's presence because she wanted to talk in private. A part of Elenora was curious to test that theory now that she was alone—assuming a baby didn't count as an unwanted spectator—but she quickly changed her mind. She might be more comfortable around spirits now, after her trial by fire with a wide cast of ghosts at the old house, but she was tired and emotionally fragile and could easily lose it. It was a bad time for a face-to-face with a blood-soaked spirit carrying its head on its hip like a soccer ball, even if curiosity weighed heavily in the balance.

Aubrey started fussing, her arms shooting and twirling urgently at the lot as they walked past it on the opposite side-walk. The timing was uncanny, and the baby's obvious desire to go there was disturbing.

A dreadful thought shook Elenora: was Aubrey aware of Mary's ghost and wanted something with her?

Or did her daughter just remember being at the lot with her and Yukiko, and she was attracted to it for a reason that followed baby logic?

Either way, Elenora didn't have the bandwidth to run into a spectral being right now. "Not today, love. Mommy has some serious recovering to do first." She kissed the top of her daughter's head, stared straight ahead, and kept walking.

But then, a balmy breeze caressed her bare arms and legs, sending a warm chill through her.

Crap.

She slowed to a stop and stood there for a moment, wondering what to do. Aubrey started wriggling again. Elenora sighed and turned to face the lot.

The space was quiet. At first, she saw nothing—until a faint shimmering caught her eye.

Another warm chill followed.

Elenora sighed again. "Hi, Mary. May I please take a rain check? Now's not a good time. I'll be back later. I promise."

Double crap. Why did she have to promise?

Maybe the ghost didn't hear her. How good was their hearing, anyway? It wasn't like Elenora had screamed her promise. And there was street and city noise. Maybe Mary didn't hear.

As if in response, the shimmering and the warm chills ceased, leaving goosebumps on Elenora's skin in their wake.

"Thank you for understanding," she mumbled, grateful there was no one else on the sidewalk to see the crazy lady talking to herself.

She headed to her car, wondering what she had gotten herself into.

THANK YOU FOR READING!

Elenora, the gang, and the little boy at the bottom of the river will return.

In the meantime, check out *Shade of Evil*, a deliciously creepy short paranormal mystery featuring Pierre as a budding detective. Get it for free when you sign up for my newsletter or buy it from your favorite retailer. Visit www.jacinthedessureault.com to subscribe.

If you enjoyed this book, please consider leaving a review.

A THOUSAND THANKS

I'd like to thank my wonderful husband, especially for putting up with me while I wrote (and rewrote, and revised, and reread, and rewrote, and revised, and reread, and tweaked for the last time, I swear) this book.

Thank you also to my awesome family and friends for your support and words of encouragement.

A special thanks to my friend Catherine for the inspiring bizarro tidbit.

And thank you, Nadene, Bettina, and Gloria for your crucial feedback and your much-appreciated enthusiasm.

ABOUT THE AUTHOR

Jacinthe Dessureault writes paranormal mysteries and humorous fiction. She is a big fan of lemon meringue pie and the silly antics of Boonie and Jackson, her family's two adorable lop buns. She lives in Montréal, Canada with her husband and daughter.

HER BOOKS

Elenora Bello Paranormal Mysteries
Shade of Evil (short story prequel)
A Sinister Gift
Trapped Souls

Humorous Fiction
Igloo High (young adult)